RIP RIDLEY
AND THE
EVANS STREET STATION

JOE MARESCHI

Edited by Kristen Hamilton of Kristen Corrects, Inc.
Cover art design by Victoria Wolf of Red Wolf Marketing

ISBN: 978-0-578-70622-1
Published by Duderonomy Productions, LLC
First edition published 2020

Special thanks to Bryan Wasetis, M.C., and Clint Barker. A very special thanks to Kristen Hamilton of Kristen Corrects, who helped put my thoughts into ideas and provided a structure.

This book was funded by the sale of cryptocurrencies.

If you wish to contact the author, please direct any correspondence to Joeyrecords101@gmail.com.

One morning I was having tea with my wife. (She was having coffee.) And she said to me that sometimes she didn't know what character in the book she was going to wake up to.

This book is dedicated to my wife, Kitty and our son, Louis.

I can hear music

PART ONE

CHAPTER 1

It was an overcast, hungover San Francisco morning. Chief Brady chewed on the end of his cigar as he sat in the back seat of his fire department-issued red Crown Vic. His operator, Lieutenant McGuire, drove up Evans Street from Third Street in Hunters Point. With twenty-eight years on the force, Chief Brady was an old timer who believed in the operations manual and tradition—though sometimes tradition overruled the manual, but only if someone had put in their time. Chief Brady was one who had put in his time.

"What's on the agenda today?" Chief Brady asked Lieutenant McGuire. Chief Brady's gravelly voice sounded rough like sandpaper. From years on the bottle, his complexion was the color of the whiskey he liked to drink. His nickname was "the Penguin," because he had a slight waddle in his walk after a fall at a fire incident years ago, and because he was short, though nobody ever said it to his face.

"The Evans Street Station sir, Station 51. The paramedic division," Lieutenant McGuire said. As operator, Lieutenant McGuire's duties were to drive and maintain in a condition of readiness the assigned vehicle, report mechanical failures or damaged equipment, clean and service the assigned apparatus, and most importantly, follow the rules and regulations in the manual as interpreted by Chief Brady.

Lieutenant McGuire was Chief Brady's sister's kid who grew up in the Richmond District. He wrestled in high school, and always had a crew cut. He lifted weights, and never smiled because growing up he had bad teeth, until they fixed them in the Army. After his stint in the Army, Chief Brady put a good word in for him, and he was hired by the fire department.

"Fucking medics," Chief Brady said, spitting a wad of tobacco from the chewed end of his cigar out the window. "How did I ever get transferred to Battalion 10?"

"It's a promotion, sir."

"Some promotion."

Station 51, or the Evans Street Station as everyone called it, was an old brick building that was once a slaughterhouse. The grass in front of the station was overgrown like a forgotten football field. Behind the station, a coffee brewing company spewed out foul burned-coffee odors from its rooftop filters. On Phelps Street was a sewage treatment plant. The administration offices were on the second floor, along with the conference room, the weight room, and the sleeping quarters. On the ground floor were the men's and women's locker rooms, the film room, and the warehouse. Roll-up doors led from the warehouse to the yard, where the ambulances were parked. A chain link fence, topped with barbed wire, enclosed the yard.

Even though the paramedic division wasn't under the fire department's jurisdiction, the Evans Street Station was now in Chief Brady's district, and he was told to keep tabs on it by Chip Hogwash, the mayor's chief of staff, and to check up on the new paramedic chief. Chief Brady was only too glad to do so. Because of budget restraints for the new fiscal year, there were rumors that the paramedic division was going to merge with the fire department. To Chief Brady, the thought of a merger between paramedics and firemen was a bitter pill to swallow, but he wanted to keep his ear to the ground, so he knew what to expect. Maybe there was something in it for him.

"Drive around the block," Chief Brady told Lieutenant McGuire as they came to the station.

A caravan of beat-up and broken-down vans, cars, and other vehicles were parked along the side streets, mostly on Mendel and Fairfax Streets. Broken car parts, empty oil cans, stray dogs, shopping carts, and trash were everywhere.

"For Christ's sake," Chief Brady said. "What the hell is this?"

"It's a homeless encampment, sir. The medics call it Camp Willie, after the mayor proposed to have the police seize their shopping carts. It was a citywide proposal."

"Fucking politicians. Don't they ever call the cops?"

"They do, sir. But the homeless seem to find their way back again."

"Let's get some gas and pay a visit to this new paramedic chief. What's his name again?"

"Chief Ridley, sir."

"Ripley?"

"Chief Ridley, sir."

The pumps were in the yard of the station. Lieutenant McGuire drove up to the roll-away gate and put in the code on the pad on the metal stand, and the gate rattled and shook on its tracks and opened slowly.

While Lieutenant McGuire refueled the chief's vehicle, Chief Brady looked over the yard, but an expression of disdain showed on his face that something was out of place—and that something bothered him. And it wasn't the aging ambulance fleet, or the paper and plastic litter stuck in the barbed wire of the chain link fence surrounding the yard, or the broken hose nozzle in the wash area for the rigs. It was...a small metal object in the yard that seemed to glare at him in defiance.

"Look at that," Chief Brady said to Lieutenant McGuire. "Do you know what that is?"

"I think so, sir."

"Lieutenant McGuire, could you please pick that up for me?"

"Yes, sir."

Lieutenant McGuire walked over, picked up the object, and brought it to Chief Brady.

"Is it what I think it is?"

"It's a nail sir, a rusty nail."

"A fucking nail," Chief Brady said. "What was that name of the chief here again?"

"Ridley, sir."

"Ripley?"

"No, Ridley, sir. Chief Rip Ridley."

"What kind of parents would name their son Rip?"

"I don't know, sir."

"College boy?"

"San Francisco State. Film major, sir."

"What the hell does a film major do?"

"I don't know, sir. He made some training films for the paramedic division. Seems to have long hair. Hippie type. May be a pothead too."

"For Christ's sake, a pothead? A fucking pothead hippie chief?"

"Yes, sir."

"Let's go pay this Chief Ripley a visit."

"It's Chief Ridley, sir."

While Chief Brady was examining the nail found in the yard, the newly appointed paramedic chief, Rip Ridley, was completing his office furnishings on the second floor. Like Rip's personality, his office décor was a little bit of ying, a little bit of yang, and some of the memories of Laura, the lost love of his life.

Rip had received the call for his promotion from Chief of Staff Chip Hogwash the day after Mayor Brown's inauguration. It was January 9, 1996. At the time, Rip was the captain of training, working on a training film on nasal intubations in the back of the warehouse titled *Ode to the Nose*. On his twelve-inch black and white Memorex TV that he had illegally hooked up into the station's cable, Rip watched the highlights of the mayor's inaugural speech on *News at Noon*.

"We must ensure," the newly elected Mayor Brown spoke to the adoring crowd, "that every school kid has an opportunity to do exactly what Willie Brown has been able to do and the Willie Browns of yore, and we must make sure that we are never without the compassion… Our resources must never be so limited that we cannot help the helpless."

While watching the speech, the phone rang. At first Rip did not answer the call, thinking, who would be calling him anyway? The film wasn't due for another week. But Rip put the receiver to his ear.

"Hello," he said.

"This is Chip Hogwash, Chief of Staff of the mayor's office. Is this Captain Ripley?"

"It's Ridley, sir."

"As you know, your chief resigned unexpectedly."

"I heard he disappeared, sir."

"Well, Captain Ridley…you are the new chief of the paramedic division."

"Really?"

"Do you have any questions?"

"What exactly does the paramedic chief do?" Rip asked.

"He stays out of my way. And you are getting a new hire named Arne Dibble. He was number one in his class. Make sure he passes probation."

"When do I start?" Rip asked.

"Tomorrow."

"No, I mean staying out of your way."

The phone went dead.

And with that phone call, Rip Ridley became chief of the paramedic division of San Francisco. He never asked why he was appointed chief, but he always thought it had something to do with his training films. They were really quite popular.

Moving from the warehouse basement to his new office on the second floor, Rip felt like he had finally arrived. At age thirty-three, Rip was the youngest chief ever to run the paramedic division. And like any other man who looked up to and resembled Dennis Wilson of the Beach Boys, he was a little vain. And why wouldn't he be? Rip had dirty blond hair, brooding eyes, was 5'8", and was a surfer living in California. He always wanted to be a drummer in a surf rock band, and whenever in a pensive mood, would usually pick up two pencils and beat out a rhythm, mostly to surfer songs. Rip loved the Beach Boys' music, especially *Pet Sounds*, which he first heard on acid. Rip was vain to the point that, when he became chief, he moved the mirror from his old office and installed it in his new bathroom, along with an early picture of Dennis Wilson—before the drugs and alcohol had kicked in. Rip always wanted to have that Beach Boys surfer-style wave, though gray had started to creep in. Rip felt that having his own bathroom was a sign that he had finally arrived. City hall could slash his budget, cut his staff, but they couldn't take his bathroom away.

In his office, Rip hung a picture of the ocean waves beneath the Golden Gate Bridge, which he had picked up at Pier 39. He still surfed there sometimes. He hung a broken surfboard from the ceiling, and cutouts from Playland at the Beach. There was a sofa chair with a large stuffed gator, the mascot of San Francisco State, his alma mater. It was green with a purple cap and sweater, and looked feral. On the floor, near the gator, was a tuba. There was an old candy machine that Laura had given Rip for his birthday one year, that still worked. Rip filled it up with all his favorites. He loved Nestlé's Crunch, Snickers, and Milky Way. On the shelves of his bookcases were departmental manuals, EMS procedures, MCI reports, a book on the history of San Francisco, a book on the forts of the Golden State, and one titled *The Shock of the New*. On the wall to the right of Rip's desk, which sat in the middle of the room, facing the door, hung his paramedic license, along with his degree from San Francisco State. On the wall with the window that had a view of the traffic going up and down Evans Street was a framed poster that said, *This is a Drug Free Zone*, and another one that said, *Coyote Crossing*. There were empty takeout containers of Chinese food on his desk. Sweet and sour chicken with pea pods was Rip's favorite. Near his desk was a stand with a departmental color TV, as all chiefs were required to follow local events in the news. And, of course, there was the bathroom, which was in the back to the left.

Just as Rip took a seat and gently placed the picture of Laura—the lost love of his life, wearing that itsy-bitsy baby blue bikini at Ocean Beach—on his desk, facing him, Chief Brady and Lieutenant McGuire barged into his office unannounced. It took Rip by surprise because since he had become chief of the paramedic division, nobody of official capacity had come to see him or even called since he had been appointed.

Chief Brady walked up to his desk with Lieutenant McGuire by his side.

"For Christ's sake, Ripley," Chief Brady said, looking around, "what the hell have you done to your office?"

"It's Ridley, Chief Rip Ridley."

"Whatever. What is this?"

"It's my office, sir. I thought I would put a little bit of my personality. Jazz it up a bit."

"A bit?" Chief Brady snapped, still looking around amazed. Lieutenant McGuire only shook his head. "How did you ever become chief of the paramedic division?"

"I was appointed."

"Hogwash," Chief Brady said to Lieutenant McGuire. "Fucking Hogwash."

"Actually, I was quite surprised myself," Rip replied.

"Well, let me ask you a question, Ripley," Chief Brady said.

"It's Ridley."

"What the hell is this?" Chief Brady asked Rip, holding the nail up to his face, as Lieutenant McGuire, who was chewing tobacco, spit a gob in Rip's wastebasket with a splash.

"It's a nail, sir. A rusty nail."

"Yes, a rusty nail. And do you know what a rusty nail means in the yard of your station?"

"Surprise me," Rip said, throwing up his hands, not knowing where the conversation was going.

"In the manual under procedures, 'the area which is considered your workspace most be maintained at all times.' A rusty nail means that your workspace has not been swept down daily, and is not being maintained. And why is the hair on the back of your head so long? In the manual it states that 'hair will not cover the back of your collar, or the tip of your ears.' But looking around here, I don't think you ever read it."

"Well, maybe our manuals are different. Who are you again?" Rip asked, bewildered.

"I am Chief Brady of Battalion 10 of the fire department, and you are in my district. And this is my operator, Lieutenant McGuire."

"And you are here because...?"

"Because Hogwash from city hall told me to look in on you from time to time, and to see what the hell is going on around here. And from everything I can see, it's something that would never happen in the fire department."

"Well Chief Brady, the paramedic division is not in the fire department."

"Don't you know anything, Ripley?"

"It's Ridley, and obviously not."

Lieutenant McGuire spit another gob of chewing tobacco, but this time it missed, hit the side of the wastebasket, and ran down to the carpet.

"There are rumors floating around city hall," Chief Brady said, leaning over Rip's desk to make his point, "that in the new fiscal year, the paramedic division will merge with the fire department."

"Rumors?"

"Yes, and rumors from city hall have a tendency to come true. And you know what, Ripley? I don't like it. There's no place for medics or free thinkers in the fire department, and if I have anything to do about it, there will never be a merger. A city-run ambulance is a waste of money that would be better spent on suppression. I only hope the mayor's office gets rid of you medics and brings in the privates. At least the privates know their place."

"Well, thank you for your endorsement," Rip said sarcastically.

Lieutenant McGuire nudged Chief Brady with his elbow, and they both looked down at the picture of Laura on Rip's desk. Chief Brady picked up the picture, and with Lieutenant McGuire, looked it over.

"Not bad, Ripley. Is this your girlfriend? You do like girls, don't you?"

Rip got up from his desk and grabbed the picture from Chief Brady's hand, put it face down on his desk, then sat down again. Both the lieutenant and Chief Brady laughed.

"Don't be touchy, Ripley. This is just a meet and greet. That's all. Fire department style. But let me give you some advice: The next time we meet, you will address me by my title, Chief Brady, as you will Lieutenant McGuire. And the next time we meet, wear a tie, and for Christ's sake, get a haircut."

There was a moment of silence. Rip rubbed his chin, then looked at the picture on the wall of the waves rolling beneath the Golden Gate Bridge. Rip was a pretty good surfer, and could ride a wave or two.

"Chief Brady," Rip started, "I saw your daughter on a call the other day. I guess she's in the fire department, too. She was on Engine One with the other first responders."

"Yeah, what's your point, Ripley?"

"It's just that my father was short, but my mother was six feet tall. They never got along. But that's another story. But somehow, I never got her genes. I got my father's genes, so I'm short, too."

"What's your point?"

"My point sir, is why is your daughter so tall, and you're not?"

"You bastard," Chief Brady said, going around Rip's desk until Lieutenant McGuire came between them.

"It's not worth it, sir," the lieutenant whispered in Chief Brady's ear, who regained his composure somewhat.

"And it's *Chief Ridley*," Rip stated, "of the paramedic division."

Chief Brady gave a hard-nosed stare at Rip, then he and Lieutenant McGuire walked out of the office. The click-clack of their shoes echoed down the hallway. Watching Chief Brady leave, Rip thought to himself that he really did walk like a penguin.

After Chief Brady and Lieutenant McGuire left, Rip's phone rang. It was the mayor's office.

"Chief Ridley, this is Chip Hogwash. It's your father. He exposed himself at the mayor's press conference. The mayor was not happy."

"His penis?"

"Yes, Chief Ridley, he showed his penis at the mayor's press conference with the Gray Beavers. You *are* familiar with that radical group of female senior citizens who expose their beavers? They unjustly feel the mayor's office is trying to tear down low-cost senior housing for new condos."

"Oh, yeah, near the Ferry Building," Rip said. "I read about it in the *Chronicle*."

"At the mayor's press conference!" Hogwash screamed into the phone.

"But Mister Hogwash," Rip tried to explain, "my father is not in it for the politics. I'm sure he only joined the Gray Beavers for the sex. He's French. Or at least he thinks he is. There aren't a lot of Ridleys in France, but he speaks the language well. Taught it in school. Years ago, my mother left him for another woman. They had a bad divorce. I just think that now he's overcompensating. I'm sure it's been a while for him. I know it's been a while for me, too."

There was grumbling on the other end of the line.

"Was that an attempt at humor?" Hogwash asked.

"Yes, sir."

"Talk to him. Straighten it out."

"Yes, sir. I will talk to him."

"This is your first week here, Chief Ridley."

"Sir, I know this is my first week, but I promise it will get better," Rip proclaimed. "But sir, I just had a meeting with Chief Brady today. Very reactionary guy. Short too. Walks with a waddle. Do you happen to know anything about this fiscal year merger between the paramedic division and the fire department that everybody is talking about? I think it would be good if I was kept in the loop."

"Fix it," Hogwash said.

"But don't you think—"

The line went dead. Hogwash had hung up the phone.

CHAPTER 2

When Arne Dibble rang the buzzer at the Fairfax gate to the warehouse of the Evans Street Station, he looked more like the ZOLL salesman in his Men's Wearhouse black suit, white shirt, and black tie than the newly hired medic for the paramedic division. At twenty-four, besides working in a comic book store and flipping burgers, this was his first real job.

Arne was tall and lanky, his face was white as flour, and he still had acne that should have cleared up years ago. He resembled Ned Ryerson in *Groundhog Day*, with his awkwardness and thick black-framed glasses. Arne was first in his class in paramedic school at City College when he was hired, and though being first meant a lot to him, it didn't mean a lot to anybody else. To his fellow students, seeing the awkwardness of Arne and his tendency to sweat and be nervous during clinicals, they felt it had to be political.

His classmates called him Ichabod Crane because they thought his head looked like a pumpkin, and he was prematurely going bald. And the fact was that even though he was always punctual and did well in exams, Arne saw everything as a crisis, and then his voice would crack, and he would get nervous, and he really didn't exude confidence. It was as if Arne Dibble was born with a KICK ME sign on his ass.

After Arne came up to the Fairfax gate and rang the buzzer, he saw a warehouse worker in the yard smoking a cigarette.

"Excuse me," Arne said, "may I speak to you?"

Arne was ignored.

"Excuse me," Arne tried again, "could you please let me in? I have an appointment."

The worker's name was Effin, but he was never one to introduce himself. Though he recently turned twenty-five, he looked like a scrawny kid from the outer Sunset District who always held a grudge. He put out his cigarette only to light another.

"Why should I?" he asked, as they talked through the gated fence.

Arne was taken aback. Looking at Effin, he was small, and his pants and shirt were bigger than what they should have been. They were like hand-me-downs in a family of taller people, and he just didn't grow. And he was always tucking his shirt in his pants as a nervous habit. He wore glasses that were dirty and crooked on his nose, and his hair looked like a Nick Nolte mug shot. He smoked cigarettes constantly, but could only smoke outside in the yard because there were chemicals in the warehouse, and he had to be away from the pumps. Arne noticed that he had a smirk on his face—and it wasn't a happy smirk, either.

"Because I asked politely, and I am a good person, and I would think that is your job," Arne replied.

"What do you know about my job?" Effin asked.

"I just think that you should help me because that's how people should act."

"Maybe in your world."

Arne Dibble always became uncomfortable in any tense interactions, and he grew puzzled.

"I'm just asking."

"Well go ask somebody else."

"I would, but I don't see anyone else," Arne said with his voice rising a few octaves. "I mean, there must be some kind of management around here."

"Management, you want management? Just wait till you meet Rip Ridley. You'll meet management." Effin laughed, smoking, puffing away.

"You mean Chief Ridley. I have an appointment with the chief."

"Oh, yeah, Chief Ridley," Effin said, thinking for a minute. "You must be the rookie."

"My name is Arne. Arne Dibble, not the rookie."

"Yeah, well as of today, you are the rookie. Get used to it. But okay, Rookie, I'll let you in."

Effin flipped the switch on the side of the gate, and it rattled open.

"I'm Effin," he finally said to Arne. "You know, effin this and effin that. You'll understand later. Now if I were you, I would go up those stairs there," he said, pointing to the metal stairs leading to the second floor, "and make a left. Now leave me alone."

"How do I know which office is his?" Arne asked.

"It's the one you wouldn't think it is."

Arne had a confused look on his face when he walked away from Effin, who smirked and kept puffing on his cigarette.

"Effin medics," Effin muttered to himself.

Jesus came up to Effin after he saw him talking to Arne. Jesus was the supervisor of the warehouse, and was Effin's chain of command. His real name was Charles, but everybody called him Jesus because of his recent religious conversion while watching a Burger King commercial on TV. Jesus didn't know it at the time, but he was ripe for conversion. He was so intent in helping those without the means to help themselves, that he let Effin do whatever he wanted to. Whenever the medics complained about Effin's work habits, since he was responsible for stocking the ambulances, Jesus protected him. Being a sinner, Jesus was at the crossroads in his life and didn't think Effin was dimwitted, as everybody thought he was, just angry. But Jesus was Black, so he knew what anger was about.

"Who was that?" Jesus asked.

"The rookie."

"Really, the rookie?"

"Yep."

"Poor soul."

"Yep. Poor soul."

"Think he'll make it?"

"Not a chance," Effin said. "Not a chance."

On the second floor, Arne noticed that the hallways smelled of bathroom odors, medic boots, and burned motor oil. There was a metal chair outside of Rip's office and somebody told him to sit there and Chief Ridley would be with him, so Arne sat.

Sitting outside the office, Arne heard Rip's phone ring. Rip never closed his door, so his voice could be heard in the hallway.

"Dad."

"Bonjour!"

"Dad, don't *bonjour* me. You can't picket the mayor's office. He just gave me this job."

"You are telling me what to do, and even as a child, you always took your mother's side, especially in our divorce. And you certainly know about your mother, and her lifestyle."

"Dad, I know you think I was irresponsible as a child, but you kept speaking in French and losing your temper, and I didn't know what you were talking about. And leave Mom out of this."

"Well, you know about her lifestyle."

"Dad, she's a lesbian. Big deal. Get over it. And my adolescence was such a long time ago. Why do you keep bringing it up? And why are you involved with the Gray Beavers anyway? They are all women. You don't even have a beaver, and why are you showing off your penis?"

"For support. I call it a man's vagina. But it's the housing problem in this city that I'm concerned about," Rip's dad said, trying to sound convincing.

"Concerned? I know housing in the city is getting harder for the elderly, but you already have a house."

"And...?"

"And Dad, the mayor's office just gave me this job, and you know this housing is a big issue for him. And why the Gray Beavers? You can't even handle Mom's sexuality."

There was silence on the other end of the phone.

"Wait a minute, you're sleeping with one of them, aren't you?" Rip asked.

"Maybe."

"Dad, I know that tone of voice. You did, didn't you? Did you sleep with more than one?"

"I'm French. Since your mother was never satisfied by my performance, obviously by her life changes, then why not?"

"Dad, you're not French. You only speak it. Your penis is French, that's all. Ridley is Anglo Saxon. But don't you want me to be successful?"

"No."

"Why not?" Rip asked, hurt.

"You always took your mother's side."

"There was no side," Rip tried to explain. "Living in that house, you two were miserable together. It was amazing that you even got together and had me."

"See, there you go again. Like your mother, questioning my manhood."

"Dad, I was miserable, too."

"That's okay. Being French, we know how to live in misery."

"Not the French thing again."

"Whatever happened to that girl you used to go out with—Laura?"

"Dad, Laura's been gone for over a year. Remember Australia, and her moving to the outback to find herself? When she asked me to, I wouldn't go. I asked you if I should move to Australia, and you told me don't be crazy, that nobody moves to the outback, and she will soon be coming back running into my arms. Well she's gone, and she's not coming back, and she met somebody else, so now she's running into *his* arms."

"Well, that happens. I happen to know an older lady…"

"Dad, forget it. But will you please stop picketing the mayor with the Gray Beavers and showing off your penis. For me? Please?"

Silence.

"Dad!" Rip raised his voice. "Promise me."

"Can't do it."

"Dammit, Dad!"

The phone went dead. Rip looked at the receiver.

"These damn phones."

It took a few minutes for Rip to recover, but then he remembered that his new hire, Arne Dibble, was waiting for him, and he called him into his office. He also remembered what Hogwash had said about making sure that he passed his probation, and Rip really wanted to stay chief. When Arne came in, Rip was seated at his desk, and told Arne to take a seat across from him. Arne looked nervous.

"So," Rip said, shuffling through paperwork, "you are the rookie."

"Sir, why does everybody call me the rookie? My name is Arne."

"Well Arne, it's a little station house humor. Since you are the last one hired, you are the rookie. Then when the next person comes on, they become the rookie."

"But sir, what if you never hire anybody else?" Arne asked.

"Paramedic Dibble," Rip said, leaning over his desk, trying to get Arne's confidence, "I have talked to the chief of staff for the mayor's office. I have been assured that they have great plans for the paramedic division. The wheels are in motion."

"Does that mean hiring new people, sir?" Arne asked, no longer wanting to be called the rookie.

"Paramedic Dibble." Rip leaned back in his chair. "That's all I can say right now. But have a seat outside, and we will get you situated. We have plans for you."

"Plans, sir?" Arne asked.

"Yes, my two best medics are going to be your preceptors, and I want you to meet them. You'll enjoy it."

"Enjoy it, sir?"

"Yes. You'll enjoy working with them, Paramedic Dibble."

"Oh, okay, sir," Arne responded, not quite sure.

When the phone rang again in Rip's office, Arne got up from his seat and looked around Rip's office at the décor. Trying to take it all in, he glanced at all the signs, the pictures, the tuba, the candy machine and the feral alligator, and wondered what he had gotten himself in for. Arne only wanted to be an accountant and join the family's construction business. His dad, a well-known developer in the city, had scratched and clawed his way up the ever-changing political ladder from humble PG&E roots. He learned from getting knocked down, and getting back up again, how to make a deal with the unions, and wanted to toughen his son up a bit with some real-life experiences. Arne's father had signed Arne up for paramedic school because he saw him as soft.

As Arne was about to leave Rip's office, his eyes slowly focused on Laura's picture on Rip's desk. She was so beautiful that for a moment he couldn't take his eyes off the picture. Then he remembered his girlfriend Ashley.

Arne loved Ashley. He thought she was the prettiest girl he could ever have as a girlfriend. Ashley Green was a UC Davis student when she met Arne at an Earl Dibble political fundraiser for the mayor, where she was working for a catering company. She didn't think much of Arne until she found out who his father was. Ashley was popular in high school for all the wrong reasons. It was because of the hot dog incident, where she had used it to sexually pleasure herself, and it broke off inside of her vagina, and her mother had to drive her to the ER to have it removed. Her brother told everyone the next day at school. Her nickname at school became Oscar Meyer and then finally Relish. From all the ribbing she had to take from the boys in her high school, she really didn't like the male gender anymore. Once as a freshman in college, she had a sleepover with a girlfriend, who went down on her. Ashley acted like she was asleep, but she really wasn't, and she secretly enjoyed it—but never told anyone, especially Arne. But this hot dog incident and all the boys making fun of her in high school really stacked the cards against Arne. She took out her wrath against the male gender on him because of it. But when Arne got the job as a medic, Ashley did perform a handjob on him while wearing a rubber glove. Somehow the rubber glove really excited Arne. But remembering where he was, Arne lowered his head and took a seat outside the office.

"Hello, Chief Ridley here," Rip answered the phone.

There was no response.

"Dad, I know it's you. I can hear you breathing. Dad, answer me. And not in French. Are you going to stop this nonsense? Don't you want your son to do well?"

A dial tone came on the line.

"Why does everyone keep hanging up on me?" Rip muttered. "Dammit Dad, dammit."

CHAPTER 3

When Reed saw Jan coming out of the women's locker room with a letter in her hand, looking like the air from her psychic balloon had just been deflated, he shook his head. He was glad he had the joint in his wallet to make his day go a little easier. He would certainly need it.

Because for Jan Stein, the third Wednesday of every month was Mommy Fucking Dearest Day, when she received her mother's monthly letter. Jan had a Greenpeace *Save the Whales* sticker on her locker, along with one that said, *Arms Are for Hugging*, but all the liberal bullshit in the world couldn't calm her resentment of her mother's monthly letters, and having the same last name that meant *stone*, it reminded her that one day she might end up being just like her mother.

The secret of success is to be paranoid, her mother's letter began. *Our fault as parents was that we never made you paranoid enough. We thought it would come naturally being such a family trait, especially among the women of the family. I just don't understand how that trait passed you by. All your sisters have it. And they all married successfully. But why not you? You are smart. You could have been a doctor, or at least married one. You are fairly good looking. I thought you would have married into money like your other sisters, but instead are still not married, and have no children. Not that it is any of my business, but perhaps it is time to reevaluate some of your life decisions.*

Your father, God bless his soul, worked very hard to provide the best for our family. We all knew your father had an adventurous nature. What real man doesn't? As I get older, I have come to find these stories about his infidelities to be, at the very least, exaggerated. But he was also a man who cared about you, and the career paths you should follow. If he was alive, I'm sure he would say, "Why a paramedic? What exactly does a paramedic do? What were you thinking?" Your father, as you know, was very blunt. Helping the homeless is noble, but that is why we have charities. Lord knows how much the government takes from us, and gives to them. And our family does give money to a charity that provides the homeless with blankets, and they made their own life choices. I just hope this paramedic division supplies you with gloves, as hygiene is very important to our family.

Recently I read the article about your new chief, a Rip Ridley or something. Why would any parent name their child "Rip"? God, I hope you are not sleeping with him.

What I am asking from you is to please take this time to reflect on my advice. When you look at the homeless, always remember that we are not like other people. We give them money. Isn't that enough?

Well I have to go now because tea is being served along with those little sandwiches you always liked as a child.

God Bless. Mother Stein.

The Stein family came from old money. The kind of money in stocks and bonds that banks kept in underground impregnable vaults, like those pictured in James Bond movies. Mother Stein liked the finer things in life, which included teatime at the Fairmont and spa treatments at the Nob Hill Spa. The letter she wrote to Jan was tea-stained.

Though Mother Stein had three girls and a son, she only wrote letters to her daughters, mostly in a critical nature. The letters were therapy for Mother Stein. It helped her forget the part of her life that wasn't the storybook ending that she thought having money would have allowed her. Her letters to Jan were the most critical of all because she had an independent streak like Father Stein, which bothered Mother Stein.

"Rip wants to see us," Reed said, walking up to Jan.

"In his office?'

"He is the new chief."

"God, I hope he doesn't change."

"They always do," Reed replied.

"Does he think it's going to be forever?" Jan asked.

"He has already moved into his new office."

"Well he better not get too comfy. There was an article this morning in the *Chronicle* about us merging with the fire department."

"You mean the fire department taking us over?" Reed asked.

"Yep."

"I don't think Rip really reads newspapers."

Reed was Jan's partner in the ambulance. He was the EMT driver. His nickname was Vincent because he had one time been partnered with a Black medic named Jules, who resembled an older Samuel Jackson, and everybody played off the *Pulp Fiction* thing. Reed had shoulder-length black and gray hair, brown hazy eyes, and his wrinkled clothes always smelled of patchouli oil. Though his legs were thin, he had a pouch from late-night munchies of chocolate chip cookies and large glasses of unpasteurized raw milk, after smoking the best homegrown buds that he grew in his basement. When growing marijuana, he had the artificial lighting down and the correct ph of the soil to provide all the necessary nutrients for growth. Reed even took horticulture classes from San Francisco State, and the teacher was one of his clients.

For Jan, Reed was the perfect partner. He never said much, and he enjoyed rolling his own cigarettes and knitting in the ambulance between calls in silence. A knitted scarf from Reed during the Christmas holidays was his way of saying that you were in good standing with him. He also loved motorcycles. Choppers. Reed wore one of those storm trooper helmets because California law said he had to wear some protection on his head, while riding his chopper.

And then there was Reed's fixation with the death of Lady Di. He had this conspiracy theory that the British and French governments had something to do with her death, had secretly planned it, and then covered it up. His many letters of inquiry concerning this conspiracy to the governments of France, England, and even the United States about what he saw as inconsistences in their investigations and reporting of Lady Di's death put him on many watch lists. Somehow that didn't seem to bother him.

When Jan and Reed went to see Rip in his office, they saw an odd-looking kid sitting near the door appearing nervous. It was Arne Dibble, and when Jan and Reed passed by, he was sweating profusely. They both thought he looked like a patient. When Jan and Reed knocked and came into Rip's office, there was an air of familiarity. They had all come up in the same paramedic class, with Reed being the oldest, and Jan being the same age as Laura, two years older than Rip.

For a second, Rip looked at Jan, and remembered how her uniform made her look so rigid, and how beautiful she looked naked at night. Yes, Rip had slept with Jan a while back when Laura had left him for the outback, and Jan had just gotten another letter from her mother. Rip had wanted to forget about Laura, and Jan wanted to feel good about herself. He longed to get back together with Jan some night, even if it was just a friend thing.

And Jan was not unattractive. Just in a uniform she looked so ordinary. Her hair was short, as she refused to let it grow long. The first time Rip slept with Jan, he was surprised how attractive her body really was. Her breasts were petite, her legs long. Jan was tall, and her light brown hair had a touch of red. Rip was amazed how her stomach was so smooth and firm, when lying next to her at night. And her eyes were definitely bedroom eyes. They swirled when she was having an orgasm. Rip felt it was such a shame that a uniform could hide such beauty all day long. But then there was her temperament that was only tamed in the quiet of the night. Unfortunately, most of those hours Jan spent sleeping.

"Well," Jan asked, "what did they offer you?"

"Offer?" Rip asked.

"Yes, offer, to be the new chief of the paramedic division. You know, they never found the last guy who had the job. Remember Hard Truths Tortellini? Just packed up one day and left. Never did understand him. So, what did they give you? New ambulances, gold shield, better staffing, pay raise? No more medic to follow?"

Rip didn't say anything.

"They didn't offer you anything, did they?" Jan asked.

"Well, it's very complicated. But the wheels are in motion," Rip explained. It never occurred to him to ask for something. "There have been a lot of discussions. Lots of ideas. Lots of good things. The mayor's chief of staff already said I have his full support."

"Did you say complicated?" Jan asked, simply amazed. "You didn't get anything, did you? There is nothing complicated about getting nothing."

"Well, that may not be true," Rip said, trying to explain himself. "The station just got a new hire today. His name is Arne. Arne Dibble. Number one in his class. That's why I called you in."

"You mean that guy who looks like a patient, sitting in front of your office? He's a medic?" Jan voiced her opinion strongly.

"Yes, he is a medic. I have his paperwork here. He may be a little rough around the edges, but we were all that way once. Let me call him in." Rip raised his voice. "Paramedic Dibble, please come in here."

Arne Dibble wiped the sweat from his brow, and came into the office looking like he was about to face a firing squad. All he needed was a last cigarette and a blindfold.

"Yes, sir."

"Paramedic Dibble, I want to introduce you to my two finest employees, Paramedic Jan Stein and EMT Reed Verne. They have agreed to be your preceptors, and they will show you how to be the best paramedic you can be."

"I never agreed," Jan said, looking Arne over. Reed backed off a bit knowing it was Mommy Fucking Dearest Day.

"Well, Paramedic Dibble," Rip said, trying to put a positive spin on everything, "you'll all be working together. They will be helping you with your skills. Now go down to the supply office and ask for Jesus, and he'll fit you with a uniform."

"Jesus, sir?"

"Yes, Jesus. Charles is his real name, but everybody calls him Jesus. It's a religious conversion kind of thing. It's something that came over him while watching a Burger King commercial on TV."

"A Burger King commercial, sir?"

"Yeah, something about the Whopper. I don't get it either."

"Sir, doesn't anybody call anyone by their real names?" Arne asked.

"Sometimes. You'll get used to it. Just go downstairs, and see Jesus. It's your first day, and he'll fix you up."

Arne shook his head and walked out of the office, looking more confused than when he came in.

"No, no." Jan started protesting after Arne had left. There was anger in her eyes. Somehow she didn't look so sexy to Rip anymore.

"What?" Rip asked.

"You're not sticking him with us. Find another preceptor."

"Jan?"

"Don't *Jan* me. First you take a job with no promises except one guy with pimples who probably can't even tie his own shoes, and now you want us to train him?"

"Well, that's a negative way of looking at it," Rip said, trying to lower the temperature gauge. "Let's look at it in a more positive light. It's preceptor pay, and I trust you enough to put him in your good hands."

"Good hands my ass. Great! Fucking great! And to think I slept with you, and now you're making me babysit this, this…"

"He's a rookie." Rip tried to calm Jan down. "Rookies need to learn the ropes. We were all rookies at one time, and look how well we all turned out."

"Rookie my ass. Next time your heart is broken, don't come to my bedroom to fix it."

"Does that mean never?" Rip asked.

"Yes never. Fucking never! Great. Fucking great," Jan said. "Have a nice day, Chief Ridley. Have a nice fucking day."

Jan slammed the door as she walked out. Reed looked at Rip, but did not say a word.

"Well that didn't turn out so badly, did it?" Rip asked Reed, who just shrugged. "It was the letter, wasn't it?"

"Yeah. The letter and other things."

"Other things?"

Reed shrugged again. "The kid is kinda raw."

"Wednesdays. I got to remember the third Wednesday of every month. The day the letter arrives from her mother. Mommy Fucking Dearest Day. I should have known."

Reed just shook his head as if to say, *You should have known.*

When Arne Dibble went to see Jesus in the supply room for his uniform, he ran into Effin.

"I am here to see Charles or Jesus. I have to get my uniform," Arne told Effin.

"It's on the form in the back room with what you need," Effin replied.

Once in the back room, it took a while for Arne to figure out what he was supposed to wear. When Effin told Jesus that the rookie was in the back room, Jesus came in with Effin to help.

"Are you Jesus?" Arne asked. "I'm Paramedic Arne Dibble."

"Yes, that's what they call me around here."

"Why does everybody call you Jesus?"

"The same reason everybody calls you the rookie," Effin said, "and the same reason everybody calls me Effin. Live with it."

"Paramedic Dibble," Jesus interrupted, because he knew where the conversation was going, "please find a uniform that fits you. There is the list on the wall for everything you need. Get a pair of boots, and some pants, and a shirt, and a jacket that fits. We will get you your other stuff later. But first, go into the men's locker room, find an empty locker, get some white tape and stick it to your locker, and write your last name on it. Then after you find a uniform that fits you, change into it and go to the yard, and report to your preceptors."

"Why tape?" Arne asked.

"Because it's easier to rip off." Effin smirked.

"Why would anyone want to take it off?"

"For the next guy."

"Give him a break," Jesus finally said to Effin. "It's his first day."

"Everybody has a first day." Effin walked away. Jesus was the only one who Effin listened to. Jesus and Rip. Jesus refused to write him up for the many complaints received from the medics, and when Rip was captain, he told Effin that he should smoke more marijuana to control his anger.

"Do you have any?" Effin had asked Rip.

"No," Rip said, "I get mine from Reed. Maybe you should be a little nicer to him and Jan."

Effin thought about it.

After Arne found a locker, he taped his last name on it, and found a uniform that fit and changed into it. There was a long mirror in the locker room. Arne felt a sense of pride walking past that mirror and looking at himself in uniform. He did like a sense of order. If only he could get through the day, he thought to himself. But as he went outside in the yard, he walked up to Jan and Reed, and that sense of order did not last very long.

"Okay, Rookie, this is your first lecture," Jan told him.

"Lecture?"

"Yes, lecture."

After hearing Jan's lectures before, Reed was all smiles. Everybody in the yard stopped what they were doing. It was dress down Arne day.

"Listen up, Rookie. Let's get something straight," Jan said to Arne, pointing her finger. "This is my ambulance. This is Reed's ambulance. You don't have an ambulance. You are a guest. Unwelcomed, but still a guest. This is the Evans Street

Station, ground zero, and you are sort of like an alien observer. Did you believe in flying saucers?"

"I don't know."

"Well I do. And this one has just landed. And the Evans Street Station is a strange and mysterious place, and sometimes it consumes your body and your soul and changes how you see the world. And sometimes not for the better. Sometimes you are no longer in the land of the living. Are you following me?"

"No," Arne said.

"Good. Now our job here is to pick up these aliens that some people call homeless, and take them to hospitals, where they try to put them back into human form. Now I'm not saying they are all going to be aliens, but this is San Francisco, so you will treat a lot of them. Do you believe in aliens, Rookie?"

"I think so."

"Doesn't matter, Rookie, 'cause after this job, you will. And do you know what, Rookie?"

"What," Arne said, looking at the ground knowing he was being dressed down.

"No matter how many times we transport these aliens, sometimes they still don't come back in human form. That means we have to pick them up all over again. That's the hardest part of the job, Rookie. Taking the same patient to the same hospital with the same problems, and they never get better. All the bad shit that they have been doing has possessed their body and their soul, and they are no longer in human form. Sort of like..."

"*Invasion of the Body Snatchers*," Reed chimed in.

"Thank you," Jan acknowledged Reed. "But we try, Rookie, we try. Do you understand?"

"I think so. I'll try."

"Good again. Trying is good. But let me put it in better terms. Even though they are aliens, treat them like human beings. 'Cause in your worst moment, theirs is usually a lot worse. Do you get it, Rookie?"

"I think so."

"Good. Your job today is to observe and obey. If I ask you to get a gurney, then you get it. If I ask you to start an IV, then you start it. You do know how to start an IV, right?"

"I was first in my class."

"That means nothing here. You deserve what you get by the medic you are. Your job is to become more human instead of starting to resent the people you have been sent here to help. It happens, Rookie. Is that clear enough?"

"I think so."

"Good."

"What if I have any questions?" Arne asked.

"Questions? Questions like what?" Jan snapped back at him as if saying, *I'll ask the questions.*

"What do you want me to do first?"

"Talk to Effin. He's only half alien. He'll tell you what to do. How to stock my ambulance. How to stay out of my way. Oh, and lecture number two: Don't fuck up my ambulance when you stock it. Can you do that?"

"I think so."

"Good. Now go find Effin."

Arne went to see Effin, who was standing in back with the rest of the crowd during dress down Arne day.

"You had to do the alien lecture, didn't you?" Reed asked Jan.

"Don't start with me today."

Reed shook his head. "He had to come on Mommy Fucking Dearest Day," he said under his breath.

"What was that?" Jan asked, annoyed.

Reed walked away smiling.

Arne walked up to Effin. "Is she like this all the time?"

"Mostly, but especially the third Wednesday of every month. You'll learn the pattern."

"Gee, thanks."

"Don't mention it. I guess you found the chief's office, Rookie."

"How do I stop them from calling me Rookie?"

"You file a grievance."

"Will that stop them?"

"No, they will only do it more because they know it bothers you. I've filed lots of grievances. Now my boss Jesus tells me I can only file one grievance a week. I got to pick my moments."

"Has it helped?" Arne asked.

"What?"

"The grievances."

"No. I still hate the medics, and they still call me Effin. Did Jan call me a half alien?"

"Yes."

"Well fuck Jan, and fuck her lectures, and fuck her ambulance," Effin said, louder than he should have. "I mean effin Jan, and her effin ambulance, and her effin lectures."

"So that's how you got your name?"

"Yeah, they were going to write me up for saying fuckin' medics all the time so I changed it to effin. Effin medics, effin ambulances, effin Jan, especially effin Jan. Can't find effin in the dictionary."

"Will you help me restock her ambulance?" Arne asked. He looked a little beat down and desperate, even for Effin.

"Sure. Tough day, eh?" Effin said. Usually it was him being picked on. "But I'll help you. See, I'm not that bad. People say I'm angry, and maybe I am. But effin Jan ain't going to tell me how to stock her effin ambulance."

"So, you are angry?"

"Well, maybe just a bit."

While Arne and Effin were stocking Jan's ambulance, RC Suzy Pang drove up to the pumps, and got out to fill up her RC vehicle. The RC was the rescue captain of the day, which meant she was the supervisor of the medics in the field. RC Pang was Chinese, petite but sturdy, had short black hair, oval eyes, and was known for her great derriere, and she softly— though not with the look of an angel—glanced over at Arne.

"See her?" Effin nudged Arne. "That's RC Suzy Pang. They call her Grasshopper. Grasshopper Pang. But she is really a praying mantis."

"A praying mantis? Why?"

"Because she bites men's heads off after having sex with them. Have you ever had sex, Rookie?"

"I have a girlfriend."

"That's not what I asked."

"We are saving ourselves for marriage."

"So, you're a virgin?"

"Like I said, we are saving ourselves."

"What if you never get married? Ever think of that?" Effin asked. "Heavy petty?"

"Sometimes."

"What's her name?"

"Ashley," Arne said. His mind started to drift how beautiful she was.

"Sounds rich to me. When Jesus was Charlie," Effin began, taking Arne's mind away from Ashley, "he used to meet a lot of girls, and sometimes he would take me along with him. But now Jesus is Jesus, and he ain't a lot of fun. But don't let Grasshopper Pang know that you're a virgin. She preys on rookies like you. Sooner or later, before you know it, she'll be biting your head off, too."

"I have made a commitment."

"Yeah, so have a lot of others. Nobody gets away from Grasshopper Pang."

While her vehicle was filling up, RC Suzy Pang walked over to Arne. "So, you're the rookie? I'm Captain Pang, or Suzy. Welcome to the Evans Street Station. Is everybody treating you right?"

"I'm Arne Dibble. Sure. I guess so."

"I see you are working with Paramedic Stein. Did you get the alien lecture?"

"Yeah."

"Don't worry about it," RC Pang said, trying to reassure Arne, "you'll get used to it, and you'll get used to your nickname too. Everybody goes through it. But why don't I just call you Paramedic Dibble or maybe Arne. I think that's a lot better too. If you need anything, let me know. We have a ride along soon."

"A ride along?"

"Yes, a ride along. It's part of your training. You will see how the RCs can support the crews during the course of a working day. I'm looking forward to it. But take care, Paramedic Dibble, and don't let them get to you. And don't make yourself a stranger either."

As RC Suzy Pang walked back to her vehicle, Effin couldn't help watching Arne watch her walk away. And RC Pang was worth checking out, especially from behind. Inadvertently, over dinner at the station house, she let it be known that the movie *Jade* was one of her favorites. And she did look a little like an Asian Linda Fiorentino. Because of her adventurous nature, and her quick rise to the top—a captain in two years— it was said, with a little sarcasm, that RC Suzy Pang had backed her way into getting her promotions.

"Grasshopper," Effin whispered to Arne, as they watched her from behind, "Grasshopper."

CHAPTER 4

When Rip received the news from Hogwash that he was the new chief of the paramedic division, he went through the locker of the last paramedic chief, "Hard Truths" Tortellini, and found his gold shield. Temporary chiefs did not get gold shields, but Rip knew that the old chief didn't want any memories, and certainly would not have cared. It was easy to find. Wearing his Class A uniform and pinning on the gold shield, Rip looked admiringly at himself in the mirror of his bathroom, then fixed his hair Beach Boys surfer-style. Rip then drove out to the old neighborhood on Delmar Street near Ashbury Market, to the old Victorian where he was raised. The house had changed since Rip lived there with his parents. After their divorce, the house was sold and renovated by the new owners. Rip hardly recognized it.

When he was a kid, Rip's parents were dysfunctional. They certainly were no Ozzie and Harriet. He had no brothers or sisters, and there was very little discipline placed upon him. They had bought the house when the neighborhood was run down, and the prices were low. But then the hippies left along with the wannabes, and the drug addicts and homeless. When the neighborhood started to improve, housing prices started to rise, and people with money started moving in and fixing up the old Victorians. But the Ridley house never changed. There were very few curtains, and the roof leaked into the attic. Weeds took over the lawn, and the paint was peeling off the facade. There was a weathered beaten rowboat in the side yard, and a family of raccoons that lived underneath the house. The

Ridley family was known in the neighborhood as the Addams Family. Neighbors avoided them, and the Ridleys preferred it that way.

But on that day, when Rip walked into Ashbury Market wearing his Class A uniform and his gold shield, everybody recognized him. There had even been a newspaper article in the *Chronicle* about his promotion. Some of the old timers nodded their heads in acknowledgement. There were little whispers behind him as he walked around the store. Rip thought those whispers were about him. Rip was happy that day because he walked into Ashbury Market and acted like it was the most natural thing in the world for him to be in uniform, and do some shopping. It wasn't like he needed anything. Rip just wanted to be seen.

From the top shelf, Rip put a bottle of red wine in his basket. He also got some candles. He passed the meat and frozen food section. He picked up a can of tomato sauce and some dry pasta. In the cheese section, Rip got a container of shredded imported Parmesan. He went to the vegetables and got a head of romaine lettuce. He picked up an overpriced bottle of olive oil.

When Rip was finished shopping, Walter himself, the owner, rang him up on the register. It was certainly not like the old days, when Ashbury Market was where his dad was sometimes seen going through the garbage dumpster. "Just because," his dad would say, "a tomato doesn't look good enough to sell, doesn't mean you can't eat it," and Rip was once kicked out for shoplifting cigarettes. But on that day, he was no longer the kid with the long hair and the crazy parents, living in their broken-down house, with a broken-down boat in the yard, and with a family of raccoons living underneath the house. Today he was Chief Rip Ridley of the paramedic division.

As Rip was growing up, his parents had their own set of issues, most obvious being they should have never been together. Rip's dad was a French high school teacher who drove a twenty-year-old Audi. He was a small man who wore a sweater over a sweater when it was foggy and a scarf and a cap.

Whether it was foggy or not, he always wore the cap over his Wavey Gravey white hair. He had a love for wine ordinaire, Gitanes cigarettes, the movies of Jerry Lewis, and had a tendency to throw childish tantrums.

Rip's mother was of English descent, took the Muni bus for transportation, and taught English literature in a private middle school. She had aristocratic facial features with high cheekbones, and a pale complexion. She was tall, and always dressed in black with a scarf on her head. There were days when riding the Muni that fellow passengers had mistaken her for a nun, and offered her their seats when the bus was too crowded, as she always looked to be in mourning. Needless to say, when Rip's parents were married, they slept in different rooms and barely spoke to one another. After their divorce, while Rip was in high school, she became a quilter and a lesbian.

At an early age, Rip started hearing voices. They weren't demonic or boogiemen-underneath-the-bed or in-the-closet voices, but voices that were trying to ask the questions he was subconsciously asking himself. For Rip, as the Ridley family had no interaction, it was almost therapeutic.

Duderonomy was Rip's name for these voices that popped inside his head. Whenever hearing these voices, he would scream out, "Duderonomy," to the point in school where it became his nickname because he said it all the time. Nobody knew what it meant, and it certainly wasn't biblical, but when Rip said it, it was funny. In a survival sort of way, the voices in his head helped Rip in school, because instead of being beaten up, he just said the crazy things that came into his head, and made the bullies laugh. There was no filter. Where had these voices come from? Even Rip didn't know. Later, when Rip found the reefer, the voices started to visualize themselves when Rip was high.

Naturally popping off in school, and saying whatever came into his head, complaints came in from his teachers. They claimed that Rip was a disruption in class, had the habit of going from one thought to another in mid-sentence, of never finishing a task or a book assignment, and saying whatever he was thinking at the time. Rip was ADHD before they had the good drugs for it. It drove his teachers crazy, always complaining that Rip was unable to comprehend a thought or an idea for any definite period of time.

After so many of these complaints from the teachers, usually in letter form, Rip's mother finally brought him to a doctor, who hooked Rip's brain up to electrodes from a machine that made buzzing noises and looked to Rip as if it came from a 1950s sci-fi movie. According to the doctor's analysis, the strip of Rip's brain patterns showed bursts of electrical activity that could not be explained. After questioning his mother on Rip's home life, and questioning Rip on the voices that he was hearing in his head, the doctor came to the conclusion that maybe the voices came from the deprivation of any social interaction at home. "Subconscious manifestations," he called them, scaring the hell out of Rip's mother. The doctor went on to conclude that the voices may stop if there was more of a social family life. There were more tests, with more unexplained brain activity, and it was recommended to Rip's mother that she seek help from a medical specialist to examine her son's abnormal coping behavior.

But Rip's dad refused, throwing a tantrum and calling it nonsense. "Stupid American doctors," he called them. "And what is normal in American life anyway?" Since Rip's parents did not agree on anything, nothing was ever done. Rip never went back to the doctors, and the teachers' complaints of Rip's behavior were ignored, and the voices remained.

When Rip received the call from Hogwash that he was promoted to chief of the paramedic division, he had four things on his mind: seeing his old neighborhood while showing off his Class A uniform, surfing, getting a burrito, and smoking a good joint. He usually went to Reed for his pot, but after receiving the call to be chief, he wanted to keep everything on the down low.

After visiting the old neighborhood, Rip went to the parking lot at Fort Point in the Presidio so he could surf beneath the Golden Gate Bridge. "It was a fort," Rip liked to say, "where a shot was never fired in anger." The Pride of the Pacific, until it fell into disarray. He changed into his wetsuit in the parking lot, and grabbed his surfboard to catch a wave or two. Besides the surfing, Rip liked Fort Point because *Vertigo* was shot there, and Kim Novak's character jumped into the bay near Fort Point, only to be saved by Jimmy Stewart. Rip always wanted to play the role of the hero. He thought it fit him well. Now Rip was surfing in the same waters.

After surfing, Rip unzipped his wetsuit and changed, this time into his Bahama Mama shirt and khaki shorts and old sandals, and hung out smoking a joint with some of the locals and surfer bums. He thought about going to the Officer's Club in the Presidio—which was now open to the public—and having a drink, but it wasn't that kind of day. In the past on special occasions he would get dressed up with Laura, and they would go to the Cliff House and drink martinis and eat oysters. Then they would go for a barefoot walk on the beach, and then, of course, a night of passionate lovemaking. Once home, they wouldn't even wait to take off their clothes. It was those nights that Rip missed the most. But with Laura gone, this ride he would have to take alone.

After Rip put his yellow surfboard on the top of his light green Chevy Caprice wagon, and popped in a cassette of the greatest hits of the Beach Boys, he did what he had promised he would never do again: He went to a convenience store and bought a pack of Marlboro menthol filtered cigarettes, and smoked a few. They were Laura's favorite. She was a chain smoker. He wondered if she had quit smoking, like she had quit meat and fish and him.

"Well I'm smoking tonight," Rip proclaimed, "I'm smoking."

Rip then drove through the Presidio, down Geary Boulevard to the Great Highway. He rolled down the windows, found the remnants of a joint in the ashtray, and lit it up. The Great Highway! Civilization to the left, and the Pacific Ocean to the right. All the windows were down, and the ocean breeze carried the smoke from the joint into…the cosmic universe where all the planets were aligned that day. For Rip, it just couldn't have been better.

And then, with a puff, Duderonomy showed up. Duderonomy sat on his shoulder trying to get some of that secondhand smoke from Rip's joint.

In Rip's mind, Duderonomy started out as that hippie surfing dude he always wanted to be, no bigger than Tom Thumb who looked like a smarter Jeff Spicoli in *Fast Times at Ridgemont High*, who actually read the books. As Rip got older, his world expanded, and his thought patterns did too. It was only natural that Duderonomy would follow that path, and be a touch more sophisticated. Like Rip, he even developed a grooming disorder.

"Very good day, Bwana. Very good day," Duderonomy said, whispering in his ear. Duderonomy was wearing a Hawaiian shirt, shorts, and sandals. Bwana was Duderonomy's nickname for Rip.

"Very good indeed," Rip said.

"You want it, don't you? This chief thing, Bwana," Duderonomy said, as Rip was driving down the Great Highway. "Come on, say it."

"No, no."

"You know you want to be chief. It's a big deal, right?"

"I just accept what comes along."

"Yeah. Some big deal. You know you always wanted to be more successful than your dad. To show him you went a little further than he did in life," Duderonomy said, analyzing.

"That's not true."

"Come on, Bwana."

"Okay, I'll give you that."

"And?"

"Okay, Laura. To show her that she never should have left me for him."

"Tarzan?"

"Yes, Tarzan. But I can do a lot of good for the department."

"Yeah, maybe," Duderonomy said. "But remember the last chief. He wrote his resignation on a bar napkin. It said, *I quit.* And then he signed and dated it, and that was all he wrote."

"This time it's going to be different," Rip said, trying to explain. "How hard can it be? I have an office on the second floor with my own bathroom. You know how hard it is to have your own bathroom. If anything, I thought you would be on my side. I'm the new chief of the paramedic division."

"So, the bathroom is the big perk."

"It's important. And I got changes in mind," Rip said reassuringly.

"Changes?"

"Yes, changes. The wheels are in motion."

"Wheels?"

Rip finished his joint, and threw the roach out the window. "Yes, the wheels are in motion. I'm on a roll today, and I don't need your doubts or negativity. I'm on a pretty good high."

"Fair enough. To be continued," Duderonomy said, and then like the puff of smoke from Rip's joint, disappeared.

As darkness began to fall, and the fog started to roll in from the ocean, and the sun started to drop into the horizon of the deep blue sea, like a coin in an old Wall-O-Matic jukebox, Rip went to Mission Street and got himself a burrito.

"Black bean, rice, spinach tortilla, extra guacamole, extra salsa, extra hot sauce," he ordered.

All the workers at the Burrito Supremo knew Rip. Lalo was behind the counter, and took Rip's order. He handled the money for the owner, and sold dope on the side. There was a sticker on the menu board over the counter that said, NO ILLEGALS, NO BURRITOS – SORRY AMERICA.

"What's up, Rip?" Lalo asked.

"You think you can add one to my order?"

"Sure thing. You will like this stuff, *amigo*. I promise."

"I know I will."

Lalo handed over the bag with the burrito and the joint, and Rip handed over the cash.

Burrito Supremo was a cash-only operation.

"Where you off to tonight?" Lalo asked.

"Evans Street Station."

"Oh yes," Lalo said, remembering the article in the newspaper. It was in the Spanish newspapers too. "Big deal for a local boy."

"Yeah it is," Rip said. "Catch you later."

"I know you will."

Driving, Rip wanted to see the Evans Street Station at night. And the Evans Street Station may have just been an old broken-down building, with overgrown grass in front, and dim lights in the yard that reflected off the white tops of the dated ambulances fleet, with the mist of fog coming down, but now Rip was the chief of the paramedic division, and somehow it looked a little different to him. It didn't look so bad. A beacon of hope in Rip's stagnant career. Well, maybe.

But what stood out that night around the Evans Street Station wasn't the seedier side of Hunters Point where the station was located...not the drug addicts or the drug dealers or the gangs...not even the homeless encampment of Camp Willie with its broken-down vans and cars that filled the neighborhood. What stood out that night was Rip Ridley driving in his light green Chevy Caprice wagon with the simulated woodgrain exterior trim, all the windows open, and the yellow surfboard strapped on top, driving around Hunters Point while he finished off the joint that he had gotten from Lalo. The Beach Boys' song "I Get Around" blared out from the cassette player in the car. Hell, even the drug dealers on the corners and the drug addicts hanging out in the shadows stopped what they were doing to watch him go by. When Rip passed the Evans Street Station, he hit the horn, banged the outside of the car door with his free hand, then went around the block and did it again.

Rip then drove down Cargo Way, past the Bay Railroad, a short-line railroad that operated out of the Port of San Francisco, with its tracks a few blocks from the station. There was a goat pen in the back that the railroad raised to make ends meet for clear-cutting large areas of weeds and grass. Rip used to come by sometimes and feed the goats when he made the acquaintance of Paco, the only burrito-eating goat he had ever seen. When his wagon pulled up, Paco came right up to the fence, and Rip got out with his burrito. As he was eating it, Rip took little pieces of the burrito and fed it to him. Duderonomy showed back up on his shoulder.

"Hogwash," Duderonomy whispered in Rip's ear.

"Hogwash?" Rip asked.

"Yeah, Chief of Staff Chip Hogwash. His enemies call him the mayor's henchman, and he's got a lot of them."

"Nicknames?"

"No, enemies."

"How do you know this?" Rip asked. Even Paco was listening.

"You know all those newspapers you leave on your desk? Well I actually read them. There are more than just comics. What else can a figment of your imagination do? I can't have sex. I can only live through you. The most I can hope for is residual effect from you smoking one of your joints."

"What about this Hogwash?" Rip asked.

"He's the mayor's enforcer, one of the most powerful people in city government who avoids the limelight. He is the Shadow Master, the Heartless Henchman. He's an obstacle kind of guy. I'm just saying that he may be using you. Remember, it wasn't long ago when you were making training films."

"Hey, they were quite popular, I want you to know."

"Be it as it may, Bwana, but people like Hogwash don't have time to watch films on medical procedures. I think that being chief may be more difficult than what you expect. You are now in his political arena."

"Are you sure we're talking about the same person? He just told me to stay out of his way."

"They all say that, until they need something done. Someone as powerful as Hogwash always has an agenda. It could be this merger they're talking about. Maybe he only hired you to babysit, until it goes through. I'm just saying, Bwana, be aware.

And always remember that he can destroy you," Duderonomy warned.

"Why would he do that?"

"Because he can. That's the way these people roll, Bwana."

"And how do I survive this Shadow Master?" Rip asked. Even Paco looked up waiting for Duderonomy's answer.

"You ride the harmonic waves of instinct. It's a sensory kind of existence," Duderonomy said, walking back and forth on Rip's shoulder, pointing his finger in the air. "People like Hogwash foster fights to justify their existence. All I am saying is don't be another casualty waiting to happen. Don't be the fall guy."

"Are you saying that this Hogwash would hire me, just to fire me, so he can justify his existence?"

"Maybe."

"But he just hired me," Rip tried to explain.

"Well who knows? But he had to hire you for a reason. What better one could it be than to destroy you? I think we need to be one step ahead of this Shadow Master. Never forget that crisis can be the path to peace and harmony if problems are properly engaged. We need to figure this one out."

"We?" Rip asked. "Maybe he hired me for my skills. And maybe I can figure things out for myself."

"Really?" Duderonomy asked. "Remember Laura? You were the last one to figure out that she was going to leave you. Even I knew."

"I was blinded by love," Rip said, finishing his burrito with Paco, then patting him on the head. "And who else knew that Laura was going to leave me?"

"Everybody knew, Bwana."

"Everybody?" Rip asked.

"Afraid so, Bwana... Afraid so."

Even Paco nodded.

CHAPTER 5

Ambulance 54 was Jan and Reed's favorite in the fleet. The heater worked, the seats were reasonably comfortable, the transmission didn't grind, and when Reed stepped on the brakes, the ambulance came to a stop. Everybody knew that Ambulance 54 was their ambulance, and most crews knew, if they ever took it out, it better come back the same way. Nothing was to be left out of place.

But now there was something in Ambulance 54 that was out of place. Reed knew it, though it wasn't in his nature to say anything. But Jan knew it too. And it wasn't in her nature to be quiet about it. Her feelings were bound to come out. It all pointed to the physical presence of Arne being there.

And usually it was the little things that bothered Jan about working with Arne, like not having enough backup batteries for the defibrillator, or not turning in the narcotics at the end of the shift, or not having the proper count. Then there was Arne and Effin not stocking the ambulance with the medical supplies the way Jan wanted it stocked. It would piss Jan off when her ambulance was not stocked to her standards, and she would have to go through it, just to make sure everything was the way she wanted it, before taking it out. Depending on Jan's mood, it could be a long day for Arne if there was something he should have known, but didn't do.

But after a week of working together, what bothered Jan the most about Arne was the look of fear he had on his face when he started his shift. Usually rookies work through it, but with

Arne, it didn't go away. For Arne it was the fear of the unknown, that maybe the next call would be something he couldn't handle, and he would look bad in front of his peers. Jan saw right through him, and she had had enough. She just couldn't hold back her feelings anymore.

On that day, they were posted in the Sunset District on Judah and 34th near the N line. Jan was in the passenger seat, Reed in the driver's seat, and Arne was in the rear jump seat attached to the steel wall behind the driver's seat, facing the back of the ambulance.

"Okay, Rookie, spit it out," Jan said, turning around in her seat to speak to Arne.

"What?" Arne whimpered.

"Spit it out. How did you ever get hired for this job? And don't give me that bullshit about being first in your class."

Arne hemmed and hawed, but then blurted it out. "My father is a friend of the mayor. He's in construction."

"I knew it," Jan said triumphantly, "Dibble Construction. Is that your father in those commercials? The guy who looks like Bud White in *LA Confidential*? What happened to you?"

Arne nodded his head, yes.

"Does your mother look like Kim Basinger too?" Jan asked.

Arne nodded again.

"Come on, Rookie. Why a medic? Why don't you go work for your father?"

"My father was a boxer growing up in the Sunset, and thought I grew up too privileged. He thought if I became a medic, it would toughen me up a bit."

"Toughen you up for what?"

"To work for the family business."

"So, you never lived up to your family's expectations?"

"No," said Arne, lowering his head.

"Well at least we have something in common. Do they ever write you letters how disappointed they are in you?"

"No."

"They will," Jan said. "They will."

As the day went on, Jan calmed down a bit and even almost took pity on Arne, and he got his chance to evaluate a patient on Clement Street, near the Tee Off. It was a seventy-year-old Russian named Yuri Trosky. To the medics he was a regular known as "the Russian" because of his thick Russian accent, his love for vodka, and his numerous transports because of his drunkenness.

But what Arne didn't know—and what Jan and Reed weren't about to tell him—was when treating Yuri, he didn't like to go to hospitals. They reminded him of the sanitariums in his Mother Russia. Places where fellow Russians went to dry out or even die if you found yourself in displeasure with the government. Getting Yuri in the ambulance to the hospital was such a struggle that most medics would just give him an IV, have him sign the *Against Medical Advice* on the back of the Patient Care Report, and drive him back to his apartment, and then move on. Yuri would try to get the medics to stop by the liquor store before driving him home, and with his booming voice would sing them Red Army patriotic songs, if they did. Yuri was very animated singing these songs from his Cold War past, sticking out his chest and swinging his right fist and his forearm back and forth as he sang. Some days, when he really had it going, he would show them his goosestep. Most of the medics took him up on it. It broke up the monotony of slow days.

But not knowing his history, once assessing the patient, Arne tried his best to coax Yuri into the ambulance.

"Sir, you are making this extremely difficult for me to treat you." Arne tried talking to Yuri. "You are drunk, and according to your statements you drink every day. I palpated your liver, and it is swollen. Sir, you need to go to the hospital."

"I came to America to do what I want. Land of the free. I no die," Yuri proclaimed. "In Russia nobody does what they want. Everybody is weak. They go to sanitariums and never come back. But America is strong, and I am strong too."

"Sir, unfortunately your liver doesn't feel that way," Arne pleaded.

As Arne tried to convince Yuri to get into the ambulance, an RC vehicle pulled up to the scene. It was RC Jules Diamond. Jules had a faint resemblance to Samuel Jackson with a few pounds added on. Before Jules was an RC, he worked as a medic on the ambulance with Reed, who everybody started calling Vincent. It was a *Pulp Fiction* kind of thing. Watching Arne, RC Jules Diamond walked up to Jan and Reed, who were near the ambulance waiting for Arne to finish his assessment.

"So, this is the rookie, eh?" he asked.

"Seems that way," Jan remarked sarcastically. "We're taking bets if the rookie is able to convince the Russian to get in the ambulance and go to the hospital, or if the Russian goes to the nearest liquor store instead."

"Who has the rookie?" Jules asked.

"We both have the Russian."

Jules shook his head and walked up to Arne.

"Okay, Rookie, twenty dollars," Jules said to him.

"Sir?"

"I'll bet you twenty bucks I can convince Yuri here to get into the ambulance, and go to the hospital."

"But he doesn't want to go."

"Twenty bucks. Or do you want to look bad in front of your preceptors? Yes or no?" Jules asked.

"I guess so," Arne replied rather sheepishly.

"Good," Jules said, and then he turned his attention to Yuri. "Okay, my Russian friend, let me ask you a question. Are you a tough guy?"

"Yes, like Gary Cooper."

"Bodybuilder?"

"When I was younger."

"Red Army?"

"A colonel."

"Okay, I'll make you a deal. I'll arm-wrestle you in the back of the ambulance. If you win, you don't have to go to the hospital, and we will give you a ride to the nearest liquor store and then home. But if I win, you go to the hospital."

"Arm-wrestle?" Yuri asked. He looked interested. Yuri nodded yes, and pounded his chest with his fist.

"Sir, I have a problem with this," Arne said, getting nervous.

"Listen Rookie, I'm the RC here, and that makes me your chain of command. And as your chain of command, what I say goes. Now, me and my Russian friend here are going to arm-wrestle. Do you have any issues with this?"

"No, sir."

"Good. Now you are going to listen to me, Rookie, because unlike Jan, I don't repeat my lectures. Your job here is to take Yuri to the hospital. If he doesn't go to the hospital then something bad may happen to him. And if you fail to convince him to go to the hospital then something bad may happen to you. I don't mean health wise—I mean paper wise. Filling out forms. *Inattention to Duty* and all that other good shit. Now I don't make the rules, Rookie, and I know the EMS agency are a bunch of assholes, but assholes or not, he has got to go. And I don't need any complications. I am what you call an easy-going RC who likes his days nice and uncomplicated. Which means I don't like filling out forms. Do you get that, Rookie?"

"I think so, sir."

"Good."

RC Diamond turned to Yuri.

"Okay, these are the rules. If you agree, we will arm-wrestle. It will be a tournament of strength, just like in the Cold War. Good versus evil. If you win you don't have to go to the hospital, and we will drive you to the liquor store and then home. If I win, you're going to the hospital. Understand?"

"Am I the good or the evil?" Yuri asked.

"Whatever you want."

"I be the good," Yuri said, sticking out his chest.

"Good enough. Let's do it."

"Okay, Shaft. Let's do it."

"Shaft?"

"Intimidation."

"Fair enough," Jules said. He had certainly been called worse.

Jules and Yuri shook hands, went into the back of the ambulance, and a space was set up for the match. They kneeled across from each other with their elbows elevated on the large metal med box, and their right hands clenched together in what seemed like a Cold War death match. Jan, Reed, and Arne watched.

"Okay, Rookie, say it. On your mark, get set, go," Jules told him.

"Sir, I don't think…"

"Come on, say it, Rookie."

"On your mark, get set, go."

The renewal of the Cold War was on.

Yuri began strong, but the years of abuse on his liver had taken a toll on his overall agility. His muscles had pretty much turned into mush. Jules' arm hardly moved. Then the Russian started sweating from his forehead and on his arms and the palms of his hands. And they were dirty liver sweats. The proud Red Army cadet that Yuri once was, was now gone. At the most he looked like a border guard, waiting for his pension. As for Jules, he didn't like the sweating of the Russian's palms against his hands. Which was why he had become an RC instead of staying on an ambulance. Jules didn't really care much for patient contact. He liked to manage from a distance. When the Russian's sweat started to run down his face, Jules already had enough, and with one big push, he forced Yuri's hand toward him and then down. The Russian looked exhausted. The Cold War had officially ended.

"Okay, Yuri," Jules said, getting a handful of sanitary wipes and cleaning his hands, "you're gone. And Rookie, that will be twenty bucks. He's all yours. And when you speak of me, speak of me kindly. Good luck, Rookie."

"Gee…thanks, sir," Arne said, not too enthusiastically though. For Arne it was another day, and another humiliation. He reluctantly took out his wallet and handed over twenty dollars to Jules. Yuri sat back in the ambulance while Arne put his wallet back into his pocket, minus the twenty dollars, started an IV on Yuri, and got him ready for transport.

When the ambulance left, RC Suzy Pang drove up to Jules in her RC vehicle. He was just about to leave when she got out of her vehicle and walked over to him.

"RC Pang. Did you come to see me or maybe observe how our new employee is doing?" Jules asked.

"Little bit of both. Was it the Russian?"

"Yep."

"You didn't do the arm-wrestling thing, did you?"

"Hey, he had to get into the ambulance."

"How much did you take from Arne?"

"Just twenty. I let him off easy."

"It's nice to know you are doing your job, RC Diamond."

"Every little bit counts. But I have been meaning to ask you a question." Jules' expression looked like he really did have a question he wanted to ask RC Pang. His lips started to move, and then he stopped.

"Come on, RC Diamond. Out with it."

RC Pang and Jules were good friends. They both knew the rules of making their job easier. It even surprised Jules that they hadn't slept together. But there was nothing for RC Suzy Pang to gain and Jules knew it, and the opportunity for sex just never presented itself.

"Okay," Jules started in, "what I don't get, RC Pang, is that the head of the Chinatown Business Association is a relative of yours. They supported the mayor. Word around the campfire is that your family has even done business with the mayor's people. Why is it that you are not Chief Pang of the paramedic division? Come on, Chief Rip Ridley? Even the Black Firefighters Union didn't know who he was, along with the rest of the players at city hall. He wasn't even on their radar."

"I'm sure the mayor has his reasons," RC Pang said with confidence in her voice, "and my father is just doing some business deals with some of the mayor's friends. That's all."

"Does it have anything to do with the mayor's plans for new condos along the Ferry Building? Maybe knocking down some of the old hotels and other low-cost housing. Maybe even moving out some of the elderly. Hence the Gray Beavers."

"I wouldn't go that far. But yes, they have been showing up at the mayor's press conference showing their... Well, their gray beavers. They don't shave, you know."

"Then why Rip?" Jules asked, a little bewildered.

"Because, RC Diamond, Rip is harmless. Chip Hogwash saw him one time at some EMS outing, and thought he would be the perfect guy. And when the new fiscal year begins there may not be enough money for the paramedic division to go solo."

"So, we'll be under the fire department's umbrella."

"Well that's the word out there. Everybody thought that someone like Chief Ridley couldn't do any harm, so why not make him chief?"

"And his future?"

"He'll be compensated."

"Does he know?"

"Everybody who wants to know, knows."

"Still, it will be hard for him to give it up. He is a little vain."

"It always is," RC Pang answered like a player. "City hall thinks after the merger that Planning and Development would be a good job for him. All he has to do is stay out of the way, and do what he's told. His office would have a nice view of the ocean. What more would he need?"

"Well, RC Pang, if this merger does happen, please don't forget me when you become chief of EMS or some other department. And I don't want any PIO job either. Airport chief would be nice. I mean how many Black airport chiefs have we ever had?"

"The press would probably say not enough. But when the time comes, I am sure they will keep you in mind."

"They, huh? RC Pang, you have become a player in your own right. I saw your name on the schedule to do a ride along with the rookie."

"Just doing my job."

"He'll never be the same, you know that."

"They never are, RC Diamond, they never are. He'll have to learn some time."

"Just be gentle."

"I always am, but unlike you and the rest of the department, I see a bright future for Arne Dibble. The captain's test should be coming out next year, and he was first in his class."

"Don't tell me," Jules said. "His father does business with your father who does business with the mayor's office, and they want to build those condos. I think I get it."

"I think you do, RC Diamond. I think you do. Have a good day."

RC Pang went back to her vehicle.

"Don't forget me," Jules yelled as she got into her RC vehicle and started it up. "Remember, diversity is the keystone to any successful department."

RC Pang waved as she drove away.

"Please don't forget me," Jules said, halfheartedly waving. "Please?"

RC Pang never looked back.

CHAPTER 6

Before Jesus was Jesus, he was known as Charlie Wilson, a bodybuilder who lifted weights in Golden Gate Park. He was tall, Black, well-built and looked a little like Don Cheadle with those *Boogie Nights* eyes, when nobody would give him a chance lending him money when he tried to open up his stereo shop. When Jesus was Charlie, he liked to oil his well-built, shaved upper body whenever working out in the park, so his shirtless muscular skin would glisten in the sun, and everybody could see him. When girls passed by he would blow them kisses. Sometimes they blew back.

From one of his bodybuilder friends, Charlie got a job with the city in the maintenance department. He found it to be boring, and since everyone was Irish, he didn't have any friends. When an opening came up at the Evans Street Station for the position of supply clerk for less money, he applied. At the interview process, when asked why he would take a job for less money, he told the panel that he wanted to work, and did not enjoy standing around all day. He got the job.

And even if working in supply was a thankless job with lots of paperwork, Charlie worked hard. His boss was George Miller, who everybody called Henry because of his resemblance to Henry Orbit, the superintendent in *The Jetsons*. George wore a cap with white hair sticking out of both sides of his head, and had a big white mustache. He always had a tool belt around his waist filled with tools, though he rarely used them.

But unfortunately, Henry liked to drink a little too much on the job. Empty airport bottles of booze were found throughout the warehouse. But Charlie covered for him, was willing to put in overtime, had no complaints, made sure orders came in and out on time, and when his boss was finally forced to retired because of his drinking, Charlie Wilson was offered the job as head supervisor of supply. He was doing the job anyway, so administration thought why not promote him, since they had so many problems with the other guy before.

Being promoted was the first time that Charlie was ever appreciated for anything he had ever done in his life. With the demands of his job, he quit going to the park and lifting weights and blowing kisses to the girls. Because of the promotion, he was also able to rent a nicer room in a Tenderloin hotel that was closer to the bus line, and had a lot of older longtime tenants, so it didn't have that transient feel to it. Charlie was even in good terms with the manager who worked for Orkin during the day, which meant he would take home pesticides so the hotel didn't have any major cockroach or rodent problems.

But one night, Charlie was eating his favorite fast food, a Whopper with fries and a Diet Coke smothered with those little packages of ketchup, and watching *Family Feud* with Richard Dawson hosting. When watching *Family Feud* Charlie always rooted for the Black family, and he loved eating fast food. It was during a commercial for Burger King that Charlie felt the presence of God come over him, like the first time he had smelled fast food cooking in his local Burger King. Charlie felt that the presence of God was around and within him. While God's presence came over him, the TV screen became a blinding light, like a spark from the Muni rail line. Seeing the light, tears came streaming down his face, and he started to cry. Then he heard a voice that was so faint he could hardly make it out. It was like the first time Kevin Costner had heard the voice in *Field of Dreams*. But Charlie didn't care about baseball, and didn't give a damn about Shoeless Joe Jackson, so it had to be something else.

"Help the..." the voice commanded.

"What did the voice say?" Charlie asked himself in bewilderment. But now the blinding light was gone and Richard Dawson was back on the TV. Wiping the tears from his face, Charlie felt good inside.

"But why me?" Charlie asked himself. "Why me?"

There was no answer.

Charlie had always been a sinner, who loved fornication and fast food, so why did he feel the presence of God come over him while watching a Burger King commercial and eating a Whopper? And then there was the blinding light from the TV.

What does God want from me, he asked himself, *and who am I supposed to help?*

There was still no answer.

So, Charlie turned to reading the Bible, and listening to religious programs on the radio. He remembered that his mother would read to him from the Bible when he was just a boy. She used to say to him, "Fast, anoint your head, and wash your face."

Then one night, while listening to the religious programs on the radio in his Tenderloin apartment, Charlie heard the voice of Preacher Dan. All the lights were off, and there was only the glow of the TV on with the sound muted. And in that room, Charlie felt that Preacher Dan was talking just to him, asking to give himself to the Lord God.

Preacher Dan was from the ministry of The Church of God's Guiding Light in Yazoo County, Mississippi. His ministry started as a small church, with an office in the back and a tall antenna where Preacher Dan's voice would go out on the radio, and could be heard all over the South preaching the gospel. Preacher Dan's voice was so soothing. He talked about how people would put nickels and dimes and quarters in little envelopes with handwritten letters, and sent them to the ministry and asked Preacher Dan to please pray for them. And please build a bigger church where they all could come and give greater glory to God. And yes, the envelopes kept coming and the antenna got bigger too.

"When praising God," Preacher Dan said over the radio, "our hearts and minds can only become greater. If you are listening on the radio, then you are looking for something more in life. Faith in God will help you overcome your hardships. He will help you overcome your fears. If you are looking to talk to somebody about what the presence of our Lord God can do for you in your life, just pick up the phone and call. And maybe you have a few extra nickels or dimes, too."

And that's what Charlie did. He called so many times he was able to talk to Preacher Dan himself. Charlie confessed to him that he wanted to give himself, as Preacher Dan asked, to the greatness and glory of God. He told Preacher Dan that he had felt God's presence in his heart one night while watching TV. At first, he didn't bring up feeling His presence when the Burger King commercial came on, or the voices that he heard, or the blinding light from the TV. But as the calls became more frequent, he opened up. And Charlie did tell Preacher Dan that he had come to the realization, from listening to him speak on the radio, that he wanted to become a preacher too. He even sent away for Preacher Dan's cassette, *Following God's Guiding Light*. It was a big hit in the congregation.

Preacher Dan told Charlie that if he worked hard, and didn't waver in his convictions, that he too could be ordained a preacher. That The Church of God's Guiding Light had mail order correspondence classes set up by the elders of the church, and by Preacher Dan himself. Charlie was relieved because he thought he would have to go to some big university, and he could never afford that. But he learned from Preacher Dan that just by calling The Church of God's Guiding Light's call center, that Preacher Dan's people would walk him through the process. There was always some kind of fee, but for Charlie that money was for God. Even Effin would bring up the money part. But Charlie knew that if you have never been touched by the presence of God, you would never understand. So, he never tried to explain. But Charlie had been moved deeply and spiritually.

After Charlie signed up for the mail order correspondence classes, Preacher Dan called him, and they talked about the ordainment process. Preacher Dan even brought up his name on the radio.

"Let us all pray for Brother Charles Wilson in San Francisco," Preacher Dan said out on the radio. "That he will follow God's guiding light, and find the strength to let us help him through the process." Then Preacher Dan told Charlie to ask forgiveness for all his past digressions, and to start fasting. "It is important to cleanse the body and the soul." Preacher Dan raised his voice mightily. "No more poisons are to be put into your body. No more alcohol, no more tobacco, no more fast food. And every day should be another fast."

So, Charlie followed the advice of Preacher Dan. One day his fasting was for his sins of pride, another day for arrogance, another day for past fornications. He had a lot of them. But Charlie was intent in trying to live a purer life. At first it wasn't easy because he missed fornication, and he scratched himself hard on his forearms whenever those thoughts crept into his head. But in his fasting, Charlie followed Preacher Dan's teachings by only eating foods that came from the earth. Roots and nuts and vegetables, but no pork and no more Whoppers. Well, sometimes in a moment of weakness he had a Whopper. Who could blame him with Effin around always hounding him to go to Burger King for lunch?

From all his fasting, Charlie lost weight. Those muscles he once showed off in the park were no longer obvious. Effin told him that he was starting to look more like the homeless who slept in their vans in Camp Willie. That his chest looked like one of those arcade skeletons that came out of the haunted hidden doorways to scare little children.

But Charlie didn't mind. For the first time, he had a purpose, and a meaning in his life more than just working in supply, and he was determined to follow it. And there would be setbacks. But a phone call to Preacher Dan usually put him back on the righteous path. Of course, he had to go through the call center because Preacher Dan was a popular preacher, and spreading the word of God made him a busy man. And it usually took a few days for Preacher Dan to get back to him. But Preacher Dan would always call him back and talk, and Charlie would listen.

When Charlie started losing weight, and talking about finding God, and wanting to be a messenger like Jesus, and listening to Preacher Dan's cassette in the warehouse... Well, that was enough for people at the Evans Street Station to start calling him Jesus. First the supply people whom he managed, and then everybody else. Somebody who claimed to have felt the presence of God while eating a Whopper, and watching a fast food commercial, was enough to get some kind of a nickname. But he didn't mind being called Jesus because He was a messenger, and Jesus wanted to be a messenger too.

One night, Jesus had a dream. He had a dream that the real Jesus had come to him and touched him, and told him that his mission in life was to be a messenger, and to help the homeless. The dream made Jesus feel good inside, and he came to work that morning with an illuminated smile on his face. But when Effin was helping Arne stock Jan's ambulance, he saw that smile, and it surprised him. Jesus wasn't a smiler. He was a sufferer.

"What's with the smiling? Did you hear any more voices? Any more guiding lights?" Effin asked, going up to him. Jesus and Effin were friends more than work mates, and it didn't bother Jesus that Effin asked questions in his usual sarcastic nature. It was just Effin being Effin. He even asked Jesus one day if The Church of God's Guiding Light had been a soap opera because his mother always watched it on TV. That made Jesus laugh. They both had very few friends in the department for their own reasons—Effin because he was angry, and Jesus because he had always been a loner.

"I had a dream," Jesus said.

They walked outside in the yard away from everyone.

"About God?"

"This time it was about Jesus."

59

"So, Jesus had a dream about Jesus," Effin laughed to himself. "What about the words? Help the…"

"Jesus came to me in a dream and told me to help the homeless."

"So, Jesus really said, 'Help the homeless.'"

"Yes. You don't believe me?"

"No. Jesus doesn't come in dreams, he comes in signs. Like Moses in the desert, burning bushes, loaves and fishes, water into wine. Hey, I learned catechism in school too. I never heard anything about dreams."

"Well Jesus also speaks through dreams, too. Sometimes they come in visions. I learned it in my class."

"Oh, from that mail order ministry you joined to be a preacher?" Effin asked.

"Yes."

"Cost you money, didn't it?"

"Render to Caesar what is his."

"Yeah, yeah…"

"You laugh all you want, but when I pass my classes, I'll be a certified preacher and be able to teach the word of God, and just like Jesus, I'll be a messenger, too."

"So that's what you want to be?" Effin was finally coming to the conclusion that maybe Jesus was serious about what Effin didn't want to believe. "Is there a final in your courses you are taking?"

"No," Jesus said, "but after I complete my courses, I'll go down to Mississippi, and if they find me worthy, Preacher Dan himself will baptize me in the river."

"So, they dunk you."

"I'll be baptized."

"Will you get a certificate?" Effin asked.

"Yes, they will give me a certificate."

"Who is they?"

"The elders and Preacher Dan."

"Yeah, the ones you're sending the money to."

"It's their church," Jesus proclaimed. "It's mine too."

"Okay. So, tell me about the dream," Effin asked.

"First I saw Jesus with his arms open, and then He told me to help the homeless."

"The real Jesus?"

"Yes."

"Are you sure it was Him?"

"Of course, I'm sure. I know what Jesus looks like."

"Did He have a beard?"

"Yes, He had a beard."

"Did He have light brown hair?"

"Sort of."

"Did He have blue eyes?"

"I didn't look into His eyes."

"How could you not look into His eyes?"

"Well I didn't."

"Okay. Did He look like Charlton Heston?"

"I don't even know who Charlton Heston is."

"Well, my mother loved Charlton Heston," Effin proclaimed. "She loved *Ben Hur*, and he played Moses in *The Ten Commandments*. Come on. *Planet of the Apes*? Everybody has seen his movies."

"You're comparing my dreams with *Planet of the Apes*?" Jesus asked.

"Hey, it was a great movie, and if I had a dream about Jesus, I would think He would look like Charlton Heston. He had that rugged look, like he could save souls, and my mother loved those blue eyes. If He didn't look like Charlton Heston, then yours could have just been some other guy dressed up who looked like Jesus, but didn't get the part, and now he's in your dreams. That's why I would have rather had a sign."

"This was not a movie. It was a dream. You sure talk a lot of nonsense."

"Yeah, well I'm not the one hearing voices and seeing blinding lights," Effin replied matter-of-factly. "And how are you supposed to help the homeless? Get them a job?"

"I'll do whatever I have to do to help them find the grace of God."

Jesus never minded confiding in Effin. He didn't even see him as dumb. To Jesus he was just Effin, another angry soul.

"Maybe you will be lucky enough to have it happen to you," Jesus said.

"What?" Effin asked.

"Find the grace of God."

Effin shrugged. "What else was the dream about?" he asked.

"That was it. And it wasn't Charlton Heston. But when I woke up it came to me."

"What?"

"After Jesus came to me in a dream, I thought that once I become a certified preacher, I can help the homeless by opening a storefront church on Third Street."

"Why?"

"I can give them coffee, a warm place to spend some time off the streets, and they can hear the word of God."

"I don't know," Effin said, shaking his head. "Storefronts cost money. How you going to pay the rent?"

"I'm going to turn in my contributions from my pension," Jesus said.

"Wait, you mean cashing out your pension?" Effin asked, choking on the smoke from a cigarette he had just lit. He took out a Hall's cough drop from his pocket and sucked on it. "Do you realize you're talking about giving up your pension? People say that I'm not smart, but even I know your pension is all you got. You know Burger King is right around the corner. I think you need a Whopper. This fasting is going to your brain."

"There is nothing wrong with my brain," Jesus tried to explain, "but I think it is my calling to help the homeless."

"But you don't need a storefront for that. And if you cash out your pension, soon you'll be preaching to yourself, because you'll be homeless too. Dude. Dude. Charlie, listen to me…" Effin tried to reason. He really did care about Jesus. "People accuse me of being crazy and angry and maybe I am. But you're the one talking nonsense. When I feel crazy, and I get mad, I go and see Rip. He makes me feel better. 'Cause he's not like

62

everybody else around here, he doesn't judge me. One time, when he was a captain, I asked him if he thought that I was not very smart 'cause Jan kept calling me a stupid alien, and he just said that I was a little angry, and that it didn't matter what Jan thought, and then he told Jan not to call me a stupid alien anymore, and she stopped. He also got me to stop saying, 'Fucking medics,' too, and didn't write me up. And you know why I stopped saying it? 'Cause nobody ever told me that it didn't matter what other people thought about me. That was kind of nice. And then he told me whenever I started feeling angry, to come see him, and just talk. And maybe I should smoke a joint and get stoned. Imagine that! Management telling me to just talk, and get stoned whenever I feel angry."

"I don't need to see management, and I don't need any drugs."

"Charlie, it's Rip, and he ain't management. He's Rip. Go see him. For me! Maybe he can talk some sense into you."

"Why would I see him?" Jesus asked.

"Because I'm asking you. No one gives up their pension. And for the homeless?"

"What if I do see him?"

"Then I'll never bring it up again about your dreams, and the voices you're hearing, and cashing out your pension, and paying those Preacher Dan people to get your certificate."

"Promise?"

"Promise."

"Okay, I'll see him," Jesus finally agreed, "but no more comparing Jesus with Charlton Heston."

"I didn't compare him. I just thought that if I saw Jesus, He would look like Charlton Heston, that's all. And hey, Moses was a cool dude too, you know, and it was a cool movie. Remember when he parted the Red Sea. It was really cool to see all those chariots get blasted when the water came back again. And who can forget the burning bush? See, you're not the only one who knows something about religion."

"How do you think up this stuff?" Jesus asked Effin.

"It just comes to me."

"Just don't compare them."

"I'm not. But it was a cool movie."

Jesus gave Effin a look as if to say, *Are you done yet?*

"Okay," Effin said, "I'm done."

"Good," Jesus said. "Good."

"So, you will see Rip for me?"

"I said I would."

"Okay." Effin nodded. "Can we go for a Whopper now?"

"Maybe."

"I'll buy."

"Okay," Jesus said, knowing he was falling to temptation. "But just this one time."

"Sure thing," Effin said. "Sure thing."

CHAPTER 7

Crack Addict Eddy was a forty-five-year-old bag of bones drug addict that looked a lot older than he really was. He had some teeth missing, and lived in a broken-down, off white Ford van that was parked on the side streets of Camp Willie that surrounded the Evans Street Station. Though Eddy was no more than 5'7", he had a big head which was bald on top, with gray hair on the sides, and had a long gray ponytail, which he tied with a thick red rubber band. He kind of looked like Ron Howard's brother, Clint, when he was running away, handcuffed, from the police car in *Seinfeld.* The windows of his van were smudged from years of collected dirt and grime, and the curtains inside were flowered but torn. Eddy liked to watch from his van the ambulances that came and went from the station, and he liked to hear the sound of the sirens. Those sirens helped put him to sleep at night or early morning. Sometimes when he smoked too much crack and drank too much Royal Gate, Eddy would forget to wear clothes, and walked around the streets naked playing his guitar and singing songs. He sang mostly cowboy songs, remembering his forty-five-record collection when he was a boy. He liked songs about honky tonk women, and lost love, and six packs of beer and yes, at times, he was so lonesome he could cry.

Whenever Eddy was on one of his binges where he had been up for days on crack, the medics from the Evans Street Station would take him on a 5150 to San Francisco General Hospital, and he would dry out, then come back again sober, but it never lasted very long. His demons were always close by.

And since Eddy was one of the easier ones—which meant that he really didn't put up too much of a fight—the medics would wrap him up in a blanket, and let him bring his guitar to the hospital, and Eddy would sing to them. And Eddy really wasn't that bad of a singer for a crack addict. He was no Hank Williams, but who was?

With his sad eyes, Crack Addict Eddy came up to the Fairfax gate with his shopping cart looking for any empty bottles and cans or scrap metal to sell at the recycling center. Seeing Jesus, he asked one morning if he could go through the two big dumpsters for the station house. They were just inside the gate. Eddy had his head down, and didn't look Jesus in the face when he made his request. Because of the dumpsters, the Evans Street Station was considered the motherlode for dumpster diving, though it was a locked-down facility and unauthorized personnel were not allowed in.

For Eddy it was good timing. He had come around when Jesus was going through a transitional period in his life, and had come to the conclusion that he wanted to be a messenger of God and help the homeless.

"Okay," Jesus told Eddy, "but always come to me."

Then Jesus opened the gate and waited till Eddy was done with his dumpster diving, and escorted him off the premises. That first day, Eddy ended up with a shopping cart full of empty bottles and cans and other materials which he took to the recycling center on Third Street past the Third Street Bridge, which was known for its art deco-style bridge tender's house. Eddy usually arrived around four o'clock, but that day he was there by noon.

One day, Crack Addict Eddy came by the station to go through the dumpsters to collect the empty bottles and cans, but Jesus noticed that Eddy wasn't looking too good. Being a crack addict, Eddy never looked good to begin with, but this day was different. He looked like he had been up all night, maybe even a few nights. His face was yellow and brown like a catcher's mitt, and the pupils of his eyes were small like a pinhead. Jesus brought him into the yard, and over the objections of Eddy, called it in to dispatch so they could assign an ambulance from the Evans Street Station. Jesus told Eddy he would look after his van, and make sure that it was locked up, and even told him he could leave his shopping cart in the yard. But Jesus made it clear to Eddy that he had to go to the ER to at least be checked out. Eddy didn't want to go, but from the kindness Jesus showed him, didn't put up much resistance. Engine One from the fire department were the first responders, and as they were around the corner on a false alarm, they showed up quickly. The ambulance that was assigned had just begun their shift.

With all the commotion in the yard, people from the station gathered around. Rip came out to the yard as Engine One was pulling up. Rip didn't pay much attention until the captain of Engine One approached him. It was Captain Barbara "JoJo" Brady, the daughter of Chief Brady. She was tall and quite beautiful. She had green eyes and little freckles around her nose. Her helmet was in her hands instead of on her head, and Rip noticed her hair was brown with a tint of gold and held in the back with a scrunchie. In her turnout gear she looked like a tomboy, only sexier. To Rip, she looked a bit mysterious, like Ingrid Bergman in *Casablanca* with freckles. He always loved that movie.

Looking at JoJo, Rip thought that she had a confidence about her, like a wild horse who could only be tamed when she wanted to be, and looked like she could run with the best of them, which in the fire department was important to hold your own. Even in the fire department, Daddy can't protect you all the time. But after meeting her father, Rip knew his place. Rip saw her a few times on medical scenes before, and though they exchanged glances, nothing ever came of it. He did, though, find out that her nickname was JoJo. Everybody in the fire department, and even in the paramedic division had a nickname. Rip's was "Hippie Chief" when he got promoted. Before that it was "Surfer Boy." But after first noticing her, Rip did look her up in the city's directory called HRMS. She was younger than Rip, twenty-eight years old, and Rip was at the point in his life when he was getting a little sensitive about his age. The gray that started to show up in his hair certainly didn't help. And though he did feel an attraction toward her, Rip still thought that Laura, the lost love of his life, would come back to him.

"So, I heard you met my dad," JoJo said, getting Rip's attention.

Rip felt a little uncomfortable, and looked away and didn't reply. He had heard her voice before, and did feel a little spark inside. She was known for her humor, which made her more appealing. But she was still Chief Brady's daughter. She was an Eliot Ness, as they say in the fire department. An untouchable.

"Don't worry," JoJo told him, "his bark is worse than his bite."

"Captain Brady," Rip asked, "why does everybody call you JoJo?" Rip never got the JoJo connection. "I thought your name was Barbara."

"My dad is the Penguin, so I'm the Joker. It's okay. Just call me JoJo. Everybody else does. And since you're the new chief of the paramedic division, call me anytime you want."

Her crew was standing behind her, and with all eyes on Rip, they all laughed. Rip was a little embarrassed, and turned red. He saw it as another fire department joke at the expense of the medics.

"I'm sorry," JoJo said. "I didn't know you were so sensitive."

"I'm not sensitive, I just hear it all the time. I just can't get involved," Rip said as Eddy was being taken away in the ambulance.

"Not even with me?" JoJo said loud enough so her engine crew could hear. They laughed again.

"Another joke at my expense?" Rip asked as he walked away.

"Maybe it wasn't a joke," JoJo said, looking playful.

"Give her a chance," a voice came from the back of the engine crew. Usually they would never talk to a chief that way, but Rip was a chief of the paramedic division, and to the members of the fire department, that really didn't mean a lot. Nobody was going to get in trouble. Rip let it slide, and walked back to the station.

"Don't be a stranger now," JoJo said. But she said it in a lower voice, as if it wasn't so much a joke anymore.

Walking away, Duderonomy showed up on Rip's shoulder, wearing Bogie's trench coat and fedora. "You had a toke today, didn't you?" he asked.

"Just a little."

"In your department bathroom?"

"No, no. In my car driving to work."

"Makes you a little sensitive, you know."

"Maybe."

"But she likes you."

"Yeah sure. Get involved with the daughter of the chief who hates me. You and your great ideas. And what's with the outfit?"

"Of all the fire stations in all the towns in all the world, why did she have to walk into mine? Play it, Sam. If she can take it so can I," Duderonomy said, imitating Bogie.

"Okay, that's enough."

"Hey, you were the one who watched that movie so many times. Especially when Laura left you. Word for word it's all up here." Duderonomy pointed to his brain. "I think this JoJo can make you forget Laura."

"Laura is going to come back to me one day," Rip proclaimed proudly.

"I don't know. Have you forgot about her boyfriend? The one you call Tarzan? He may have a say in it."

The mention of Laura to Rip was a sensitive subject.

"Well, even if she never comes back, I'm not getting involved with Chief Brady's daughter," Rip said, looking more dejected.

"Well you never know. There is always a positive side to everything."

"What positive side could it be getting involved with the daughter of a chief who hates me, and has it in for me?"

"Look back," Duderonomy said.

"What?"

"Just look back."

Rip did and JoJo was still looking at Rip, watching him walk away.

"Positivity is the key to possibility. Or do you want to be like Bogie and just suffer in your drink?"

"Laura will come back to me, you'll see," Rip snapped arrogantly, shaking his head, and flicked Duderonomy off his shoulder.

"Hey, that wasn't cool," Duderonomy said before he disappeared.

When Rip looked back again, Engine One had left the yard.

CHAPTER 8

It took a while for Jesus to go see Rip. He didn't want to go, but had promised Effin, who kept bringing it up. And usually Effin didn't have the attention span to bring up anything more than once or twice, except when it came to lunchtime, or eating Whoppers, or even how much he hated stocking Jan's ambulance. But Jesus seeing Rip and talking about giving up his pension was something that Effin wasn't about to let go.

"Did you see Rip yet?" Effin asked Jesus one morning in the yard.

"Who?"

"Rip! Remember? Did you go see him?"

"I said I would."

"It's been a week."

"I can tell time."

"But can you tell days?" Effin asked.

Jesus walked away, but knew that he had to keep his promise. If he was going to be a man of the cloth, then his word meant everything and he had made a promise. When Jesus finally did go, Rip was going through papers that Hogwash's staff had sent him in the weekly report from dispatch on response times. Hogwash lived by the numbers. And in this report, dispatch monitored response times of the ambulance crews for calls received from their post to the patient, and then on scene to the hospital. When response times were not met, the system backed up, and it was called medic to follow, which meant that patients had a longer wait time for an ambulance.

And for people like Hogwash, response times mattered, because when they were good, the press wasn't snooping around asking questions about the paramedic division, and he could use his staff to focus on other problems. When response times weren't good, it meant the paramedic division wasn't doing their job, and patient complaints had a way of finding themselves in print. When getting the weekly report of response times from Hogwash, his staff would highlight in red the unacceptable response times while Hogwash would add remarks like: *Why? Look into this! What is going on? What was the crew doing? Straighten it out!* Hogwash rated Rip's first weekly report on response times from dispatch with a big C minus in red, and three heavy lines underneath the grade to accent it even more.

For Rip's part, he learned quickly that the reports were just another way for the Hogwashes of the world to control him. It wasn't hard to figure out that without adequate staffing and a workable fleet, it was like Humpty Dumpty falling off the wall. Not all days were going to be good, and not all the pieces of Humpty Dumpty were going to be put back together again after he fell. But Rip put up with it because he loved being chief. On a chief's salary he could now afford new rental digs in the Presidio, overlooking the Golden Gate Bridge and the Pacific Ocean. Looking at himself in the mirror of his own bathroom in his office at work, Rip liked wearing his chief's uniform, always making sure his hair had that Beach Boys surfer-style wave.

"Admit it," Duderonomy would say. "You love it. You love being chief."

Rip knew it, but didn't want to admit that being chief was a whole lot better than making training films in the back office of the warehouse, which was cold and moldy even with a space heater. And in his new job, Rip enjoyed signing documents approving neighborhood groups and schools requesting medics to teach first aid and CPR. Helping these neighborhood groups made Rip feel good inside because he actually felt that he was doing something constructive that he could control, and this was where he could make a difference. When Rip saw Jesus at his office door, he was happy for the interruption and pushed Hogwash's papers aside.

"Come on in, Jesus," Rip said. "Sit down. If you'd rather, I'll call you Charlie. I really haven't gotten used to this chief thing yet. You know we really don't talk enough. What can I do for you?"

Jesus sat down but looked extremely uncomfortable squirming in his seat. Rip found that unusual because when Rip worked in the back room of the warehouse making films, they could always talk. Rip found Jesus a little too serious sometimes, and one day at work, to the annoyance of Jesus, he followed Jesus around with a camera and made a short film called *The Life of Charlie Wilson*. It was a big hit in the station house, and it broke the ice between them. Jesus was a bit embarrassed by the attention, but the film did make him laugh a little at himself. At first it was hard for Jesus to accept Rip's demeanor of having no filter whatsoever, whenever they had a conversation. But he got used to it, and at times Rip could even make him laugh. There was also Jesus' way of always calling uniformed members of the paramedic division "sir," which Rip tried to break him of.

"You know Jesus, you have lost a lot of weight," Rip said, looking Jesus over.

"Sir, it's my penance. I sacrifice. I used to... Well, I had a lot of sins to make up for. I am trying to be a messenger of God."

"Oh right. I heard about that. Every day another sacrifice. And all this over a Burger King commercial."

"Yes, God works in mysterious ways."

"But Burger King? I have to admit that I'm not a big Burger King fan."

"It grows on you, sir. Even with my fasting I'm not supposed to be eating them but sometimes I do. Me and Effin are big Whopper fans. We tried Quarter Pounders and Big Macs but we always go back to the Whopper. Effin swears it's the flame-broiled beef patties. Whenever I break my fast, we go and have a Whopper."

"Jesus, you can call me Rip. Remember we worked together downstairs?"

"Yes, sir."

"What is your sacrifice today?"

"Past fornications."

"Past fornications? You know, Jesus, I don't want to sound disrespectful—and I know your religious beliefs are important to you—but I think that fornication is a good thing. God, I really miss it."

"Well my church says it's not, outside of marriage, and I'm trying to find my way into Heaven."

Rip was slowly coming to the conclusion that Jesus didn't come up to his office to ask the normal request. Jesus was not looking directly at Rip, and his arms were folded as he sat in the chair.

"If there is no fornication…" Rip asked, thinking about the old times when Jesus was so serious and Rip would try to make him laugh, "How about surfing? Do you think Jesus would have liked surfing, or would He have been too busy saving souls?"

"Saving souls, sir."

"Yeah, but there has to be some down time."

"Sir, I mean Rip, I would think it would be a twenty-four-hour job. Which is why I came to talk to you. I want to give my life to saving souls."

"All or just a few?" Rip asked.

"All sir, or whoever will follow me."

"Is masturbation allowed, or do you have to sacrifice for that one too?" Rip asked. He wanted to tread lightly, but still found it irresistible to ask, "I don't really think that it's a sin. I mean, everybody does it. You're not hurting anyone, and it can't kill you. I would even think that some of your religious leaders do it. I know nuns do."

"I try not to think about it."

"Not to be insensitive, but scientific research says that masturbation is a good thing for your body, and it also relieves stress. Scientific research and my dad."

"Your father, sir?"

"Yeah," Rip confided, "he's got this older sexual revolution thing going on. Thinks he's back in the sixties again. He's hanging out with the Gray Beavers. It's driving city hall crazy."

"And you approve of his behavior?" Jesus asked.

"Well, he's better now than he used to be. But you really don't mind people calling you Jesus?"

"No, sir. He was a messenger, and I want to be a messenger too."

"Wouldn't it be cool if Jesus was like Superman?" Rip asked. Rip was a comic book kind of guy. Growing up, he spent a lot of lonely nights in the Ridley house, so it was only natural that his imagination would turn to comic books and superheroes as an escape.

"Superman?" Jesus asked, looking a little confused.

"Yeah, Superman. Jumping over tall buildings in a single leap, and he's always saving people."

"Jesus saves people too," Jesus replied.

"Oh yeah. Sorry. I forgot," Rip said, coming to the conclusion that Jesus wasn't going to lighten up. Not even a smile.

"What can I do for you?" Rip finally asked. "We have worked together. You have always done a good job, so whatever you need. Time off?"

"Well sir, Rip, I just want to ask you…"

There was a moment of silence.

"Charlie, it's me, Rip. Ask me anything. Please!"

"Okay, me and Effin have this thing going on, and I had a dream about opening my own church, but I don't have a lot of money. Matter of fact, I don't have any money. But I had a dream, and Jesus was in it."

"So, Jesus was in your dream?" Rip asked, taken back a bit.

"Yes."

"Was it you or the real Jesus?"

"The real one."

"What did He look like?"

"Not like Charlton Heston."

"Why would he look like Charlton Heston?" Rip asked.

"Because Effin said he would."

"But didn't he play Moses?"

"I know."

As they made small talk, Jesus noticed, from the side angle where he was sitting, Laura's picture in her itsy-bitsy baby blue bikini and his eyes wandered. Rip's eyes followed too. Then they shook themselves out of Laura's trance.

"I know about the relationship you had with that girl who left you, when you wouldn't follow her to Australia. Everybody knows about her."

"Yes. Laura," Rip said.

"Why didn't you give up everything for her? I mean your pension. Would you have cashed it out?"

"Jesus," Rip said, getting somewhat serious, "if I cashed out my pension, I wouldn't have anything left. You're not thinking...?"

This was no longer about time off.

"No, no... Well you know...I was just asking... Maybe?"

"If I could bring her back, well who knows. But when she wanted me to, I just couldn't. I thought about it, but I guess there are some things you never get over, like comfort. I couldn't see myself living in some outback. But what is this all about?" Rip asked.

"Sir, I want to open up my own church in a storefront on Third Street and save souls. I want the homeless to have a place where anyone can come, get a cup a coffee, and maybe read some scriptures. But I need money, and I thought maybe... I'm also taking classes now to become a preacher."

Wow, thought Rip. That really sunk in. *Nobody ever cashes out their pension.* There was another moment of silence.

"What is it tomorrow?" Rip asked.

"What do you mean?" Jesus asked.

"Your sacrifice."

"Pride, sir, pride. I mean Rip."

"Well, say a prayer for me, Jesus. At least that I keep my job."

"I will. Are you a believer?"

"That I'll keep my job? Every day it changes."

"No, I mean a believer...in God."

"Sometimes I am. When I need something, I believe or at least try to. But when things are going well, I really don't think about it. I used to chant a mantra, but that was just a Laura thing, and I never quite understood it. But are you really thinking about giving up your pension?"

"Maybe."

"That's a big sacrifice."

"I know."

"It's certainly a calling all right. To be honest I thought Laura was a calling once too. I thought I would have followed her anywhere, but when it got down to it, I didn't want to live in the outback eating berries and sleeping with all those insects flying around at night. And I kind of like running water on a daily basis. And there is nothing better than Chinese takeout food and burritos. Laura used to love Chinese food. God I still miss her."

"Well, I promised Effin I would ask what you thought about it. Just to get another opinion. It seemed to have helped him when he talked to you about his problems with Jan."

Jesus thought it best not to mention Rip's advice to Effin to smoke more dope when he got angry at something.

"Jesus," Rip said, leaning over a bit on his elbows to get his attention, "I can't really tell you what to do. Sometimes I can't even tell myself what to do. But even I know that cashing out your pension is a big step."

"Yes, I know. Do you ever think of her?"

"Not much," Rip replied. "Just every day."

Slowly both Rip and Jesus went back to staring at the picture of Laura. Rip started feeling that old urge for Laura again, and Jesus started thinking about how he too missed being with a woman. Laura had that aura about her. She could stir men's hearts, and other things. Finally, looking embarrassed that the picture had conjured up such strong feelings inside, Jesus looked away.

"Well sir, Rip, I think I should be going."

"Yeah, yeah," Rip said, lost in his thoughts. "Are you really going to do it?"

"I don't know. Do you think you'll ever get over her? If you don't mind me asking."

"I don't know. Everything was just so free and easy when she was around. Laura once told me that my worst enemy could not harm me as much as my unguarded thoughts."

"What does that mean?"

"I have no idea, Jesus. I really don't know."

"Well," Jesus said again, "I think I should be going."

He got up to leave.

"Hey Jesus, just a thought," Rip said.

"What?"

"Why don't you just help out your friend, who collects the cans from the dumpsters, find religion instead of giving up your pension? I mean, if you want to help the homeless, we got a lot of them here. And if you want a place to meet, they all have vans. Then you can keep your pension."

"Eddy, huh?"

"Think about it. If anything, he could use the attention. Living in that van all day, I'm sure he gets kind of lonely."

"I never thought about it," Jesus said.

Seeing Jesus leave his office, Rip felt bad for him, but then thinking again about Laura, he knew he still had it bad for her, too.

Before Jesus could think about saving Eddy, the thought of Laura played on his mind. It was the image of her on the beach in her little itsy-bitsy baby blue bikini, her smooth tanned skin and her supple breasts and her long flowing blonde hair. And she really did look like Christie Brinkley had a sister, and Jesus always had a thing for Christie Brinkley. Who didn't? During his weight lifting period, he had her *Sports Illustrated* sexy wall poster tacked to his ceiling over his bed. He found it again, and tacked it back up. All the sacrificing in the world could not deny the fact that he missed fornication.

After a while, temptations started to creep in. Jesus quit fasting, and at night was back on the Whoppers and fries and

Diet Cokes along with piles of squeezed-out packages of ketchup. Then came the masturbation, something Rip said wasn't really a sin, but Jesus still felt guilty. He even went to a strip club, and spent his rent money. More and more he found himself going to the corner liquor store for pints of Royal Gate vodka. The true alcoholic's delight. He even quit shaving, and started coming to work late in the same clothes. Jesus was sinking.

In his guilt, Jesus tried to stay away from everybody, even Effin. But Effin would have none of it. His radar was up. And the smell of fast food on Jesus' clothes was too much to hide. At first Effin held back a bit. Jesus was his only real friend at work, and even Effin knew enough to give him some space. Whenever Effin tried to approach him, Jesus would turn away. His humiliation was too much for him. One morning Jesus had his head down on his desk sleeping, when Effin came in and woke him up.

"So, going to see Rip didn't really help you out?" Effin asked.

"Yeah, gee, thanks a lot," Jesus said. There was disappointment in his voice.

"What do you mean?"

"Well we got to talking, and then he brought up…"

"What? What?"

"Masturbation. How he didn't think it was a sin, and then I started looking at the picture of his ex Laura on his desk, and she reminded me of Christie Brinkley. I couldn't get her out of my mind. I even tacked up the Christie Brinkley *Sports Illustrated* poster on my ceiling. The one where she's all wet."

"You still have the poster?" Effin asked, amazed.

"Yeah, some things you never give away. Then I had another dream, but it wasn't Charlton Heston."

"You mean…?"

"Yes, a wet dream. I couldn't control it."

"Did you snap a picture of Laura from Rip's desk?"

"No, I just couldn't do it."

"Well I did when Rip wasn't there. I just couldn't resist it."

"You don't understand," Jesus tried to explain, "I tried so hard to get these impure thoughts out of my mind, and then there they were again. I dreamed we were all on the beach. Me, Laura, Christie, surf, sand, and oh yeah sex."

"Gosh, I wish I had dreams like that."

"Now I have to do more penance. I was so embarrassed I didn't even call Preacher Dan."

"Don't worry about it," Effin said, trying to reassure him. "All great religious leaders have moments of doubt. Look at Gandhi. But are you still going to cash out your pension to start your church?"

"I don't know. Rip brought up something."

"What?"

"He said instead of cashing out my pension, I should stay here and try to convert Eddy, and maybe some of the other homeless. He said we had enough homeless here that I can help."

"Really! See, I told you to see Rip. That's a great idea. Why not start your church here? It's not like they are going anywhere, and if they do, they'll just come back again anyway."

"Listen, don't mention this to anybody," Jesus pleaded. "Okay?"

"What?"

"The wet dream."

"Christie Brinkley and Laura? What a great dream! But don't worry. I won't say nothing. Nobody talks to me anyway. But I would think about what Rip said. Where would you meet? Did you give it any thought?"

"Rip said that maybe Eddy was a little lonely, and maybe we can meet in his van?"

"I don't know," Effin said. "I know you got to meet somewhere, but crack addicts' vans are kind of fucked up."

"What if I helped him clean it up?" Jesus asked.

It was a stretch.

"Well lonely or not, I'm not sure," Effin said. "I mean he does do drugs all the time. I'm just saying, I don't know if he's willing to go down that road. And it would have to be cleaned

up. But there is an extra mattress in the sleeping quarters upstairs that's still in the plastic. Hell, I was going to take it. Maybe
that would fit nicely in Eddy's van. It's been there for a while,
and who would notice?"

"Well I don't want to take…" Jesus started.

"You don't have to take anything. I'll take the mattress and
leave it outside near the gate. Just let me know when you need
it. Either you give it to Eddy or I'm taking it."

"Maybe I could talk to Eddy about the meeting, and we can
clean out his van," Jesus said, thinking out loud. "I can get him
new bed sheets at Goodwill."

"Yeah," Effin added, "and we got lots of bleach around
here. You'd have to clean out all those aluminum foil crack
pipes, and wash those windows. Gosh, those windows are terrible. I don't even know why he has curtains. Nobody can see
inside."

"But Eddy may not go for these meetings," Jesus said, starting to doubt himself.

"Well, maybe if you brought some food to these meetings,
it would be okay."

"Food?"

"Yeah, maybe some Whoppers."

"Whoppers?" Jesus asked.

"Yeah, Eddy is always at Burger King. He likes the same
shit that we do when it comes to fast food. Whoppers, fries,
Diet Coke, and lots of ketchup. Hell, all of Camp Willie goes
there. And Eddy has friends. They got to eat too. That could
be the kick. Why wouldn't somebody come for a Whopper?
But it means that you're going to have to break your fast."

"What do you mean?"

"You know you can't buy a Whopper for Eddy, and not
have one yourself. That can even be the name of your
church—Whoppers for Jesus. What a great name! See, I have
my moments, Whoppers for Jesus. It has a nice ring to it. Who
would have thunk it?"

"I'm not calling it Whoppers for Jesus."

"Hey, have it your way," Effin said. "But if you bring the Whoppers they will come."

It took a few days for Jesus to get back to his religious ways, and the thought of Laura and Christie Brinkley started leaving him. Okay, more than a few days. But then he finally broke down and called Preacher Dan, and confessed his sins, and even brought up his idea of trying to start a meeting place for the homeless who lived in the vans that surrounded the station. He didn't bring up the word congregation because he hadn't been ordained yet, but Preacher Dan was a smart man. He knew, and with his kind words Jesus' religious convictions were restored. And instead of impure thoughts of Christie and Laura, the thought of starting his church at Camp Willie stayed with him.

CHAPTER 9

Before Jesus could begin building the foundation of his congregation at Camp Willie, Chief Brady and Lieutenant McGuire showed up to see Rip in his office. And Chief Brady wasn't one to call beforehand. With Chief Brady, it was always the pop in. Chief Brady and Lieutenant McGuire didn't even bother to knock before entering Rip's office. They just walked right in. Rip, sitting at his desk, reviewing the daily schedule, heard their footsteps in the hallway, and knew they were coming. He looked up, and there they were, standing over him, arms folded, both showing that fire department grin as if to say, *Our lives are so much better than yours.*

"Chief Brady," Rip said sarcastically, "what do I owe this pleasure?"

"Looking at the daily schedule, eh Chief Ripley?"

"It's Ridley, sir."

"It's a bit thin, isn't it? Do you have enough staff?"

"It's never enough. I'm hoping for a slow day."

"We all are, Chief Ripley, but you can't ask for slow days all the time. But what can you do? Start a homeless plan like the last guy? That would certainly get Hogwash's attention. Who was your last chief? Chief Tortellini? He started a homeless plan, and was the golden boy of the city for a while. Even got his name in the newspaper—until as always, city hall fights back. They don't like new ideas, Ripley. Never did, and never will. Unless of course they thought of it first. I don't know why you paramedics can't just follow the plan."

"And what plan is that, sir?"

"Don't matter what the plan is, Chief Ripley," Chief Brady said, poking his index finger in the air to accent his words. "City hall will tell you. All you have to do is follow it. I heard that your last chief just left one day. Got up, signed the papers for his retirement, and was gone by lunch. But you don't have enough years in yet, do you?"

"I'm not quite sure, sir," Rip said, sitting back in his chair. He knew Chief Brady had him. "I haven't gone over the numbers yet."

"Yeah, well when you do, let me know. You may come up a little short. Heard you spoke to my daughter the other day. The crew said you were all over her with your hippie charm," Chief Brady growled in a lower tone. Lieutenant McGuire gave Rip the firehouse stare down.

"I barely said a word."

"I know how you work, Ripley. Just don't get any ideas."

"It never crossed my mind."

"Good." Chief Brady nodded, backing away from Rip's desk, and even Lieutenant McGuire backed off a bit. "At least we got that straight. But when I came here today to gas up, there was some homeless guy going through the dumpster, and some guy from your supply was watching him."

"That would be Jesus," Rip said.

"Jesus? That's his name?" Chief Brady said, looking amazed then frustrated. Lieutenant McGuire just shook his head.

"His real name is Charlie but everybody calls him Jesus. He has this religious conversion thing going on," Rip tried to explain. "Claims to have heard the voice of God during a Burger King commercial. Now it's about a new sacrifice every day. I guess today was help the homeless day."

"For Christ's sake, Ripley! What kind of station house are you running around here? And you approve of the homeless going through your dumpsters?" Chief Brady asked, driving up his blood pressure. "And why aren't you calling the cops to roust these homeless who seem to be occupying your neighborhood? Get a few red lines drawn on the curb so they can't park their vehicles around the station house anymore. Even if you got to paint the lines yourself. Just get it done. If I were you, I would call the press in. That would really stick one up Hogwash's ass."

Chief Brady looked at Lieutenant McGuire, and they both smirked knowing that Rip would never go that far.

"I'm trying to keep my job, sir."

"Not from what I hear, Chief Ripley. I hear differently. You don't even go to any of the commission meetings, do you?"

"I haven't paid much attention to them since I was appointed."

"Well if I were you, I would start," Chief Brady said. "Don't you think showing up would be a good political move, considering they're always bringing up the paramedic division? Seems like Hogwash has it in his head that in the beginning of the fiscal year, he wants to merge the paramedic division with the fire department. Trust me, I'm against it too. But I like to be on the winning side of whatever comes down—and Ripley, I don't even think you have a side. The fact that Hogwash is not parading you out in front of the press kind of means that they don't have any plans for you if this merger goes through. You were a captain before, weren't you Chief Ripley?"

"Yes, Chief."

"You made those training films, didn't you?"

"I did."

"My daughter said they were very entertaining. But do you think Hogwash found them entertaining, or just another waste of taxpayers' money? Does city hall even call you anymore? And with all that paperwork on your desk, Ripley, they are burying you."

"And the reason you came by…"

"I just wanted to come by and say hello. That's the kind of guy I am. You could learn a lot from someone like me, but I think you're too much like the last paramedic chief, a free thinker."

"And what could I learn from you, Chief Brady?"

"Play the game, Chief Ripley. Play the politics. Be a good soldier. Make them not have to worry about you. And slowly you get what you want. But I'm afraid that, like the last chief, you think it's beneath you. I've seen it so many times. When will you get it into your head that since you can't beat city hall, you might as well join them? But look outside the next few days, and you'll see what true leadership is about."

"What do you mean?" Rip asked. Now he was interested.

"You'll see. Have a good day, Chief Ripley, crunching those numbers... Let's go," Chief Brady said to Lieutenant McGuire, and they walked out of Rip's office. Rip could hear those same heavy footsteps walking away down the hall.

In two days' time, Chief Brady showed Rip his version of "true leadership." Chief Brady pulled a few strings and contacted some of his old friends in the police department, and they rousted all the homeless from Camp Willie with tow trucks from City Tow and sanitation workers right behind them, first moving along the vehicles that were able to start, towing the rest, and sanitation picking up the debris left behind. It was an operation where even Rip was impressed. By the end of the day, the streets surrounding the Evans Street Station looked like a different neighborhood. Chief Brady couldn't wait to call Rip.

"So, how did you like my little operation, Chief Ripley?"

"You made your point, sir." Rip had to admit it.

"You don't get it, do you? All it took was a few phone calls and a few cases of beer, and that's how you get things done. I heard when Hogwash found out, he almost grinned. That bastard! Favors, Ripley, favors. I just called a few of them in. And I did the right thing. Do you know what the right thing is?"

Rip didn't answer.

"It's learning how to get things done. Play the game, Ripley," Chief Brady said with authority.

Rip felt like the Coppertone girl with the puppy pulling down her swim trunks. He had been showed up and dressed down.

For a while the homeless stayed away, which kind of screwed up Jesus' plan to start his congregation with Eddie and the homeless in Camp Willie. All his future parishioners were gone. But slowly, the beat-up vans and cars rolled back into the neighborhood again, some barely being able to park before they broke down, mostly in the middle of the night, testing the area. When there was no resistance, the neighborhood started filling up again with old broken-down vans, cars, and other vehicles.

When Jesus saw Eddie's van, he made a special space for him right next to the Fairfax gate. That was prime real estate in Camp Willie. There were the lights at night in the yard of the station house, and the traffic from the ambulances going in and out kept the shadier elements of the neighborhood away. The closer you were to the station, the safer you were.

When Eddy came back, Jesus let him go dumpster diving again for empty bottles and cans. Jesus even brought Eddy strings for his guitar, which even Effin thought was a nice gesture. Eddy only said, "Thanks," but slowly he opened up.

"I wasn't always a crack addict," Eddy divulged to Jesus one morning. "I wasn't always an alien. But then things happened so quickly, and I just couldn't go back. If I could do it again..." Eddy never completed his sentence, but that was enough for Jesus to try to get Eddy to open up a bit. It was hard at first. But slowly Eddy told Jesus that it was the loneliness and the boredom that drove him to the pipe, and for salvation he played his guitar. Every day Eddy stayed a little longer while Jesus asked him questions about himself. Finally, Jesus brought up to Eddy that maybe he would like to fix up the inside of his van. The station house was getting rid of a mattress that would fit nicely inside.

"What do I have to do?" Eddy asked. Nobody had ever given anything to him for free.

"Nothing," Jesus said. "You would be helping me out. But it would be better to do it on a Saturday when no one is around."

"My van is not very clean," Eddy told Jesus.

"We can fix that."

Eddy hesitated. "Okay."

On Saturday, Jesus had two Whoppers and two orders of fries and two Diet Cokes and lots of packets of ketchup for the both of them when he tapped on Eddy's van to get him up. There was also a nice mattress, still in the plastic, near the roll-up doors. Effin had kept his word and left it out the night before, inside the gate.

When Eddy came out, Jesus gave him a plastic bag with new bed sheets for the mattress. Eddy was almost in tears. They both sat down on the curb near the Fairfax gate and ate their Whoppers. Then Jesus opened up to Eddy.

"Here," Jesus said to Eddy as they were eating. It was a Bible. "I haven't been really honest to you, but I'm studying to be a preacher, and I thought that maybe like me, you too could use a little salvation. I'm trying to be a messenger of God."

"Why me?" Eddy asked.

"You were talking the other day if things were different, and I used to have the same feeling until one day, He came to me."

"Who?"

"The spirit of God."

"Really? What did He say to you?"

"He told me to buy Eddy a Whopper."

They both laughed.

"But I was wondering, after we clean up your van, if sometimes we can have a meeting there. It won't be preaching; it will be like friends talking. I know I need it sometimes. And if you know someone else who wants to do it, they can come too."

"In my van?" Eddy asked.

"I just thought it would be easier that way. We can fix it up. And if it doesn't work out, then we won't do it."

As Eddy was finishing off his Whopper, he looked over at the two dumpsters that Jesus let him pick through. They were prime real estate in the dumpster diving business.

"And I'll bring Whoppers and fries too," Jesus said.

"Whoppers?" Eddy asked, surprised.

"For anybody who wants one."

"Okay," Eddy finally said.

"Well let's get to work cleaning out your van."

So, they did.

Eddy may have been a crack addict, but he was not lazy. And he really wasn't against this religious thing either. It was just that the pipe always got in the way. Eddy's mother used to read the Bible to him growing up, and one could say that his father was somewhat of an Old Testament man. He never spared the rod.

Jesus gave Eddy some rubber gloves and they took out the old mattress, tossed it in one of the dumpsters, swept out the aluminum foil crack pipes, burned matchsticks and empty fast food wrappers, put them in plastic bags, and threw them in the dumpster, too. Then Jesus told Eddy to gather up his washables, and Jesus put them in the station house washing machine, and gave everything a nice once-over. Then Jesus mixed nine cups of water to one cup bleach, and they mopped down the inside of Eddy's van. They even cleaned the windows. There was a lot of dirt and grime, but Jesus and Eddy cleaned it well, and when they were satisfied, they put in the new mattress with the new bed sheets they had gotten out of the dryer, along with the other washables, and the van looked different inside. They even washed the curtains, though the flowers had faded. But the van looked better. Cleaner. To Eddy it looked like it was almost new. With all the goings-on, Flat Nose Joey and his girlfriend Sequoia came over.

"What the fuck is going on?" Flat Nose Joey asked Eddy.

Joey was called Flat Nose Joey because somebody had beaten the crap out of his face, and flattened his nose when he was living on the street. He was thin and wiry and always told everyone he was from the East Coast. His girlfriend Sequoia, who always wore those long patch dresses that she sewed herself, painted murals on the outside of the concrete walls of the Evans Street Station. It looked like a religious Berlin Wall. Sequoia painted hands together in prayer, a guiding light, a watchtower—anything that was spiritual. When Chief Brady came by and saw the murals on the walls of the Evans Street Station, he called BOE and had them painted over. But Sequoia didn't mind her murals being painted over, and just painted them again. She even planted a small garden in a section outside the Fairfax gate of flowers that she had stolen from some of the houses in the neighborhood. Flat Nose Joey and Sequoia both lived in Camp Willie in the same van, and shared the same weaknesses.

Sequoia also had a drug-addicted cat named Mumbles. Mumbles lived in their van, and with all the drug residue everywhere, well, he had to ingest it some way. When going across the yard, Mumbles shook a lot, and some of the lesbian medics at the Evans Street Station put cat food out for him. Every once in a while he would even catch a rat. Mumbles became a favorite at the station house. Watching Mumbles walk across the yard in his jittery addicted way, who couldn't love him?

"Cleaning my van," Eddy said to Flat Nose Joey.

"With a new mattress?" Flat Nose Joey asked.

"Yes," Jesus replied. "We are going to have meetings."

"Meetings about what?" Flat Nose Joey asked. "Are you some kind of preacher?"

"I'm trying to be."

"Is there going to be any food?"

"Whoppers."

"Whoppers?"

"Yes," Jesus said. "But all we're going to do in these meetings is talk. Sometimes I need it, and I thought that maybe sometimes others may need it too."

"Well I ain't going to no fucking meetings," Flat Nose Joey snapped, getting all defensive. "People have always tried to meet me to death."

"But I want to go," Sequoia said.

"Shut the fuck up," Flat Nose Joey said to her. "We ain't going."

"Well, I can go if I want to go," Sequoia yelled.

"No, you can't."

"I'm going." Sequoia walked off.

"Fuck," Flat Nose Joey said. "Fuck. Now I got to put up with this shit."

He walked off to catch up to Sequoia, trying to convince her not to go, but she locked herself in their van, and since Flat Nose Joey didn't bring any keys, she wouldn't let him in. He banged on the side of the van loudly and started screaming to "open up the fucking van," but Sequoia wasn't opening up, and then a cop car rolled by, so he stopped. Finally, though Flat Nose Joey wasn't happy, he settled down, and reluctantly agreed to go.

At the first meeting in Eddy's van, there was Jesus, Eddy, Flat Nose Joey, and Sequoia. Jesus sat in the front of the van, behind the front seats, on an empty milk crate, and Eddy and Flat Nose Joey sat facing him on the mattress, leaning against opposite sides of the van. Sequoia sat in the middle of the mattress with her hands folded as if in prayer. Flat Nose Joey told Eddy that he didn't want to come, but Sequoia wouldn't shut the fuck up about it, and she kept locking him out of their van until he promised to go. So, he came. Jesus brought Whoppers and fries and Diet Cokes for everyone. He was thrilled. It was his first congregation.

Through the slurping of the Diet Cokes from the plastic straws, Jesus first read scriptures, then asked everyone to talk about themselves. At first nobody said anything, so Jesus started talking about his own binges with alcohol and sex, though none of his homeless congregation thought the sex thing was a sin. Then Jesus opened up about his revelation about feeling the presence of God while watching a Burger King commercial on TV, and how his sacrificing led him to Eddy, and now to Joey and Sequoia. Jesus didn't think it was right to call Joey "Flat Nose." Sequoia said "Hallelujah" after each confession until Flat Nose Joey told her to shut the fuck up, but she kept saying it anyway. Then Jesus made sure that everybody was nice to each other in the meetings, and made sure Joey talked nicer to Sequoia, and quit telling her to shut the fuck up.

Finally, Flat Nose Joey did calm down, and even talked about his nose being messed up and how he couldn't look in the mirror anymore. Sequoia talked about how the spirit of God was inside every living creature no matter how small.

"Even an ant has got the spirit of God in him," she told everybody in the van.

"An ant ain't got no fucking soul," Flat Nose Joey said to her, but then he looked at Jesus and didn't say anything else. When it was Eddy's turn to talk, he never raised his head, and quietly talked about his father, and how he was once a Marine, and how he used to come home drunk at night, stinking of cheap booze, and beat the shit out of his mother. As a young boy, living in a small town in Oklahoma, Eddy would lie in bed at night and hear the screams of his mother while his father beat her. When his father passed out, Eddy would hear his mother's sobs. As he got older, Eddy would try to protect her. Then he would get it, too. One day after a bad beating, Eddy just left for the streets of Los Angeles. From Los Angeles, he made his way to San Francisco, getting hooked on various drugs and alcohol. But while others used needles, Eddy liked the pipe. When he heard that his father had finally taken his own life, Eddy scraped up enough money and made it back for the funeral. All that his father left for him was a samurai sword that he had picked up as a Marine in the Far East, and a coin collection with a few silver dollars that Eddy sold for drugs.

Eddy kept the samurai sword and had it clamped to the back wall of the inside of his van over the rear window. Eddy loved that sword, and never allowed anyone to get near it. Those were the rules he lived by. When Eddy sat in the Whoppers for Jesus meetings, the sword was always on the wall behind him. Eddy could never say he loved his father, but he could say he loved that sword.

"Not exactly the first apostles," Effin said to Jesus after he saw him coming out of Eddy's van. Jesus liked to schedule his meetings in the late afternoon. Nobody at the Evans Street Station seemed to mind, and certainly not Rip. Camp Willie was the rock where Jesus was going to build his church.

"So, are you going to save Crack Addict Eddy?" Effin asked Jesus.

"His name is Eddy and we talked."

"Did you bring Whoppers for everybody?"

"Yes."

"Did you have a Whopper too?"

"My sacrifices in life have led me to believe that I am here to try to help Eddy," Jesus said proudly.

"So, you had one too, didn't you?"

"Yes, I did."

"What is Preacher Dan going to say?"

"I called Preacher Dan, and he said sometimes you have to bring the sinners to you."

"Is that why his congregation has bingo once a week?"

"Preacher Dan's church doesn't have bingo."

"What kind of church doesn't have bingo?" Effin asked. "But are you back on the Whoppers?"

"Yeah, I guess so."

"And the rest of the fasting?"

"Preacher Dan said now is the time for moderation. He said I passed the first test."

"Which was…?"

"Trying to help somebody else."

"Yeah, but Preacher Dan doesn't know Eddy."

"Eddy is going to be fine."

"Will you be able to get him off the pipe?"

"That's what I hope for."

"I don't know. Crack pipes always come out of the shadows, and will whisper to you when you are at your weakest moments."

"That's crazy. Crack pipes don't talk."

"Oh yes they do," Effin argued, and he believed it too. "Just ask any crackhead. They got a whisper to them. It's like me and cigarettes. 'Just have one,' Lucky Strikes whispers to me. 'One ain't going to kill you,' and when I'm done with that one, there's another one around the corner saying the same thing. They just keep whispering to you. 'Take a puff. Take another puff,'" Effin said, putting out one cigarette, then lighting another one. "Same thing with crack pipes."

"So, they whisper?"

"Yeah, crack pipes whisper. You don't hear it 'cause you're not hooked, but they do. But to tell you the truth, I didn't think you would get this far. I'm kind of proud of you."

"Thank you," Jesus said.

"Is it true about Eddy having a real samurai sword in his van?" Effin asked.

"You sure know a lot of what's going on around here."

"I got my pipeline. You never know what you need around here. A crack addict fixed my car the other day, and he was talking about it. Fixed it for pocket money. Crack addicts can be good mechanics because something is always going wrong with their vehicles. It's not like they have the money to bring it to anyone who can fix it. But is it true about the sword?"

"Yes. It's in the back of his van. But he won't let anybody near it."

"I would love to get my hands on that sword."

"You just leave Eddy and his sword alone. Okay?"

"Okay," Effin said, backing off a bit. It wasn't like he was going to steal it, but sometimes things happen.

"There are two things that he holds dear and I intend to keep it that way. He even named them. Eddy calls his guitar Mercy, and his sword Redemption."

"Redemption?" Effin asked.

"Yes, Redemption."

PART TWO

CHAPTER 10

It was the call that Rip had been waiting for, ever since Laura had left him over a year ago. The call where Laura would say she was coming back to him. That she was wrong for leaving him, and that she had made a mistake. Well, maybe it wasn't exactly that call. But she did call collect.

Actually, Rip was surprised that Laura even had access to a phone since she was living in the outback. But there was an outpost where Laura and her boyfriend—Tarzan, as Rip called him—would pick up supplies when they needed them, and they had a pay phone.

When asked if Rip would accept charges, he said, "Sure," telling himself, *Let Hogwash and city hall foot the bill.*

"Rip, it's me, Laura."

For Rip, the beauty of her voice had not changed.

In that one moment, Rip gazed at the picture of her on the beach that was on his desk. He could almost hear the sound of the surf against the sands, and feel the breeze blow through his hair, and the warmth of her body in his arms.

No matter how much pain Laura had caused him by her leaving, Rip still felt an excitement hearing her voice. The song "Surfer Girl" by the Beach Boys played inside his head.

"Play nice, Bwana," Duderonomy said, appearing on his shoulder with a *Crocodile Dundee* hat. Rip gave him that side look like *What the hell are you wearing?*

"Play the part, be the part," Duderonomy replied. "But don't let the demons in. Come on Bwana, you can do it. You're a chief now. Of the paramedic division! You can win her back with your love."

"So, Laura, you are calling," Rip said, not knowing what else to say.

"Yes, I am calling you. I'm coming to San Francisco. I want to see you."

"I don't understand. Alone or with Tarzan?"

"He has a name, you know. It's Sydney. And yes, he is coming too."

There was silence.

"Come on Bwana. Play nice, PLAY NICE," Duderonomy pleaded with Rip.

"You're still mad at me, aren't you?" Laura asked.

"No, I'm not mad. I'm not mad. Of course, I'm still mad," Rip said, feeling his heart beat like Dennis Wilson beating a drum stick on a snare drum. "Is he legal yet?"

Duderonomy shook his head. "Come on, Bwana. Focus!"

"Yes, and he has a name."

"I know he has a name, but I don't want to say it."

"Can't we move past this?" Laura asked.

"Can we?" Duderonomy asked, holding up his hands, waiting for an answer.

"No, we can't," Rip replied.

Rip's demons had won. Little Poseidon, the Greek god of the sea holding a trident, pushed Duderonomy off of Rip's shoulder, and took his place. Little Poseidon was another one of Rip's demons that was fluid, and a troublemaker. He was an obstructionist when it came to crossing those rough seas of Laura. And Laura was the siren whose sweet song had wrecked Rip's heart.

"Well I'm coming to San Francisco next week, and I want to see you. What happened to the Rip I used to know?"

"The Rip you used to know is now the chief of the paramedic division. I have a badge, and hoping to get a company car, and I'm very busy. The wheels are in motion. And I got duties. Lots of duties."

"Duties?" Laura asked.

"Yes, duties. I run a department. That's a duty. Then there is this Chief Brady who keeps showing up, and he's got this grooming issue thing going on. And he gets his orders from a guy named Hogwash, the chief of staff of the mayor's office, who is not very fond of me either. And I am not a caged bird that sings. Yes, I remember you saying that once too."

"I thought that maybe you two could bond together."

"Bond? Him and me?" *With Elmer's glue*, Rip thought.

There was a quiet moment.

"I just thought you would be coming alone. Why did you want to move to the outback anyway?"

Little Poseidon was standing firm on Rip's shoulder, holding his trident, smiling.

"We already had that discussion."

"Well it never made sense to me."

"I'm sorry Rip, I've forgotten this side of you."

"Well it's there," Rip tried to explain. "Hidden, but it's there. I don't know why, but it just comes out. Smoking dope helps hide it, but now they're talking about drug testing. But I do seem to remember you writing to me about how you loved living in the wild, eating fruits and nuts and berries, and milking your own goats and raising your own eggs. And yes, I do know eggs come from chickens and not from Ashbury Market. I also remember how you told me that you met somebody who made you feel more like a woman than any other man ever did, and that was why you changed your name."

"I thought that we might have some closure. It's important to me," Laura said.

"Closure?"

Now Rip understood why Odysseus had his men tie him to the mast, so he would not succumb to the song of the sirens.

"Do you ever think of me?" Laura's voice was so lovely to Rip, like soothing waves on the beach receding back to the ocean.

"Every day. Okay?" Rip said, unable to hide his true feelings.

"Then you'll meet me?"

"Is he going to be there?"

"Yes. But do it for me. Remember, you didn't want to go with me, so I met Sydney."

"Sydney, eh? Laura, I'm a chief now. When you left I had just become a captain. What was I supposed to do? Drop everything? Was I supposed to give up my job and my pension to live in the outback eating berries?"

"It sounds like you are being a little hostile now, Rip."

"Me, hostile? Okay, I am being hostile. I just don't handle rejection well. And you know I'm full of self-doubt, and I don't even know if I'm going to be good at being a chief. I mean as a captain I made films, and everybody liked them. But I know that I'm only good at being Rip, and I thought that we were pretty good together. And yes, I still have your picture on my desk. The one with you on the beach. Remember we used to go to that special place near the ruins of Sutro Baths, and that Japanese tourist got all embarrassed 'cause he was hiking through, and he almost caught us? He didn't speak a word of English, but he knew what we were doing. Then we asked him to take a picture of us on my old camera. I still have that picture, too."

"Well, I can see you haven't changed, but Rip, you didn't go, and I was hurt, and then I met Sydney and my life has changed and so has yours. But can't we see each other, and put the past aside?"

Laura's voice was drawing Rip in, and turning his insides into jello. On Rip's shoulder, Little Poseidon crossed his arms and started violently shaking his head no. Knowing the power of her song, he poked Rip in the head with his trident just to snap him out of her trance. But like a mosquito in his ear, Rip swatted him aside with his hand, and Little Poseidon disappeared.

"You know I always had problems saying no to you," Rip said.

"Just this one time?"

"Okay, one time."

"With Sydney?"

When Laura asked, Rip knew he was defeated.

"Maybe."

"Will you play nice?"

"I can't say... Okay, I'll try. But not at Golden Gate Park. We will meet at the station. And I'm wearing my uniform. And tell Tarzan no flip flops. We can have a Coke or something."

"Rip, you know I don't eat processed sugar."

"Sorry, we ran out of sprouts."

"Come on Rip, can't we put everything behind us?"

"Okay, we will meet, but I'm not good at putting things behind me. You know that. Do you still think of me?"

"I called, didn't I? I'll call you when I get there. Please try to put the past behind us."

"Laura, I liked the past. I miss you too."

Rip was pouring out his heart.

"Rip, I just had to move on."

"Laura, I never wanted to move on. I only wanted things to be the way they used to be."

"So, we will meet together? All three of us, right?" Laura asked, trying to change the subject.

"Yeah," Rip said. "Okay."

Rip put the phone down and stared at the papers on his desk. What had he gotten himself into? Laura was coming back, but only to say goodbye again. It wasn't going to end in perfect harmony. The Beach Boys had packed up their guitars and their mikes and their drum kit, and had gone home.

Rip had always wondered why he never fell in love until he met Laura. Growing up he had his lovers, he had his flings, but nothing that really moved him inside. And Rip always wanted to be moved emotionally. But Rip was always afraid that maybe from the residual effect of watching his parents' painful relationship, he would always have problems maintaining a love relationship.

But it was not until Rip first saw Laura that he really fell in love. It was at the beach, and Rip was surfing and Laura was wearing that itsy-bitsy baby blue bikini, and she had stepped on some glass and cut her foot. Rip, being a paramedic, jumped into action. He held her foot. He cleaned it. He wrapped it up. He let her wear his San Francisco State sweater and drove her to the Emergency Room.

And Laura was beautiful. From their conversation in the ER, he found out that Laura was two years older than he was, had gone to Mills College, and from everything she said was trying to save the world. From her medical record Rip nonchalantly saw that Laura was on the pill. Good sign.

Rip hung out in the waiting room, and once her ER visit was over, took her for Chinese takeout food near Ocean Beach, and they ate while watching the sun go down. Then underneath the moonlight they had sex on the beach. For Rip it was butterflies in his stomach, and sand in their hair and everywhere else. After sex on the beach, they ran—or in Laura's case, limped—into the ocean naked to wash away all of the sand. Then they embraced again. It made Rip feel real good inside. He felt a purpose. He always had surfing as his spiritual enlightenment, but now came Laura. Beach Laura, bikini Laura, Chinese takeout food Laura, sex on the beach Laura, and Zen Laura. Yes, Laura believed in her Zen.

And since Laura believed in Zen, and Rip loved Laura, that meant Rip had to be a believer too…sort of. Laura even gave Rip a book called *Zen and the Art of Surfing*. As always, he didn't finish it. Rip came to the realization one day that he liked the part of Zen of living for the moment when it suited him, but being Zen all the time was hard work. He never saw the deeper nature of things as defined by Laura, but was certainly willing to go along. At times it was a very exciting ride. But to Rip, a flute was just a flute and a donut was just a donut. He never felt the need to interpret why they had holes in them. But Laura saw the difference, and since Rip loved her, and certainly enjoyed having sex with her, he learned the buzzwords because he was willing to convert to any philosophy so they could be together. Rip even read most of the book *Zen for Dummies*, and that was enough for him to get by. He also thought it was a great way to learn.

But along with being beautiful, Laura was also a very complex and strong-willed woman. She really did look like Christie Brinkley had a younger sister in her modeling days. Laura had the same blue eyes, the same silky blonde hair. Laura was athletic in high school, and radical in college. She went to Mills College for Women and majored in Political Activism. Mills College had a motto that you will be empowered to make a statement, and she did. She marched, she protested, she chanted, she took over administrative offices, she did sit-downs, die-ins, picketed the lunchroom to have healthier lunches, and even did radical cheerleading.

And Laura always took the liberal stand. She was against logging, and for saving the rainforests, and the dolphins, and the whales, and whatever else was on the endangered list that week. When it came to the government, everything was a conspiracy: the Kennedy assassinations, the King assassination, the Warren Report, Julius and Ethel Rosenberg, aliens, Area 51, Roswell, the Iraq war—well, the first one… It went on and on. When it came to government conspiracies, Laura was a political walking encyclopedia. And nobody, except maybe the most radical liberals, ever wanted to get her started on global warming. Laura always laughed when she thought Rip only saw her as his little surfer girl. But Laura loved Rip because he never questioned her convictions, and he loved her.

After dating for a while, Rip and Laura moved into an upper floor apartment on Oak Street with a balcony. When there was sun, she would sunbathe topless. It didn't matter that the neighbors saw. While Rip went to work for the paramedic division, Laura worked as a secretary in a law firm. Laura hated working there, and always wanted something more fulfilling, so she took night courses at San Francisco State on yoga and courses about the lives of the indigenous people in Australia. She was moved by the injustices they had faced throughout their lives. But for Rip, living with Laura was all he ever wanted, and that was enough for him. He had his blinders on, and he was happy. But Laura always wanted Rip to be more involved in the issues that mattered to her the most. But Rip was never an issue kind of guy.

So, it was a surprise to Rip that one day out of the blue, Laura decided she wanted to move to Australia, and live in the outback like the Aborigines. When she was a young girl, she had lived in Australia with her parents for a while, and being nature enthusiasts, they would take long rides through the most rugged areas. Like her family, Laura was all in with everything she did. It was the first time that Rip had ever asked her, "Why?" And Rip never asked why. Usually he would just go along when it came to what Laura wanted.

"It was the classes, wasn't it?" Rip asked.

"They certainly had something to do with it," Laura said, as she was making a stand for her convictions, "and I remember how happy I was living there as a child."

"But aren't you happy now?" Rip asked.

Laura always needed more. Rip then remembered that Laura had a fondness for the teacher of her yoga class. The younger, granola-eating, sandal-wearing, shoulder-length brown-haired guy was also big on the suffering of indigenous people, and had backpacked in the outback for a while. Rip also remembered he had given Laura an article about some group of artists who moved to the outback to start their own self-sufficient communities. At the time Rip thought, *Why would anybody ever go there?* But for Laura it planted a seed. Laura and her teacher also went to protest rallies together for whatever was the current cause of the day. Rip wondered, during these discussions over her leaving, if Laura had ever slept with the yoga teacher. He never brought it up because he didn't want to know the answer, and he seemed to be on the losing side of wanting her to stay.

But for her side, Laura wanted Rip to give up everything for her, and live off the land in the outback, and start a community of artists who would express themselves through nature. Laura was quite surprised, and felt abandoned when Rip wouldn't go. But Rip was too much the hippie surfing dude to leave California. He liked the Bay Area, and working for the paramedic division. He liked running water. He liked hot showers and comfortable beds at night. Those were important. Rip had expected Laura and himself to get married one day, and move to Marin, and drive a Subaru, and have little blond-haired surfer kids with blue eyes. It was hard for Rip to argue with anybody because of his dad's tantrums, but they talked about it till there was nothing more to say. Laura was leaving, but Rip always thought that this outback thing was just one of her phases, and once getting a taste of it, would come running back to him.

But while backpacking in the outback, Laura met a boy barely eighteen years old named Sydney, while she was in her early thirties, and once they had gotten together, she had never felt so free. Laura had fallen in love. And when Laura fell in love, she wrote a letter telling Rip how she had met someone else, and how she felt about him, and how happy she was living off the land, and never felt better about her life. She also said she wasn't sure if she would ever be coming back again. Then there was another scribbled note that looked like it was written on tree bark, saying that she had changed her name to Morningstar and wasn't coming back, and it broke his heart even more.

After Laura left, Rip saw this Sydney as a muscle-bound Tarzan, swinging in a loincloth with Laura in his arms, from tree to tree, even though there was mostly scrub and brush in the outback, and the trees were not nearly as massive as the ones in the deepest of Africa. But in Rip's mind, he was sure that Laura had become a princess to the Aborigine locals who came from afar to worship her blue eyes and blonde hair. Instead of cheetah, Rip thought they probably had a dingo. As time went on, Rip always held on to the hope that Laura would get tired of living in the outback, and would come back to him, and she would forget about Tarzan, and together they would feel the same magic as when they first met on the beach.

"Do you love me?" Rip hummed when thinking about her. "My sweet surfer girl."

CHAPTER 11

It was the one Wednesday of the year when Jan received her invitation from Mother Stein for the upcoming annual Stein Family Reunion. Most of the time, on the third Wednesday of every month when Jan would receive her letter from Mother Stein, it only had the effect of a mild earthquake, a roller. But not today. It was 1906 all over again, and not enough water to put out the flames.

Everybody stayed away. Reed called in sick for the whole week knowing from the past the exact Wednesday of the year when the family reunion invitation would arrive. But it was also a good time for Reed to call in sick, as the invitation coincided with the need for pruning the buds of his marijuana plants.

And it was a grand family reunion invitation. The invitation looked as if it had come from the president of the United States, if he was Republican, and it was for an inauguration more than a reunion of family members. At the heading of the invitation was written *The Stein Family Reunion* with Roman numerals for the year, in gold leaf. The backdrop of the invitation was a picture of a horse-drawn carriage, ridden by a coachman with two passengers: a man with a top hat and a woman wearing a bonnet, sitting in cushioned seats riding by the old San Francisco Mint in the 1800s.

The reunion was to be held in San Diego at the Hotel del Coronado. Why San Diego, you may ask? Well, Jan's brothers and sisters lived in the San Diego area, and Mrs. Stein never wanted the grandchildren to fly, considering her husband died in a plane crash on a big game hunting expedition in Africa. He was in the Ernest Hemingway phase of his life, and he wanted to see Mount Kilimanjaro. Unfortunately, he saw it a little too closely, as the plane crashed into the mountain, and he was killed in a fiery crash. In times of need, after receiving the invitation, Jan went to Rip.

"Family reunions! I hate them! I hate them! Everybody is going to be judging me," Jan said, coming into Rip's office, pacing back and forth, as Rip sat at his desk, watching *News at Noon* on TV. Since he had become a chief, cable was now provided by the department, along with a color TV. The newscasters were making jokes on the air that the Gray Beavers were planning another rally at city hall.

"It's going to be a big one," one of the newscasters said.

"How do you arrest a Gray Beaver?" the other newscaster asked. There was laughter.

"Damn Gray Beavers," Rip muttered. "I'm going to hear it from Hogwash again."

"What?" Jan said, waving her hands. "You're talking about beavers. I wish the only problem I had with my family was them exposing themselves instead of these damn reunions."

"Why go?" Rip finally asked. "My family never had reunions even when they were together. They weren't even together when they were together. And nobody else from the family wanted to invite us if they ever had one anyway."

"Rip, this is my family," Jan said, looking a little heartfelt.

"Jan, with your mother's letters and everything? Why put yourself through this?"

"Because," Jan said, turning off the TV and pulling up a chair, and sitting across from Rip. "There was always a part of me that wanted my mother's approval. Her acceptance. I never got it, so every year I always hoped it would be different. I always thought that one day I'd be accepted for who I am, and every year they let me down. And then there is my creepy Cousin Billy, and his stupid Jerry Lewis imitation."

That certainly got Rip's attention. "Come again?"

"I got this creepy Cousin Billy who emcees the event. We used to call him Pudgy Billy growing up. Tortured him until we made him cry. Well, after his stint in rehab, he thought for some reason that he was a comedian, and he always had this Jerry Lewis infatuation. So, at the reunion, after dinner, he goes up on this makeshift stage, imitating Jerry Lewis, and does this stupid stand-up routine, and just tears into everybody. You could call it payback."

"Really...like, 'Hey, lady' Jerry Lewis? Somehow getting to know your family makes my family almost look good again."

"Haha. Make all the stupid jokes you want. But what do you think about going with me?"

"What?" Rip asked, taken aback, thinking, *I have enough problems with my own family, and now you want me to get involved in yours?* But knowing Jan, and her *sensitivity*, to put it mildly, on all issues concerning her family—especially the Stein Family Reunion—he thought it best not to go that way. He took a deep breath, and leaned back to soften the rejection.

"Jan, I know how difficult it can be dealing with families, but I have a lot of things going on around here. I got Hogwash, Chief Brady, this merger everyone is talking about, and my dad and his Gray Beaver fixation, and...somebody called me."

"Somebody? Who? Was it my mother?"

"It was Laura," Rip said, and he wasn't smiling.

"You mean outback, hippie, Morningstar Laura?"

"Yes, Laura."

"What did she say?"

"She is coming to San Francisco."

"Alone, or with Tarzan?"

"With Tarzan. She wants closure."

"More like torture than closure. I'm sure you stood up to her, and said no."

"Did you stand up to your mother?"

"Okay. Good point. Where are you meeting her?"

"Well, we are not going to meet in Golden Gate Park. I made that clear. I don't want nature boy enjoying himself."

"So, you're bringing them here?" Jan asked, looking around his office.

"There's nothing wrong with Station 51. And my office is fine. We come here every day."

"You want her to see you in your chief's uniform, don't you?" Jan asked knowingly.

"I just told her that Tarzan can't wear flip flops. But of course, I'll be wearing my uniform."

"Are you going to wear the tie?"

"Maybe."

"Please don't wear the tie. But now you need me more than ever," Jan said.

"How do I need you?"

"Rip, I am a woman," Jan said, pushing up her breasts a little teasingly. "If you promise to go with me to this reunion, then I'll make sure you can have some alone time with Laura."

"Jan, Laura is bringing Tarzan."

"Leave it to me. I'll figure it out."

"What, are you going to sleep with him?"

"No, stupid. Distract him while you have some alone time with Laura."

"I don't know," Rip said.

"Come on. You stuck me with Dibble. You owe me."

"He needed to make it. I figure if he couldn't make it with you…"

"Great. Somehow I hear a compliment in there."

"That was a compliment…sort of."

"Come on. Come with me to the reunion, and I'll help you with Laura," Jan asked pleadingly.

"How much alone time with Laura are we talking about?" Rip asked.

Jan leaned over and gave Rip the look that she only reserved for the nighttime. Rip just loved her bedroom eyes, and wondered why they didn't sleep together more often.

"How much alone time do you need?" Jan asked.

"Oh well, hmm. Being alone with Laura, uh? Really?"

"So, you're going to the reunion with me?" Jan asked.

"Well…maybe."

"By the way, it's in San Diego."

"San Diego?"

"I'll pay for the flight, and the room, and there's great fish tacos."

"Fish tacos? Are we doing doubles or sharing a king size bed?"

"That depends how well this reunion goes," Jan said, leaving those bedroom eyes open.

"But you have to book the room beforehand."

"Well you'll just have to find that out for yourself."

"Okay, fine. As long as I get some alone time with Laura. Maybe if she saw what she has been missing..." Rip said, not finishing his sentence.

"And...?"

"And I'll be sweet and nice and deal with Cousin Billy and Mother Stein, and whoever else shows up."

"Promise?"

"Yes. Promise. Everything will be fine. I'll turn on the old Rip Ridley charm. I can even wear my uniform."

"You are not wearing your uniform. I need you looking California smart."

"California smart?"

"I'll tell you what to wear. I'll pick it out for you. I've seen your closet before."

"And I'll get my alone time with Laura?"

"Yes. I said I'll deal with Tarzan."

"Okay. Deal."

When Jan left, Rip started dialing.

"Hello Dad, it's me, Rip."

"Are you going to lecture me about the Gray Beavers again?" Rip's dad asked.

"Dad, I saw the news, and it's all over the TV that there is going to be another rally with the Gray Beavers at city hall, and this one is going to be bigger than the others before. I haven't heard from the mayor's office yet, but I'm sure it's coming."

For once, Rip's dad did not reply.

"Do you know about it?" Rip asked.

"I heard."

"I heard. That's it. You're not going, are you?"

"This protesting got to be a lot of hard work."

"Wait a minute," Rip said. "You are not having sex with any of them, are you?"

"Well… They said I was politically inept. I mean first they protest this, then they protest that, and I kept forgetting where I was supposed to be, and what I'm supposed to be protesting, and it takes a lot of time. But I want to make it clear that they never complained about the sex. But for me, without the sex, well there really wasn't a reason."

"Fantastic."

"Don't you want to know about the beautiful woman I met at the bookstore today?"

"No," Rip said, "no."

"She's French."

"Yeah, just like you. Goodbye."

Rip hung up the phone.

When Rip finished the call, Arne Dibble was at his door.

"Chief Ridley sir, can I speak with you?" Arne asked, looking like a choir boy.

"Paramedic Dibble, come on in. Sit down. Hope you still don't mind the rookie tag. We all get it. What do you need today?"

Rip was upbeat now. Jan promised he was going to get some alone time with Laura, and his dad was going to stop hanging out with the Gray Beavers and exposing his penis in public.

Arne sat across from Rip, as if he was in a confessional booth not quite knowing what sins he had committed, but always feeling that he had to do penance.

"Sir," Arne started, "I don't think I should be working with Jan this week. I heard about her family reunion. Everybody is talking about it. Even Reed called in sick. I feel something bad is going to happen."

"Bad? I just talked to her. Everything is going to be fine. And I'm going with her to the reunion to make everything nice.

It's in San Diego, and they have pretty good fish tacos. Have you been having any problems with her?"

"No, sir," Arne said, sitting up. "Not if I don't talk to her, and I do everything she asks me to do, and I never make eye contact, then we are fine."

"See, everything is working out."

"Sir, I really don't see that as working out."

"Well, I just got a call from my ex-girlfriend Laura, and she used to tell me that in the world of Zen when two negative ions collide, sometimes a positive outcome occurs."

"Sir, I took science, and I never learned that."

"Well, you never met Laura. At the time I was sleeping with her, if the price for sex was to believe in Zen, then it was well worth it. Of course, there was some meditation that went along with it which usually put me to sleep. But I got a good feeling that you and Jan are overdue for a positive outcome."

"Sir, I don't really see a positive outcome. Do you still see her?" Arne asked Rip.

"Who?"

"Your ex-girlfriend, sir."

"Laura? No, she's left me, Arne. She left me. She left me to go to the outback with mud huts and dingoes, and met some young boy of eighteen who I call Tarzan. I'm sure he's almost twenty by now. But funny you should ask because she's coming back with Tarzan to see me for closure."

"Sir, it doesn't sound promising."

"At first, I thought so too, but now, well maybe…"

"Sir, that's good, but I don't really think that anything positive can come from working with Jan this week."

"Look at it this way," Rip confided, "I know Jan is not the easiest person to be with at times, but perhaps the animosity that you say Jan shows you is temporary. It can't be all negative. Trust me, Jan does have a better side. And as Laura used to tell me, when I felt a little down, 'Even the smallest seed sometimes turns into a beautiful flower.' Laura was good that way. God, I miss sleeping with her."

"Sir, it's not temporary with Jan. It's all the time. I have never seen her good side. But if you don't mind me asking, what does seeing your ex-girlfriend have to do with me working with Jan?"

"It doesn't, Arne. It doesn't. But I just thought I would put another spin on it. Another perspective. I guess you can say I'm a little excited about seeing Laura again. Funny, just thinking about Laura, and hearing her voice again, brings back all that Zen stuff."

"But sir, you said she was coming here with her boyfriend."

"I may have that covered," Rip said, thinking of Jan's idea.

"So you are saying, sir…"

"I am saying that maybe if I get some alone time with Laura, we could talk about the good times we once had together. Then maybe she will see what she is missing, and she'll want to stay, and we can pick up the pieces."

"Sir, do you really think she will?"

"I don't know, Arne. I really don't know," Rip had to admit.

"Sir, so am I still working with Jan?" Arne asked, looking totally defeated.

"Arne," Rip said reassuringly, riding the Laura wave, still thinking about her, "Laura used to say to me that enlightenment can be attained through intuition, and I have a good feeling about you working with Jan this week, and I want you to have that same feeling, too."

"But sir, your intuition is not based on the past."

"It never is. But according to Laura, it doesn't have to be. Everything is for the moment. That's what makes Zen so great."

"Sir, do you really know Zen?"

"At times."

"You still love her, sir, don't you?" Arne asked.

"Well, love is a strong word—but yes, madly. We used to eat at the Hare Krishna temple in Berkeley every Thursday night, and jump around a lot and chant over and over, 'Hare Krishna,' and eat with the homeless people because they were giving away free food. Not bad either. But I could never give up meat. And I was never crazy about their clothes. Lots of rags and loosely fitting robes, and that white chalk they put on their faces. Is this helping any?"

"Not at all, sir."

"Let me put it another way," Rip said, almost giddy, thinking about alone time with Laura. "I didn't have a good feeling about seeing Laura again, but then something came up, and now I do. I think it's going to work out for the both of us, me and you. Though for different reasons. I really think it's going to work out. Let's just see what happens."

"So, I'll still be working with Jan, sir?" Arne asked one last time, sounding like a plea for help.

"Arne," Rip began, "if there is a problem working with Jan, let me know and I will talk to her."

"I thought that's what I was doing, sir."

"Arne, I will talk to her. I will. But with Jan, let her cool down a bit over this reunion thing. It's only once a year, and Reed will be back in a week. And while Reed is gone, you are actually working with a great guy named Dean Manuel. He has a nickname, Cherry Pie, but I wouldn't call him that. Little sensitive in that area."

"Cherry Pie, sir?"

"Yeah, yeah, Cherry Pie. But call him Dean. Or Paramedic Manuel in your case. I'm sure he will warm up to you in no time."

"In no time, sir?"

"Yes, Arne, in no time. Trust me. The wheels are in motion."

"In motion, sir?"

"Everything will work out with Laura…I mean Jan. Trust me, Arne."

Rip ignored Arne, and picked up the picture of Laura, remembering the intimate times they had together—especially the times when they first met—and his heart started thumping.

Dejected, Arne got up and left Rip's office to stock Ambulance 54 for the day.

"Glad we could have this talk," Rip said as Arne walked down the hall.

Rip gazed at Laura's picture in his hand, and after putting a quarter in his mental jukebox, started humming the opening bars to "Wouldn't it Be Nice."

CHAPTER 12

Dean Manuel was a seasoned veteran in the medic world, and was certainly no wilting flower. His nickname, though never to his face, was Cherry Pie. That was because being bald and overweight, and being known for his quick temper whenever he got angry, a rim of red surrounded his face, making him look like a cherry pie. Though not known for his sense of humor, Dean was known for his sarcastic wit when dealing with patients. At times it bordered on being inappropriate. He had a pattern, as management liked to say. There were write-ups, but even when he was wrong, Dean Manuel never backed down from authority.

And Dean was gay. Radically gay. His claim to fame was that he had never slept with a woman, and he was proud of it. Growing up in New Mexico with parents of Mexican descent where Spanish was spoken at home, after graduating from high school, Dean came home wearing a dress to the shock of his family. His father, wanting to make a man out of him, shipped him off to the Navy. But Dean found that he liked the structure of the Navy, and was especially fond of the uniforms. He learned his medic skills in the Navy, and found the first love of his life, the Navy chaplain. Being in love with the chaplain, Dean found himself going to services more often. His parents, being stanch Christians, saw that as a good sign. He also found a love for poetry after the chaplain introduced him to "Leaves of Grass" by Walt Whitman.

Along with the beauty of the poems, the chaplain tried to teach Dean the lessons Walt Whitman taught: to always be kind, and to be helpful to the sick and the poor. That only worked for a while until Dean became a medic at the Evans Street Station, and saw too many patients throughout the years with the same ailments, and the same problems, and the same attitudes. His compassion eroded like an old Jesus statue in the backyard that had been left out too long in inclement weather. The paint of Dean's compassion had been chipped, and the metal was discolored. Dean Manuel was not the Walt Whitman that the chaplain wanted him to be. Instead he became Cherry Pie, with his sarcastic wit.

With Jan and Dean in Ambulance 54, and Arne as their intern, the day started off like any other. Jan didn't talk to Arne, and only made small talk with Dean. Dean acted as if Arne didn't exist. He had no time for rookies. Arne was on guard because he knew it could be a teapot kind of day. Which meant that the teapot was on the stove, and it was just a matter of time when it was going to boil over if he wasn't careful. And there was no whistle on this teapot to alert him when the boiling point had been reached.

While Dean drove, Jan sat in the passenger seat. Arne sat in silence in the jump seat in the back, and never said a word.

Their first call was a kid who fell off his skateboard, chipped his tooth and scraped his knee, tearing his jeans. They let Arne clean him up. His mother looked like an ex-hippie who had come into some money by marrying a rich older lawyer, and now they had a nice house in the Richmond District on California Street. She was a bit hysterical, but settled down so they packed up the kid, with the mother in tow, and took him to CalPac.

The next call was an elderly lady who lost her keys, couldn't get into her house, and started to have heart palpitations. Even though the woman reminded Jan of her mother, she calmed her down, and had one of the engine crew climb into a half-open window to get inside the house and open the front door. Jan even wrote it up as a no merit, which meant that the patient would not get billed. By midafternoon, even Arne was starting to breathe a little easier, and was no longer using his asthma inhaler, which he sometimes used when having anxiety attacks. During a break, they had coffee at Peet's, and Arne, knowing his place, paid. Jan gave Arne a disapproving eye when he only left a quarter tip, so he upped it to a dollar.

But the life of a medic is not about negative ions colliding and creating positive outcomes as Rip said, quoting Laura. It's about getting a call, going on scene, assessing the situation, and being prepared for what happens next. The only things that collide are personalities. Jan understood that. Dean understood that. And now Arne was about to learn it.

And everything may have worked out just fine that day, if only Arne had listened to Dean. It was a call at Market and Castro that started out innocent enough. Two guys in their thirties, both a bit pudgy, one wearing a red Hawaiian short-sleeve shirt, and the other wearing a blue Hawaiian short-sleeve shirt, were drinking in a gay bar. With their Burt Reynolds hair-cuts, they started arguing about whatever drunken lovers argue about. The bartender told them to take it outside because he had seen their act before, and didn't want to hear it again.

At first the two guys put up a stink about how they had rights, and they were allowed to drink anywhere they wanted. But the bartender had had enough and told them to go.

"Your rights start at the curb. Not in here. Take it outside."

He took their drinks away and pointed to the door, and reluctantly they were out on the street.

But now, being tossed out of the bar and away from their drinks, the two guys became angrier, and their argument continued. The effect of the alcohol went to their heads, and while crossing the street, the guy with the blue Hawaiian shirt tripped on the shoe of the guy with the red Hawaiian shirt, and then stumbled and went down, scraping his elbow. Blue Hawaiian shirt guy's elbow was now red with blood from his fall that mixed with the ocean blue of his Hawaiian shirt. The bartender, watching the event, called for an ambulance.

When Ambulance 54 arrived, everybody in the bar watched, but then their attention went back to their drinks in front of them. The bartender just shook his head, turned away from the window, and turned the volume up on the TV. They were watching a tape of an English soap opera.

"Okay, Rookie," Dean told Arne as they got out of the ambulance, "it's your time to shine. Clean Hawaiian shirt guy up, and get him into the back of the ambulance."

Dean observed Arne cleaning up blue Hawaiian shirt's elbow, and then went back into the ambulance. Arne wrapped it and told blue Hawaiian shirt guy to please get into the back of the ambulance, so they could transport him to the hospital.

"I have a bad ankle, too," blue Hawaiian shirt guy replied, sitting on the curb. "I think it is swollen."

"Well, sir, if you follow me to the ambulance…"

"My ankle hurts. I can't get up. I took a first aid class, and took classes to be a paramedic. I know my rights. I want a stair chair."

"But sir, I think you can walk. I think your ankle is fine," Arne said, trying to be professional.

"I know my rights. I want a stair chair."

"But…"

"My rights."

Arne, not knowing what to do, walked over to Dean, who was sitting in the driver's seat, and told him about blue Hawaiian shirt guy's request.

"Jesus, Rookie," Dean said. "A stair chair? Tell him to get in the back of the ambulance, or we are leaving. We are not carrying this guy."

Arne went back to blue Hawaiian shirt guy and tried to coax him into getting into the back of the ambulance on his own, but he wasn't moving. And now blue Hawaiian shirt guy was also getting a little belligerent. A small crowd started to form. There was a kid from City College who was doing a video on the history of the Castro and had borrowed a recorder from film class, and he started to film the incident, which at first was no big deal, but now was becoming one.

Arne, noticing people starting to mingle around, went back to Dean, and told him what was going on.

"Really, Rookie? You can't handle this? You got a crowd out there now?" Dean Manuel said, starting to boil. His face started turning red.

"He won't budge until we get a stair chair."

"And you can't convince him?"

"I tried."

"Fuck," Dean said, getting out of the ambulance obviously irritated. In front of the crowd that had formed, Dean walked up to blue Hawaiian shirt guy, with Arne behind him.

"What is going on?" Dean asked blue Hawaiian shirt guy.

"I know my rights. If I need to get picked up, you have to do it," blue Hawaiian shirt guy said with a drunken slur.

"I'll get the stair chair," Arne told Dean.

"Don't," Dean said to Arne. "He either gets up, or he sits there all day."

"I'm on probation," Arne pleaded with Dean, "and I don't want to get into any trouble. I'll get the stair chair."

"If you get that stair chair, Rookie, then you and him are going to sit on that curb all day. Now take him by his arm, and gently get him in back of the ambulance. Lift him softly, take him by his hand if needed, but get him in back of that ambulance—now."

While Dean watched, Arne walked over to blue Hawaiian shirt guy without the stair chair, and tried to talk to him, pleading his case to the patient.

"I'm on probation. I need you to get into the back of the ambulance."

"I want the stair chair."

"Let me help you. Take my hand. Let me help you up," Arne said, starting to embarrass himself by not taking control of the scene.

"I know why," blue Hawaiian shirt guy told Arne. "I know why you're not getting the stair chair."

"Sir, please, I will help you into the ambulance."

"It's because I'm gay, isn't it?" blue Hawaiian shirt guy told Arne loudly as if making a drunken speech. "If I was straight, this was downtown, and if I was wearing a suit then you would have picked me up by now, wouldn't you? But no, I'm gay. A gay man in America. That's what I am. You can't change bigots. You just can't. Well I'm not walking. And look at all the blood on my nice blue Hawaiian shirt that I just bought yesterday. How am I going to get this out?"

"So that's it," Dean said, stepping into blue Hawaiian shirt guy's field of vision. "It's because you are gay and we are bigots."

"I call them as I see them."

Arne went to the back of the ambulance and started taking out the stair chair.

"Don't do it, Rookie. Don't do it," Jan said. She was not coming out of the ambulance for this one.

Arne pulled it out anyway, which made Dean more furious. He walked away from the patient, and now to Arne. Dean pointed his finger at him.

"Put it back, Rookie. NOW," he said.

"Sir, you are getting a little red."

"What are you saying, Rookie?"

"Your face. It's getting red."

"My face?"

"Yes, it's getting red."

"Like a cherry pie?"

"I didn't say that."

"Are you calling me Cherry Pie?" Dean screamed.

"No," Arne said, sweating. "I don't even know what that means."

"Put back the stair chair." Dean raised his voice. "I've had enough of you, and I have had enough of this guy too."

Arne, totally defeated, slowly started putting the stair chair back into the ambulance.

"You, Hawaiian shirt guy," Dean said, walking over to the patient still sitting on the curb. "Get into the back of the ambulance. I do not have time for this."

Dean was now standing over him.

But blue Hawaiian shirt guy was just too shitfaced to understand the nuances of Dean Manuel on a bad call.

"I took paramedic classes, and I know you have to do what I ask you to do if I'm injured. And I am in need of care," blue Hawaiian shirt guy blathered on.

"You took paramedic classes?" Dean asked.

"I did."

"Did you pass?"

"No."

"Well I fucking did, and I'm telling you that you don't need a stair chair, and get in the back of the ambulance or you are not going anywhere."

"You're not doing it because you're a bigot."

"So that's it. I'm a bigot? You're sticking to that again. And that's the reason you are not getting up?" Dean said with his arms folded.

While the crowd that had formed looked on, and the recorder was filming, Dean stared angrily at blue Hawaiian shirt guy, and leaned into his face.

"Well, let me tell you something and let me tell you good. I am not picking you up. You either get your ass into the back of the ambulance, or you're not going. And let me tell you something else. Gay! You talk about being GAY! Well I was gay before gays were allowed to be gay. And I am a lot older than you, and I've been sucking dick when you still didn't know how to wipe your ass. So, don't give me this gay shit. This is not amateur hour, and I have no time for all of your bullshit. There is nothing wrong with you except for a few bruises. This is my ambulance, and I am losing my patience. So, either get up and get in the ambulance, or I'm leaving."

"But you have to take me. I'm injured. That's your job," blue Hawaiian shirt guy said, looking up at Dean. It was a feeble cry.

"Oh yeah? You're telling me what my job is? Well, let me tell you something. I don't have to take you anywhere. You are talking to the wrong homosexual here." Dean then turned to Arne. "Rookie, finish putting the stair chair back into the ambulance because we are leaving. He can take a cab."

"But Paramedic Manuel…" Arne tried to say.

"What, Rookie? What are you going to tell me? How my face looks all red like a cherry pie?"

"No," Arne said, looking white as a ghost, knowing he had crossed the line, as he finished putting the stair chair back, slowly got in the back of the ambulance, and sat in his little jump seat. Dean got into the driver's seat, but he was not done with Arne yet.

"You had to push that button, Rookie, didn't you? You just couldn't keep your mouth shut, and get him in back of the ambulance. Could you? How red is my face now? Uh, Rookie? Tell me how it looks. Is it red? Say it. Is it red like a cherry pie?"

With Dean in the driver's seat, Jan in the passenger seat, and Arne sitting in the back, Ambulance 54 drove away.

"Hey," blue Hawaiian shirt guy screamed, still sitting on the curb, watching them leave, "What about me?"

"Yeah, Hawaiian shirt guy," Dean said to nobody, "what about you?"

Nobody said anything on the way back to the station. Dean wrote it up as a difficult patient with minor injuries, not wanting to get into the ambulance to be transported, and it should have been over with that. But there was too big of a crowd, and in the next few days calls started coming in complaining about a certain medic's attitude when treating a patient at Castro and Market Street. And the kid who was making his film on the Castro, and perceived what he saw as an injustice, sent a tape of the incident to the mayor's office with a letter complaining about Paramedic Dean Manuel's demeanor that read like a manifesto. After receiving the tape from the mayor, Hogwash watched it, and had it couriered to Rip's office. He even called Rip. He was not happy.

"Yes sir, I've seen it," Rip said, trying to explain to Hogwash. "Of course, like yourself, I was appalled. But then I thought that maybe Dean was just trying to express his own preferences when the incident happened, and really said nothing derogatory."

"Nothing derogatory? Are you out of your mind? I want a suspension," Hogwash demanded.

"A suspension? Sir, I was thinking about a coaching, and a sensitivity class. He can quote 'Leaves of Grass.'"

"I want a three-day suspension, and I don't give a damn about 'Leaves of Grass.'"

"But sir, they are very good poems."

"Get somebody to write it up. I want an investigation. It's in the public, dammit. Maybe the mayor picked the wrong paramedic chief."

"Does the mayor know me?" Rip asked, wondering.

Hogwash hung up the phone.

Rip, with no way out, had to assign the write-up to someone. Dean Manuel was being brought up on charges. Rip, thinking he was doing Dean a favor, assigned the write-up to RC Jules Diamond. Jules only cared about his political future, and wouldn't run with it. Which meant he wouldn't make it bigger than it really was. The write-up by RC Jules Diamond recommended three days on the beach—as suspension days were called—a sensitivity class, a week on Treasure Island for recert training, and that was the end of it for RC Jules Diamond. Like Pontius Pilate, he had washed his hands of the whole affair.

But Dean Manuel wasn't having any of it. He wasn't backing down. He went to the union, and asked for representation. He wanted a formal disciplinary hearing. The charge at first was only *Inattention to duty*. But when Hogwash found out that this medic was not going to accept the three days, and now wanted a hearing, he had Human Resources add *Failure to render care to a patient* and *Gross dereliction of duty* to the charges. Then he called Rip.

"What is wrong with your department?" Hogwash said to Rip. "How come you can't get your people in line? And who the hell is this Dean Manuel?"

"He went to the union, and has a right to a hearing," Rip said to Hogwash meekly.

"He's a friend of yours, isn't he, this Dean Manuel?"

"We came in together."

"This is a very sensitive issue for the mayor. The gay community is very important, and we want this to go away. He needs to accept the three days and move on."

"He is very strong-willed, sir."

"Well then your job, Chief Ridley, is to make him less strong-willed. It's on film. What do you think would happen if the newspapers got a copy of it? It wouldn't be too good for him or you. So, get it done. It's on you now."

"On me?" Rip asked.

"On you."

But Dean Manuel, a.k.a. Cherry Pie, had suffered the slings and arrows of his sexual preference all his life, and was having none of it.

Before Rip even tried to talk to him, Dean came up to him. "Chief, I don't care what they do to me. I want my hearing."

"Dean, they have you on film." Rip tried to reason with him. "Kind of impressive, I have to admit. Maybe think about taking the three days."

"I'll take the three days all right. But I want my hearing."

Damn! Rip thought to himself. *Maybe a gift from Reed of his new harvest*, Rip thought, *would change Dean's mind?* But Dean was too smart for that.

"It's nothing personal, Rip, but please don't try to go to Reed for his new harvest. I already have some."

"Damn," Rip groaned but this time not only to himself.

"It would have been a nice gesture, but I don't care what they do to me."

"What about?" Rip asked, trying to find a soft spot in Dean's armor.

"What about what?" Dean asked, walking away. There would be no changing his mind. Rip knew Dean was not going to back down.

"What about me?" Rip muttered when Dean had walked away, and he started thinking about the trouble he was going to have with Hogwash. "What about me?"

CHAPTER 13

Looking in the mirror of the bathroom in his office, Rip thought he looked good in his Class A uniform, straightening his tie. For one day, Rip could put behind his problems with Hogwash, and Jan's complaints about having to work with Arne, and Cherry Pie not accepting his three-day suspension and wanting a hearing with Human Resources. Today there was only Laura. Lovely, lovely Laura. Rip looked at the picture of Dennis Wilson he had near the mirror, and tried to get the Beach Boys surfer-style wave just right. He combed the front of his hair on the right side, and then did a once-over with hairspray. In his mind the Beach Boys were playing "Surfin' USA," and everybody had an ocean that day across the USA. Rip had even woken up that morning early, and took a few puffs of Reed's pot.

"So, Laura is coming. Big day, Bwana! But you can't make your tie any straighter, and your wave is fine," Duderonomy said, wearing a wetsuit and carrying a mini surfboard while sitting on Rip's shoulder, as they both looked into the mirror. With his hand, Duderonomy fanned away the smell of the hairspray. "Now remember, Bwana, don't go to the dark side. Stay positive. Be the old Bwana. The funny Bwana. The Chinese takeout food Bwana. The burrito Bwana. The Bwana Laura first fell in love with on the beach. And don't make fun of Tarzan."

"I know what I'm doing," Rip said.

"Yeah, but sometimes…" Duderonomy said, not quite finishing his sentence.

"Is there anything else?" Rip asked Duderonomy, still looking in the mirror.

"Fly low, Bwana. Fly low."

Duderonomy disappeared.

When Rip came out of the bathroom, Jan and Reed were waiting for him in his office.

"Ready for your big day?" Jan asked.

"Do you think I should wear the chief's hat?"

"Why not? Or at least hold it in your hand."

Rip didn't think it was a bad idea. *But it may mess up my hair*, he thought. Rip didn't comprehend that Jan was just kidding.

"Leave the hat," Jan finally said.

"So, everything is under control?" Rip asked. Not leaving anything to chance.

"Operation Morningstar is underway," Jan said, laughing at Rip as if he was a little kid. "Her plane has already landed."

"Where are they staying?"

"Not the best hotel. The Buena Vista. Near Ocean Beach. At least it has a hot tub."

Laura may have changed her name to Morningstar, but to Rip she would always be Laura. And when Laura's cab pulled up to the Fairfax gate of the station, Rip, Jan, and Reed were waiting.

But to Rip's surprise, when Laura and Tarzan came out of the cab, Laura didn't look like the same little surfer girl he once knew. Instead of seeing the Laura of old, with her long, flowing Christie Brinkley hair, it was all natty and Rasta and flat on one side, like she had slept on it the whole flight. And Tarzan, the one who took his love away, looked more like Keanu Reeves in one of his bad movies, after an all-night bender. Tarzan was tall and muscular, but he also had Rasta hair and a stumpy beard, and he wore sandals. For clothes, they both wore what could be considered animal skins of furs and leather that were laced together with leather straps. And they both looked a little on the dirty side.

"Laura," Rip finally said.

"Hi Rip."

At least her voice hadn't changed. Since a small crowd had been forming in the yard for the eventful moment, Jan mentioned that maybe they should take this to Rip's office. Rip agreed. All eyes stared at Laura and Tarzan as they walked through the warehouse and up the stairs.

"Jesus," Effin said after they had passed. "Looks like a Tarzan movie without the extras."

Jesus didn't say anything, but even to a man who heard the voice of God while watching a Burger King commercial, they really looked—at the very least—out of place.

Once in the office, Tarzan's eyes looked all around, fascinated by all Rip's memorabilia. He went over to the tuba.

"Don't touch the tuba, Sydney," Laura snapped at him.

He jumped back at Laura's command. He was no Johnny Weissmuller, but physically he was a specimen. His fascination of everything in Rip's office was as if he had shiny light syndrome, wanting to touch any bright object. And both of them, in their outback garb, looked like they had just come off the set of the Raquel Welch movie, *One Million Years BC*.

"Laura, well hello," Rip said, actually surprised, wondering where did the woman of his dreams go? She had to be in there somewhere.

"Rip, how are you?" Laura asked.

"Good. Working. The wheels are in motion. Lots of paperwork. Lots of ideas. Lots of doing. I'm a chief now."

"I know."

Jan looked at Laura and Tarzan and was simply amazed with what they were wearing. She tried but just couldn't hold back.

"They let you on the plane like that?" Jan asked.

"It's Aboriginal in nature. Have we met?" Laura asked.

"What happened to your hair?"

"Sydney thinks it's more natural to our surroundings."

"You could have at least gone to Ross," Jan said just loud enough for everyone to hear.

"And who are you again?" Laura asked.

"Jan."

"Oh right. Rip told me about you. You were the substitute for me when I left him to go to the outback."

"You told her?" Jan said, looking annoyed at Rip.

"It was a moment of weakness. I wrote a letter. I never thought she would get it."

"I got the letter, Rip."

"Well the letter you sent me was on bark."

"Rip, we were just communicating on different planes. But Rip, this is Sydney."

During the introduction, Sydney—or Tarzan as he would always be known to Rip—ignored them, and walked over to the candy machine, fascinated. When Reed put quarters in the machine and pulled the knob, Tarzan saw the candy falling down behind the glass. He tried to catch it, only hitting the glass with his hands, as Reed kept feeding quarters into the coin slot, and pulling the knob, and the candies kept falling. Reed pulled out a Snickers bar from the bottom of the tray, and gave it to him. Tarzan ripped off the packaging, preparing to devour it when Laura—or Morningstar—raced over and took it away from him.

"Sydney, you know you have food allergies. Don't feed him," she yelled at Reed.

"It's just a Snickers bar," Jan said.

"He has allergies. That's why we live in the wilderness."

"Don't they have Snickers in the wilderness?"

"No. He can't eat nuts."

"Maybe they should have shampoo there," Jan spoke in a lower tone of voice, but Laura heard that one too. She turned to Rip.

"Is this why you brought me here? To have your friends make fun of me?"

Rip looked at the picture of Laura, which reminded him of all the good times together in the past, then looked at the new Morningstar.

"Jan didn't mean any harm. She's a little perky. It's just a little station house humor, that's all. But I am kind of surprised by the way you look, too. You were once...so Laura."

"Rip, I'm Morningstar now. And I am very comfortable with what I wear, and how I look," she said, sending a stare to Jan. Jan backed away.

"But Laura, don't you miss hot showers and warm beds and coffee in the morning?"

"I decided to live my life being a part of nature."

"But isn't that why we have vacations?"

"Rip, it's different. Things have changed. I have changed," Laura said, worrying about her Sydney staring at the candy machine. "Don't feed him any candy," she told Reed again. Then she came up to Rip, and looked him up and down with his uniform on. "You have changed too."

"There are a lot of things that have changed since we were together." Rip looked intensely at Laura, trying to find the doorway to the past.

"Why don't we take Sydney out into the yard," Jan said, "and have him look at one of the ambulances. Would you like to see an ambulance, Sydney? You can even play with the siren."

"Maybe Sydney needs to stay close by," Laura replied.

"He'll be safe. I promise. We'll take good care of him," Jan said.

Before Laura could respond, Jan and Reed were leading Tarzan away.

"He'll be fine. Don't worry," Rip told Laura, "they are my best medics."

"It's just that Sydney has so many special needs."

"They're medics. What could go wrong?" Rip asked.

After they left, Rip finally found the words he'd been trying to say to Laura.

"Laura, how could you leave me for him?"

"It's Morningstar, and it's because he is so close to nature. I needed to get back to where I belonged. My roots."

"Roots? Laura, you grew up mostly in California. What are we talking about? Golden Gate Park?"

"Rip, you were always a little hostile to anything that was different. That's why I left you. Sydney doesn't judge me."

"It's not that I'm hostile," Rip tried to explain. "I just miss you. I miss the old Laura. I guess I don't like change or at least the part of you leaving me. I am not judging you but the out-back thing really took me by surprise."

"I have changed."

"I thought you didn't eat meat," Rip said, looking at her outback garb.

"We don't. We bought these skins from an Aborigine tribe. They waste nothing, you know."

"Do they have dingoes there too?"

"Yes, they do, Rip. Why?"

"Do they keep you up at night?"

"Sometimes. Sydney sleeps better than I do."

"See, that's what I mean, Laura. Don't you miss a good mat-tress? Remember the waterbed we used to have? Do you sleep in a tent?" Rip asked, still thinking that the old Laura had to be in there somewhere.

"No, it's a mud hut. A hut made of mud, Rip. Sydney made it. He's very good with his hands."

"Yes, you told me."

"Rip, it's not just the sex. Laura is gone. I'm Morningstar. My other life is gone. I have a new beginning."

Rip lowered his voice, and moved closer to Laura.

"But don't you miss Chinese takeout? It was our favorite. The old guy is still there. Wing something or other. Remember how we used to make fun of his broken English, and how I would speak French to him, and totally confuse the hell out of our order? Weren't those good times? He asked about you the other day. He said, 'Where is Christie Brinkley?' in broken Eng-lish. It was hilarious, but in a sad sort of way."

For a moment, talking about their past, Laura was taken aback. She softened, slightly. "Yes, they were good times, Rip. We were like kids."

"Well that's what love does to you. We can still be like kids again."

Rip put his arms on Laura's shoulder, and they embraced. Rip felt her breasts against his chest. Outback or not, she still never wore a bra. It stirred him for a moment. Then she moved back.

"No Rip, it's time to move on. Sydney and I want to build a community together."

"Community?" Rip asked, moving closer to Laura. "What, like a commune with dingoes?"

"Rip, forget the dingoes."

"But aren't you afraid that they'll steal your babies? I always thought that we would have two."

"What, dingoes?"

"No, babies."

Laura laughed at Rip being Rip, and coming up with questions nobody else would ask.

"Rip. They don't steal babies," Laura said in a quieter voice. Then she laughed. "Where did you hear that?"

"It's common knowledge. But don't you want to come back here?"

Their voices were whispers.

"Rip, I live in the outback."

"With no Chinese takeout food?"

"Yes, with no Chinese takeout food."

"In a mud hut?"

"Yes. In our community, no trees are torn down, and the huts are made from mud."

"Do you mix manure with this mud?"

"Sometimes, but Sydney does it."

"Do you take mud baths?"

"No, Rip, no."

"I really miss the old Laura," Rip said, opening up his heart.

"I'm sorry, Rip. The old Laura is gone."

"Is the old Laura gone forever?"

"I'm afraid so."

"I guess the dingoes took you away."

"Rip, please forget the dingoes," Laura whispered.

The light of love flickered for a moment in Rip's eyes. They were very close, and he just wanted to touch her.

"I guess it would be too much if I held you."

"Yes, Rip, it would be."

In the yard, Jan and Reed were showing Sydney the ambulance.

"Let's go inside, Sydney," Jan said to him. "Hop in."

They entered the ambulance through the back doors. Sydney was fascinated by all the gadgets inside. The cabinets in the ambulance were filled with medicines and syringes and bandages and Sydney wanted to take them out.

"No touchy," Jan said.

There was a gurney with a cushion that Sydney pounded his fists on like a drum.

"Don't touch anything," Jan finally admonished him. In a childlike way he lowered his head.

"Hey Sydney," Reed asked, "want to sit in the driver's seat, and turn on the siren?"

Sydney nodded as if to say, *Yes, oh boy!*

Jan went to the front compartment and told Sydney to sit in the driver's seat, while she sat in the passenger seat. Reed, close to Sydney, watched from behind.

"Okay, Sydney, this is the steering wheel," Jan told him once he had taken a seat in the front. "On the floor is the brake and the gas pedal. This is the ignition. The key is in the ignition. Turn the key."

Sydney turned the key, and the starter screamed because he kept turning.

"Okay, Sydney, let go of the key."

He didn't listen.

"LET GO OF THE KEY!" Jan yelled at him.

He let go of the key in the ignition. The engine sputtered.

"Okay," Jan said, "see that switch?"

Sydney nodded yes.

"Switch it on."

Sydney didn't know how to do it so Jan took his finger, and flipped on the switch. The lights went on, and the siren started blaring, making Sydney jump from his seat. Jan then took Sydney's finger and turned it off. Reed and Jan started laughing, and soon Sydney was laughing too.

Rip and Laura were still talking in whispers, only a few inches apart, when she heard the siren.

"What was that?" Laura moved away from Rip. "Is Sydney okay?"

"He's fine," Rip reassured her. "I told you they are my best medics. They are only showing him the siren. Nothing will go wrong."

"Well, Sydney is not used to loud noises."

"What about the animals at night? They make noises."

"It's nature, Rip, but you act like you are disappointed in me. Are you?" Laura asked.

"Laura, Morningstar… Mud huts and dingoes. I just don't know. I wanted…"

"Little surfer girl?"

"Well, yeah," Rip said.

"We are trying to get away from the outside world. We are building a community."

"Are there any other people?" Rip asked.

"There are a few other mud huts around."

"Do you have a radio?"

"We have short wave."

"No FM?"

"No."

"AOL? Internet?"

"There is one store that has it, but Sydney got thrown out for looking at porn."

"And this is what you want?" Rip asked Laura.

"Yes, I do."

"No more surfer girl?"

"No more surfer girl."

Back in the ambulance, Sydney, Reed, and Jan were having a great time playing with the lights and siren, turning them off and on. Reed leaned over between Sydney and Jan, and pulled out a brownie that he had made from his stash of pot.

"Does Sydney like chocolate?" Reed asked, showing him his homemade chocolate brownie.

Sydney's eyes got bigger, and he nodded.

"Take a piece. But just a little."

Sydney took a piece, and started chewing. Joy came over his face.

"Is it good?" Reed asked.

"Good," Sydney said. "Good."

"Have another piece," Reed said.

Sydney had another, and then another. But then the happiness on his face started to leave, and then slowly he started breathing in short breaths. Sydney threw up Reed's brownie, and started wheezing.

"Did you put nuts in that brownie?" Jan asked Reed.

"Of course. I always do."

"Fuck," Jan said. "Fuck. She said he was allergic to nuts. Get rid of the brownie. Let's get him in the back."

Reed tossed what was left of the brownie out of the ambulance and over the fence, and then putting on gloves, scooped up Sydney's vomit with all the little bits and pieces of the brownie, and tossed it too. Then they dragged Sydney out of the driver's seat to the back of the ambulance, and put him on the gurney.

Sydney was only looking worse. His blood pressure was dropping, his lips were swelling, and he developed a blue discoloration of skin.

Jan gave Sydney epi, and started to bag him, as Reed called Rip on the radio.

"Get down here now!"

When Rip and Laura came down, they saw Sydney being bagged to support his ventilation in the back of the ambulance on the gurney.

"You killed him. You killed my Sydney!" Laura screamed.

"He just found some chocolate, and ate it." Jan thought it was best not to mention it was one of Reed's homemade brownies.

"Where is it? Did it have nuts?" Laura was hysterical.

"I don't know, he finished it," Jan said, working on Sydney.

Laura started hitting Rip on the shoulder. "You killed Sydney. You killed him! This was your plan all along."

"Okay," Jan said to Laura. "Knock it off. He is not going to die. But get in the ambulance. We've got to go to the hospital. NOW! Rip, stay here."

With lights and sirens blaring, Reed drove and Jan monitored Sydney's vitals while Laura in the back of the ambulance screamed at her. "YOU KILLED SYDNEY. YOU KILLED SYDNEY. YOU FUCKING MEDICS."

Once at San Francisco General Hospital, they drove to the entrance of the ER, rolled Sydney out on the gurney, and then inside. The admission nurse, who everyone called Nurse Ingrid, came over to Jan. She had twenty years in and ten more to go. Nurse Ingrid had a kid in grade school, a deadbeat boyfriend, and a dog. The trifecta of nursing.

"He ate nuts. He's allergic. I gave him epi," Jan told Nurse Ingrid.

"They tried to kill my Sydney," Laura screamed to anyone willing to listen in the ER. Nurse Ingrid looked at Laura, and then at Sydney.

"What are they dressed in?" Nurse Ingrid asked Jan.

"It's Aborigine in nature," Jan said, shrugging. "They are from the outback. Friends of Rip. Remember Rip's Laura?"

Nurse Ingrid shook her head. "That's Laura?" she asked. "I should have known this had something to do with Rip. How did they get on the plane looking like that? They should have at least gone to Ross."

"That's what I said," Jan replied.

Laura started screaming again, "WHY ARE YOU FUCKING STANDING AROUND? DO SOMETHING!"

Nurse Ingrid took Sydney's pulse.

"His pulse is returning to normal, and his color is starting to come back. We'll put him in room 5. I'll send in the doctor. What's his name?"

"IT'S SYDNEY AND I WANT THESE TWO ARRESTED," Laura screamed, pointing at Jan and Reed.

"He ate some chocolate. It had nuts in it," Jan told Nurse Ingrid. "What were we supposed to do?"

Nurse Ingrid turned to Laura. "Do you want me to call the police because Tarzan here ate some chocolate?"

"HIS NAME IS SYDNEY, NOT TARZAN, AND YES I DO."

"Lower your voice," she said, and then turning to Jan, "Did he vomit it out?"

"Yes."

"Well Jane, there goes your evidence," Nurse Ingrid said.

Laura started screaming uncontrollably. "MY NAME IS MORNINGSTAR NOT JANE AND HIS NAME IS SYDNEY, NOT TARZAN, AND THEY TRIED TO KILL HIM."

As an attendant rolled Sydney to room 5, Nurse Ingrid called hospital security. "We got a 5150 here," she said on the phone.

When two of the hospital police came out, Officer Willy and Officer Frankie, Laura started screaming at them. She now wanted everybody to be arrested: Rip, Jan, Reed, and Nurse Ingrid. The two officers took one look at Laura in her Aborigine garb and cuffed her.

"YOU'RE ARRESTING ME? ME? YOU FUCKING PIGS!" she screamed.

That was it. Laura used the F and the P word in the same sentence, and then with the help of the police, two hospital attendants restrained her on a gurney. As Jan and Reed watched, Nurse Ingrid got the needle and stuck it in her arm to sedate her. Slowly, before Laura—Morningstar—passed out, she pointed at Jan.

"You, Amazon lady," she said to Jan, bleary eyed. "Tell that fucker I did sleep with the yoga teacher."

"Okay," Jan said as both she and Reed watched the train wreck that was once Laura pass out, and then the hospital attendants rolled her away, too.

"Room 6," Nurse Ingrid told them.

"The girl has some mouth on her," Officer Willy said.

"Shouldn't have used the F word," Officer Frankie added.

"Or the P word either."

137

"It's like a fucking Tarzan movie around here."

"What was all that shit she had in her hair?"

"We just transported her boyfriend," Jan told the officers. "He had a nut allergy. They are from the outback. Who would have guessed it?"

"Don't they have dingoes in the outback?" Officer Frankie asked.

"Why are you asking?" Officer Willy asked.

"Don't you know that dingoes steal babies when the mother is not looking, then eat them? I read it in *National Geographic*. Yep, the dingo ate my baby. It's a fact."

Both of the officers laughed.

"We got to get off this shift," Officer Frankie said, and Officer Willie agreed. Jan walked away quickly.

But it was a long day in the ER. Sydney was breathing normally, but stoned out of his mind, and under observation. Laura was sedated, and for Jan and Reed, there was a lot of paperwork to fill out. The cops didn't want anything to do with it. They didn't even fill out a report. Nurse Ingrid came up to Jan and Reed.

"Okay you two, we are going to keep them both overnight. Jane is sleeping, and I think Tarzan looks like he is stoned out of his mind. What kind of chocolate was that?" She then looked at Reed. "I don't even want to know. But one night and they're gone. So that was the famous Laura? And to think I once had a crush on Rip. Well, that was a few relationships ago. Is he still singing those Beach Boys songs? Never mind. Oh well, tell Rip I said hello. But maybe you two should finish your paperwork, and go."

Jan and Reed nodded in agreement and, looking suspicious, finished their paperwork and walked out of the ER toward the ambulance.

"I wish I hadn't thrown away the rest of that brownie," Reed said.

"Let's not talk about it, okay?"

"Well, I'm calling Rip. Maybe he's up for Chinese food."

"How can you think about Chinese food at a time like this?"

"I don't know. I'm hungry. I'm sure that Rip is hungry too."
Reed called Rip.

"Rip, Reed here. They are keeping them overnight. He'll be fine. Yeah, they arrested Laura too. You heard from Ingrid? Yeah, your Laura used the F and the P word in front of hospital security. But I'm hungry. Do you want Chinese food? We'll pick it up on our way back. Okay, the usual? Sweet and sour chicken with pea pods and rice? Right? Good. Be there shortly."

Jan and Reed got back into the ambulance.

"All in all," Reed said, "it wasn't that bad of a day."

Jan shook her head.

"What? Are you kidding? Wasn't a bad day? Reed, we almost killed Tarzan, and now they are both in the hospital. Let's just get back."

"I wouldn't say almost," Reed tried to reassure her. "He just had a bad reaction. Shit happens. Do you want some Chinese food?"

"Just pea pods."

"No rice?"

"No rice. But please drive."

Ambulance 54 rolled out of the ER.

"And let's never talk about this to anyone, ever. Okay?" Jan asked.

"Never happened. Who would believe it anyway?"

"Do you think we should tell Rip about the yoga teacher?"
Reed shook his head.

"Yeah, I think you're right," Jan said, as she stared out the passenger window.

After the brownie incident, Rip never saw or spoke to Laura again. He dreamed about her, but it was the old Laura who showed up in his dreams. The little surfer girl. The Laura who liked to take off her clothes and go skinny dipping in the ocean in the middle of the night. The sex on the beach Laura. The Laura who liked Chinese takeout food. The Laura who once loved him. That was the Laura who was locked in Rip's memory forever.

CHAPTER 14

The administrative disciplinary hearing of Paramedic Dean Manuel was held in the conference room on the second floor of the Evans Street Station, across from Rip's office. At the hearing were Dean, Arne, Jan, and a union rep named Bob; they sat across the table from Rip and a representative from Human Resources. Since all hearings were recorded, a cassette recorder was placed in the middle of the table between them. The representative from Human Resources was sent over by Hogwash. She was a short Filipina middle-aged woman with tinted short hair and glasses, named Maria. Her polyester suit was garnet in color, and Rip thought that if Chairman Mao had taken over San Francisco, that would be the official type of uniforms that all civil servants would have to wear. He imagined an army in single file of civil servants in garnet-colored polyester suits handing out one write-up at a time. Hogwash wanted his three days.

After Human Resources Lady read the charges, she showed the videotape on equipment that Rip once used in his film room, from the citizen who taped Dean's interactions with the patient. It was Dean at his best, red-faced and all. Belligerent, arrogant, and pushy. There was no Walt Whitman on that tape. No "Leaves of Grass." Only Cherry Pie. You had to love him, or at least know that if you worked with him, in the course of a day this could happen. He could turn from Dean Manuel to Cherry Pie without notice. It was always right below the surface, but this time it was on tape. Human Resources Lady had a smirk on her face watching it as if to say, *I got you.* When the tape was over, she sat back in her chair. The smirk remained.

Having no faith in Rip to follow RC Diamond's advice for a three-day suspension, Human Resources Lady ran the hearing. She had the reputation of one of Hogwash's henchmen, a pitbull.

Jan was the first one called on by Human Resources Lady to explain, "in her own words," the events concerning Paramedic Dean Manuel's behavior on the day of the incident. Jan read from a prepared statement stating that the patient was out of line, and belligerent, and his scraped elbow did not require the care that the patient requested.

"We are medics," Jan said. "There is only so much hand holding that we can do. At no time was the patient's health in jeopardy. Proper care was given."

Human Resources Lady ignored Jan's response and focused on Arne. He was called on next to give his account of the incident, and for so many reasons, everybody thought that he was going to cave in, being on probation, and being, as everybody thought, without a backbone. Arne also read from a prepared statement, and like Jan, said that the patient was difficult, and belligerent, and that proper care was rendered. But seeing weakness, which was all that Arne ever showed, Human Resources Lady was having none of it. She pounced!

The first thing Human Resources Lady said to Arne was to remind him that he was still on probation, and that the hearing would reflect on his probation. She smelled blood. Bob the union rep objected, but Human Resources Lady didn't even respond.

Rip interrupted, though, saying, "Maybe we should see this in another light," meaning that he was trying to get Human Resources Lady to just take the hearing a little slower.

"What light would you like to see it in?" Human Resources Lady responded, giving him an unwelcoming stare.

"My client has rights," Bob the union rep stated.

"Your client has been read his rights," Human Resources Lady responded.

"Did you ever see that movie with Tom Cruise...?" Rip asked.

Human Resources Lady just stared Rip down again.

"So, please tell me, Paramedic Dibble," she asked, "is it true that your fellow medics call you the rookie?"

"At times," Arne said, squirming on his chair. Jan shook her head. He was going to crack, she thought, and Dean thought so too. "But I find it to be all in good fun," he continued.

Jan and Dean looked at each other in bewilderment as if to say, *What has Arne Dibble been smoking?*

"But that is not your name, Paramedic Dibble, is that right?"

"No, but it helps me feel like I..."

"Like what, Paramedic Dibble?" Human Resources Lady interrupted.

"Like I fit in," Arne said in a weak voice. He was still vulnerable.

"Would you say your internship with the two medics involved has been difficult, especially with Paramedic Jan Stein, and do you feel any pressure not to answer my questions honestly?" Human Resources Lady asked. She was on a roll.

"I don't know what you are asking me," Arne replied.

"I am asking you to answer my questions honestly, without pressure from your peers. Tell me in your own words what happened that day."

Arne started to sweat. Everybody saw it.

"Fuck," Jan said underneath her breath, but even Human Resources Lady heard it, and had that same smirk on her face again.

A bead of sweat ran down from Arne's forehead to his nose. He paused.

"Paramedic Dibble, we are waiting for your response to what happened that day," Human Resources Lady demanded.

At first Arne stammered.

"I found," Arne said, regaining his composure, "the patient to be in a state of confrontation and his wound was cleaned and wrapped, and there was no reason for the patient to be transported."

"What about the remarks made by Paramedic Manuel?"

"If anything, the remarks made by Paramedic Manuel deflated the situation."

Jan looked at Dean and then Dean at Jan, and one of them said, "Whoa." Even Rip raised his head in astonishment.

"Deflated the situation?" Human Resources Lady asked Arne, as if he were being interrogated on a witness stand. "Are you only saying this to defend one of your coworkers? Or is it because you want to be liked and accepted, and not have to face constant name calling like Rookie, which I find offensive? Be honest. Have you been treated very well since being hired? And if not, is the only reason you are standing up for Paramedic Manuel that maybe in the hopes that you will be treated with more respect in the future?"

"I've never been treated better," Arne said.

And Arne wasn't finished.

"And I just want to say that I am well aware that I am on probation."

"But Paramedic Dibble, what about the video you just watched concerning Paramedic Dean Manuel's behavior? Didn't you find it offensive? I did. Can't you see the rage on Paramedic Manuel's face when talking to the patient? Do I need to play it again?"

"I admit, without knowledge of the circumstances," Arne said, this time in a clear voice, "you may think something different. But the circumstances show otherwise. The patient was treated, and he did not want to get into the ambulance. Not all patients are the same, and the patient's health was never in jeopardy."

"Why didn't you just bring out the stair chair? It was clear from the video that Paramedic Manuel did not want you to do it."

"Paramedic Dibble's treatment of the patient is not part of this investigation," Bob the union rep interrupted.

Human Resources Lady ignored him again.

"Because it was not needed," Arne said.

"Did the union coach you on what to say, Paramedic Dibble?"

"No, I have my own set of values."

Arne leaned back in his chair.

Wow, thought Jan and Dean. *All this from Arne Dibble.* It was like Arne was a phoenix rising from the ashes of self-doubt and insecurities, only to find himself a new set of balls. There was silence in the room. Nobody could understand it. Even Rip was amazed.

"I would like to add a statement if your interrogation of me is over," Arne said.

"This is not an interrogation," Human Resources Lady said. "Only a hearing."

"But it is being recorded."

"As are all hearings, but go on."

"I just want to say that it has been a pleasure working with Paramedic Jan Stein and Paramedic Dean Manuel. They are excellent medics. But the truth be told, difficult patients are what we face on an everyday basis. I stand by my statement."

"And you just couldn't put him in a stair chair?" Human Resources Lady asked again.

"I examined his ankle. It was not swollen. He was fine. He could walk. Are there any other questions?" Arne asked.

Nobody said a word.

Human Resources Lady shuffled her papers. She thought she had found her duck in Arne. But he had gotten away. Unbeknownst to anyone else in the room except Arne, Earl Dibble—Arne's father—had some friends in the city attorney's office, and they wrote down the questions Human Resources Lady may be asking Arne. They even had an intern meet Arne and his father at The Ramp on Illinois Street, and not only did they coach him on the questions he may be asked, they also told him what to say, made him write it down, and then questioned him again. Arne even put little post-its around his house, mostly in the bathroom near the toilet, so he could memorize his responses. He even practiced in front of a mirror.

"Did you ever wonder why the Golden Gate Bridge is painted orange?" Rip asked, breaking the silence.

Everybody in the room smiled except for Human Resources Lady. She started tapping her foot on the floor, nervously. *Probably drank a lot of coffee*, Rip thought. She dismissed Arne and Jan, telling them they could leave the room, but maybe be questioned at a further date. Left in the room were Rip, Bob the union rep, Dean, and Human Resources Lady.

"Well the video stands for itself. I am recommending a three-day suspension, which your chief will sign off on," Human Resources Lady stated.

She looked coldly at Rip.

"I will not accept a three-day suspension," Dean spoke up.

"We didn't think you would. But three days," Human Resources Lady said, looking at Rip, "is our recommendation. Right, Chief Ripley?"

"It's Ridley. Chief Ridley."

Duderonomy looked a little like Freud in his wool suit, fake beard, and round dark-framed glasses when he appeared on Rip's shoulder rubbing his chin.

"This is a very interesting dilemma," Duderonomy said. "On one side we have Dean, your friend, who you don't want to suspend, and on the other side we have Chairman Mao's handmaiden, sent by Hogwash, who demands you do it. Tough call. The question is, will suspending your friend Dean help smooth over some of the misunderstandings with Hogwash, or is the relationship beyond repair?"

A mini Chief Brady showed up on the other side of Rip's shoulder.

"For Christ's sake, Ripley, straighten up," he said, pacing. "The guy showed up in a dress in front of his own mother's house. A dress! Sign the papers. Give him the three days. If it was up to me, he'd be out of here."

"Chief Ridley," Human Resources Lady began, taking him out of his stream of consciousness, "have you made your decision?"

Rip shook off Duderonomy and mini Chief Brady and focused on the hearing again.

"I will only accept a five-day suspension," Dean said, not waiting for Rip to answer, "I need some time off to go to Burning Man."

"But we have already recommended three."

"I'm not accepting three. My vacation wasn't granted, so I want five days."

"You can't ask for a higher suspension than the one recommended." Human Resources Lady was now flustered.

"Why not?" Dean asked.

"Because we have no rules for that. And you know that any suspensions of five days or more must be reviewed before the city's commission to be approved. We are not bringing this before the commission. You must accept the three-day suspension."

"I don't have to accept anything. I want my five days. I want to go to Burning Man. And I don't mind going in front of the commission."

"We are not going in front of the commission with this video," Human Resources Lady proclaimed loudly, losing her composure.

"The patient accused me of being homophobic. I found that to be offensive," Dean stated.

"Couldn't you have brought it up in a more professional manner, Paramedic Manuel? Why did you have to be so graphic?"

"I thought I was being professional. There are standards in my community, too," Dean stated matter-of-factly.

"We are not signing off on a suspension of five days. It will not be reviewed by the commission."

"Well that's what I want."

"Paramedic Manuel, you are not going to get a five-day suspension. If reviewed by the commission, then that transcript can be requested by the public. And we are not providing this information to the public. The mayor has been embarrassed enough with the Gray Beavers. But perhaps Chief Ridley can find a solution to this."

"Why wasn't I invited to Burning Man?" Rip asked Dean, looking hurt.

"Rip, you are a chief now. We thought about it. We wanted to."

"Who are we?"

"I was hanging out with Reed, and a few others and, well…you're a chief now."

"But why?"

"Sorry, Rip. Maybe we should have."

"Paramedic Manuel, please address Chief Ridley by his title," Human Resources Lady demanded.

"He really doesn't have to," Rip responded.

"Maybe that is one of the problems with your administration," Human Resources Lady stated angrily.

"Chief Ridley's administration is not the issue of this hearing," Bob the union rep spoke up.

"Never mind," Human Resources Lady said. "Paramedic Manuel, if Chief Ridley and Human Resources sign off on the three-day suspension, you must accept it. Those are the rules. Chief Ridley, you will be signing off on it, won't you? It will not be going in front of the commission."

"I want my five days," Dean demanded.

"Laura loved Burning Man," Rip said in a low voice.

"I heard she came back," Dean said. "I'm sorry it didn't work out so well. I also heard about Tarzan."

"Yeah, that really didn't help."

"Chief Ridley, haven't you caused enough problems with your father's association with the Gray Beavers? Why are you having this conversation about Burning Man? You need to sign off on the suspension." Human Resources Lady's frustration was like the last flicker of a light bulb before it burned out. Her tinted hair looked a little frazzled, too.

"My father, for the record, is no longer associated with the Gray Beavers," Rip said to Human Resources Lady.

"It was for the sex, wasn't it?" Dean asked.

"Yeah."

"You still love her, don't you?"

"Laura? Yeah, I do."

"I'm sorry I didn't invite you."

"I understand."

"Chief Ripley—Ridley... If Paramedic Manuel does not get the three-day suspension, it will be a bad reflection on your leadership. You are going to sign the three-day suspension. Isn't that right, Chief Ridley?"

"Maybe going to Burning Man is what my father needs?" Rip said, totally disregarding Human Resources Lady.

Human Resources Lady threw down her notes. "I can't believe this. Chief Ridley, you have no respect for the process of this hearing. I will leave the paperwork for you to sign. Maybe in the mayor's office it will get the proper attention that it deserves."

Human Resources Lady had had enough. She stood up and pushed back her chair with a screeching sound. She left the write-up with Rip, took her notes, and left, slamming the conference door. Bob the union rep left to get a clarification from her concerning the suspension, and they could be heard arguing outside the door. It was just Rip and Dean left in the conference room.

"I'm sorry, Rip," Dean said after they were gone. "I didn't mean to get you in any trouble with the mayor's office."

"Then why wasn't I invited to Burning Man?"

"Rip, it's different now. We all like you. But now it's different."

"How so?" Rip really didn't understand.

"You really don't know, do you? One day they're going to make you do something that you really don't want to do. Either you love the title too much, or you end up like the last guy. Remember the last paramedic chief who just walked away."

"Chief Sam Tortellini," Rip replied.

"Yeah, Hard Truths Tortellini. Rip, everybody liked him too. But it changes you."

"Does it?"

"Yeah it does. If I were you, I would sign it. Give me the three-day suspension. I understand."

"You know what, Dean?"

"What, Rip?"

"I had a drink with Sam before he left, and you know what he said?"

"What?"

"He said, 'Well fuck it and fuck them too.' And you know what?"

"What, Rip?"

"I'm starting to come to the conclusion that they have it in for me anyway."

Dean had that look on his face like, *I know.*

"Dean, did you also know Laura was going to leave me?"

"Yes."

"Did everybody know?"

"Yes, everybody."

"Does everyone think I'm gone if the merger goes through?"

Dean nodded his head.

"Well fuck it," Rip said, "and fuck them too."

"You need to sign it," Dean told Rip. "Sorry about not inviting you to Burning Man."

But Rip didn't sign it. He was going to, but then when he had it in front of him, he just couldn't. Even Duderonomy told him one late night, when Rip was smoking a joint, that maybe he should sign it.

"Nobody would think the worst of you. And you like being chief, Bwana. It's a no-brainer," Duderonomy tried to reason with Rip, in his pot smoke-filled bedroom.

By not signing the three-day suspension, Rip stood up to all the Hogwashes of the world. But he also knew it probably meant that it was the end of him being chief of the paramedic division, and access to his own bathroom. And Rip really did like being chief.

But by Rip not following the recommendation of the mayor's office, Dean Manuel never got his suspension. His case was conveniently forgotten. It was not going to go in front of any commission. But now, after reading Human Resources Lady's report on the meeting, Hogwash had it in for Rip. He always had it in for Rip to begin with, but now Rip was on his radar.

Since Dean didn't get his suspension, he called in sick five days in a row with a fake doctor's note so he could go to Burning Man, and once there he took lots of mushrooms, ecstasy, and other hallucinogens. With his camera, Dean snapped lots of pictures for Rip, of loosely fitting gypsy-garbed women that he thought Rip would enjoy. He also took pictures of women who looked like Christie Brinkley. Since Dean was wearing a tie-dye silk robe—and the colors of the pride flag painted on his face—like a hippie gay messiah, people were taking pictures of him, too. One day, with all the hallucinogens kicking in, Dean found the mike where announcements were made, and started reciting "Leaves of Grass," or at least what he could remember. It was good for Dean to get back to who he once could be, and he even had tears in his eyes. He even received an ovation until security took the mike away.

At night, Dean looked like a fat Buddha sitting in the sand, with his legs crossed, looking at the campfires, mostly hallucinating. When the large wooden structure of Burning Man lit up the desert sky, he felt that he had reached gay nirvana, his final goal until he passed out on the desert sands, underneath the stars in his painted face and tie-dye silk robe.

The first thing that Jan said to Arne when they got back on the ambulance together was that the hearing did not change anything between them. But it did. It also changed the attitude that the other medics had toward Arne. They stopped calling him Rookie and started calling him by his first name. To them he was still a lousy medic, someone if you worked with, you had to be extra careful, but he didn't turn in Cherry Pie. Effin even confronted him in the yard one day.

"Word is that you may be a lousy medic, but you're not a rat," Effin said to Arne as they were stocking Ambulance 54. "Personally, if it were up to me, I would have turned them all in."

Arne didn't say anything, but was just happy that he had survived. Even Reed was surprised that Jan no longer showed hostility to Arne all the time. When Arne screwed up, she would take a deep breath, then tell him what he did wrong. Then she would explain how to do it better. She even took time one day to show him how to stock her ambulance. And she too started calling him Arne. One morning, Jan even paid for coffee.

CHAPTER 15

Now that Rip had gone against Human Resources Lady over Paramedic Dean Manuel's recommended suspension, it meant that he had gone against the mayor's office, which really meant he had gone against Hogwash. There had to be some payback. It mattered.

First, a few newspaper articles came out about the lackluster response times of the ambulance service. *Delays Compounding S.F. Ambulance Crisis*, read the front page of the *Chronicle*, and then the TV news picked it up. It was the usual hit piece that Hogwash got his newspaper people to send out when he was not happy with a department head of a city agency. And these hit pieces were not unusual. Everybody got one—from Muni, to the police, to Park and Rec—but this time it was Rip's turn. There were pictures of overweight people wearing robes and slippers, in dingy hotel rooms, waiting for ambulances. There were interviews with community leaders and ER nursing staffs, saying how the city was facing life-threatening emergencies waiting more than thirty minutes for an ambulance, when the standard was less than ten minutes. It was the usual hatchet job. But the accusations put Rip in a situation where he had to respond because the question about ambulance response times kept coming back to him.

"How is the paramedic chief going to fix the problem?"

He heard it from the press, and he heard it from the mayor's office. But the question never came up about where the money was going to come from to fix an aging ambulance fleet, or hire enough staff to run the calls. Hogwash had played his cards well.

"What are we going to do now, Bwana?" Duderonomy asked one night while Rip was smoking a joint contemplating the situation. "What are we going to do now?"

Rip didn't have an answer.

"But why would Hogwash have the newspapers print those articles?" Rip asked.

"Bwana," Duderonomy said, inhaling the smoke that circled him, "my theory is that in the world of Hogwashes, it is important to keep everybody in line, and throwing a few headlines to the press keeps everybody on their toes."

"But why me?" Rip asked naively.

"Because he can, and you crossed him. And maybe it was in the works."

"The works?"

He really doesn't get it, Duderonomy thought. *He's just never played at that level.* For Rip, the glass was always half filled until there was no more water left. All Duderonomy could do was shake his head at Rip's innocence. Rip was like a child who just wandered off when it came to the world of politics.

"Maybe it's the merger, Bwana. The papers said city hall is going to push it through. They already got the issues, the buzz. People get excited."

In the *Chronicle*, even Rip had to admit, the merger did sound like a good idea. A few articles came out how it was going to save money, even though it probably was going to cost more. But it made good print. Just like rearranging the chairs on the *Titanic*.

"The only thing that keeps the Hogwashes up at night," Duderonomy said, with a pensive look on his face, "are the problems they didn't know the press had gotten their hands on."

"And how do you come to these conclusions?" Rip asked.

"I read a lot."

"But where does that put me?"

Duderonomy rubbed his chin and thought for a moment. "What did the other guy do before you?"

"Yeah," Rip said in between puffs, "the other guy. Chief Sam Tortellini."

"Homeless One Program, Bwana, remember?" Duderonomy asked. "Time to dust off those old reports."

"Do you mean what I think you mean?"

"Yes. Release Chief Tortellini's Homeless One Program. Change a few words. Change the title. Jazz it up a bit. I would call it the Homeless Hope Program," Duderonomy said. "Maybe it will buy you some time."

"Some time?"

"Yeah, before they demote you."

"Thanks," Rip said, looking at the burned end of his joint.

In a puff of smoke Duderonomy conveniently disappeared.

Just reading Chief Tortellini's Homeless One Program, one would think it was the work of a genius. A mad genius, but still a genius. Chief Tortellini's program systematically revamped the homeless problem by using the resources of the paramedic division with other city agencies, instead of the patchwork political football that the homeless problem had become. Instead of just sending an ambulance on the same type of calls over and over again and taxing the 911 system and the ERs of the city, the program would send vans out with paramedics and social workers together to address individual problems. It was based on the premise that just taking the homeless to the ER or giving them a room in a dingy hotel, without addressing their needs, only compounded the habitual problem. And instead of having homeless centers only in distressed areas, the program would spread them throughout the city according to needs, no matter which district. A radical idea.

And the program would be a twenty-four-hour operation. Chief Tortellini had designed charts and graphs that showed how his program would save the city money and resources. The implementation of his program would also free up ambulances, which would lower response times.

With the help of some social workers who saw merit with the program, along with paramedics who worked at the Evans Street Station and some vans from BOE, Chief Tortellini took the initiative to start a pilot program—and it seemed to work. Social workers started knowing their patients by their needs, and fringe cases were starting to be given the supportive care that took them off the daily ambulance runs. Homeless patients in the ER actually went down, and the ambulances were not used as much by frequent flyers, so response times improved. More serious patients were identified, and their needs were actually discussed by healthcare providers, instead of being shuttled around from ER to ER, and from bed to bed. Soon the newspapers picked up Chief Tortellini's Homeless One Program and its success, and the *Bay Guardian* even mentioned that Chief Tortellini could one day be the successor to the mayor.

Unfortunately, when Chief Tortellini was called to the supervisor's meeting to discuss the program that was already beginning to be put into operations, it was already doomed. Word had leaked out to the mayor's office, from unhappy homeless advocates and city political leaders whose fragile egos had been treaded on, that there really wasn't that much support for the program, and especially how it was implemented. Why wasn't this program discussed beforehand, and didn't they have a say on how their resources were to be used? Then there were some social workers who resented going to the homeless in the streets, and not seeing them in hospital settings. It rained a lot in the fall, and San Francisco can get real cold at night.

But city hall had to be very careful dealing with Chief Tortellini. He was an optimist, and had his own ideas, which meant he could never be tolerated in any official capacity. He had to be controlled. And he had also given unauthorized interviews with *Chronicle* reporters while taking them on midnight homeless runs. He also took his program outside city limits and discussed it with the homeless advocates from other areas of the country. His nickname in the papers became "Hard Truths" Tortellini.

But officials in city hall didn't get in their positions without knowing how to crush somebody who didn't follow their plans, even if they didn't have one. It was a line that Hard Truths Tortellini had used that came back to haunt him. Speaking of the severely mentally ill, he said to a reporter, "Sometimes we have to impinge on their civil rights." It was too explosive a line for the reporter not to run with it.

And what a great line to be taken out of context. Leave out the mentally ill, and it could be used for anybody being treated by Chief Tortellini's Homeless One Program. That line itself, being reported over and over in the news, gave city hall all the ammunition that was needed to take van by van, social worker by social worker, away from Chief Tortellini, where he found himself working with a skeleton crew at night. Then officials in high places started asking why was somebody who was making a chief's salary going out at night shuttling around the homeless in vans? Shouldn't Chief Tortellini be running the paramedic division? His program was dead in the water, and it happened so fast that Chief Tortellini found himself asking what had happened. How quickly everything had turned. He went from darling to dud.

Unfortunately, Chief Tortellini was the only one who didn't see it coming. After a while, even the press didn't care. It was no longer a feel-good story, and they had already moved on to other stories to report on. Only the medics who had to go back to the old system of shuttling back and forth the same faces with the same problems suffered. It was at that moment that Chief Tortellini started to drift away. Nobody answered his calls. His nice car was taken away from him, and he was given a clunker. He was left out of meetings. And his nickname had also become a joke. Hard Truths Tortellini had just found out the hard truths of being a free thinker, and going against city hall. He drifted away one day after signing his papers for retirement from city politics and the paramedic division, and found himself a job as a chief in a one-ambulance town, in the state of Washington. One of those towns where everybody knows your name. When applying, the fact that he had worked as a

chief in a big city like San Francisco cemented the deal. It always looked good on a resume. He just wanted a simpler life,
he told the interviewer, and that was why he left San Francisco.
And from that day forward, Hard Truths Tortellini no longer
existed in San Francisco. In that one-ambulance town where
he had accepted the job, Hard Truths was known as "Chief"
and grew a beard, and put on some weight, and could be found
at the local tavern every day around five o'clock.

But Rip Ridley, in what he thought was his moment of bril-
liance, and from the advice of Duderonomy, decided to bring
back Chief Tortellini's program whenever the issue of delays
in ambulance service was brought up by city hall. It was the
same program as Chief Tortellini's, but instead Rip called it the
Homeless Hope Program and put his own name over Chief
Tortellini's, and changed the dates. It had the same charts,
same graphs, and identical requisitions for more medics, more
social workers and service vans. When Hogwash received Rip's
plan for his Homeless Hope Program, which was once Chief
Tortellini's Homeless One Program, he had one of his famous
Hogwash temper tantrums. "What if the press got hold of
this?" Hogwash screamed to whatever staff was listening. "I
don't need to go through this with Ridley, when I just went
through it with the other guy."

Rip was now politically dead. Even simple requisitions for
extra office supplies were denied, sometimes even before he
requested them. The fact that Rip did not make it public was
his only saving grace. But since there was now a report with a
homeless program floating around—which was really just a
copy of the old program—it did buy Rip some time, as Hogwash would now have to pick his moment to demote him. Rip
was able to keep his office, and his bathroom, but nobody from
the mayor's office called him, or answered his phone calls. It
was as if the chief of the paramedic division in the city of San
Francisco did not exist. But nothing is forgotten in the political
arena of San Francisco, and Hogwash put Rip's name in his file
to rein in the paramedic division, and do something about that

hippie chief. On the day he had washed his hands of him, Hogwash called Chief Brady of the San Francisco Fire Department.

"We have a problem," Hogwash told him, "with the paramedic division."

"Is it that hippie chief?" Chief Brady asked.

"Yes."

"What do you want me to do?"

"I want you to come out, and back the merger."

"Sir, with all due respect, I do not want it on my watch."

If anything, Chief Brady knew how to say so respectfully.

"What if after the merger, you were made CD1, head of the fire department, which would include the resources of the paramedic division? Imagine what that would do to your pension," Hogwash said, making his offer. "You only have a few years left. And I'm sure once your fellow members in the fire department realize that it's a done deal anyway, they would be happy to have one of their own to help them through this transitional period."

"Sir, the hippie chief would have to go. I want to see him back on an ambulance, or at least driving an RC buggy late at night in the Tenderloin."

"As the head of the fire department, you would have to do whatever is needed to be done."

"I understand," Chief Brady said, thinking of his pension. "I'll do it."

"Good," Hogwash replied. "Very well. You need to convince the benefits on all sides of this merger, mostly your own. There is always talk about cutting staffing, closing fire houses, but with the paramedics under your belt, that talk would go away. But the paramedic division needs to be reined in. And I want the streets around Station 51 cleaned up. The mayor is getting complaints that it's an eyesore. But do it quietly."

"Yes, quietly. For the time being."

"For the time being," Hogwash agreed.

Hogwash had found his man.

It didn't take long for the impending demise of Chief Rip Ridley to hang in the air like a thick fog, and the potential merger between the paramedic division and the fire department to move to a resolution. The newspapers picked it up again, and from the articles it sounded like a great idea. Chief Brady's name was mentioned as potential CD1 in the merger. He was portrayed as a seasoned pro, and an innovator. To the union representing the fire department, Chief Brady told them it was going to happen anyway, so why not have one of your own on top? Deals were made. Station houses were fixed up, and a few new trucks and engines showed up. There was some grumbling, but not publicly. The word was out. It was only a matter of time before Chief Brady called Rip. He was almost giddy.

"Well Chief Ripley, what are you going to do now?" Chief Brady asked Rip, smoking a stogie. "Got a call from the mayor's office, and yes my name was mentioned as the new CD1. That would make me your boss. This little game you played with Hard Nose Tortellini's playbook didn't go so well."

"It's Truths, sir. Hard Truths Tortellini," Rip replied.

"I remember Chief Tortellini," Chief Brady gloated. "Idealistic like you. Wanting to be his own man. But the city doesn't run that way, does it, Chief Ripley? And all this because you wouldn't give a guy named Cherry Pie a three-day suspension. Kind of sad, really. Sooner or later you have to throw down the hammer."

"So, it's going through?" Rip asked, really knowing the answer.

"Of course it's going through. What did you think? That you being chief was ever going to be long term? Just make sure when you work for me that you get your hair cut. I am even sending you over a rules and regulations manual *from the fire department.* I actually heard Hard Nose likes his one-ambulance town up there in Washington State. How old are you now, Ripley?"

"I have a few years in."

"But not enough for your pension to kick in yet, do you?"

"Not yet," Rip said. For Chief Brady it seemed to be a familiar tune bringing up Rip's lack of time in the department. "Not yet."

After the phone call, Rip sat at his desk and looked around his office. Rip really liked being chief. He really liked wearing the uniform. And he really liked having his own bathroom.

Duderonomy showed up on Rip's shoulder, sitting with his legs crossed reading an article in the *Chronicle* on the merger.

"Chief Brady?" Duderonomy asked.

Rip nodded.

"Bwana, it says in the article that once the merger goes into effect, the mayor's office is considering him for the new CD1."

"He told me. What do I do now?"

"You wait. Something will come up."

"Something like what?"

"I don't know yet."

"Thanks," Rip said. "You told me to bring back Chief Tortellini's Homeless One Program and I did and it backfired on me. I will probably get some crappy assignment. It was supposed to help me."

"It was a shot in the dark. I got to admit," Duderonomy confessed, "I didn't have anything else to give you. Reed's pot kind of fogs the mind a bit."

"Does it now?"

"Just a bit."

That night, when Rip had finally gotten to sleep, his phone rang on the nightstand. Rip didn't quite know if he was still dreaming.

"Hello."

"Do you know who this is?" It was a woman's voice.

"Mom?" Rip asked.

"It's not your mother, stupid. It's JoJo."

"Oh! How did you get this number?"

"My father is going to be CD1. I can get anybody's number I want. Do you want Hogwash's?"

"I don't think that would be a good idea."

"Yeah, I don't think so either. So, you had to bring up the report?"

"You mean my Homeless Hope Program?"

"Yes, and how did you ever come up with that name?"

"I was desperate," Rip said.

"Is that why you tried to kill Tarzan?"

"You heard? I didn't try to kill him. He just ate something."

"Yeah, you and your friends. How do you always get yourself into these things?"

"It was an accident."

"Some accident. I heard from my father that Hogwash went crazy over that report. He even called him about being CD1."

"And you are telling me this because...?" Rip asked.

"I just thought you should know. Do you still care about her?" JoJo asked. Her voice became soft like the evening breeze that blew through Rip's window.

"Laura?"

"Yes, Morningstar."

"God, you know everything."

"There are no secrets in the fire department."

"I did," Rip said, this time even admitting to himself, "the old Laura."

"Do you ever think about me?" JoJo asked. Her voice was even softer. Her vulnerability was a surprise to Rip. His family never showed those feelings.

"Sometimes."

"I also heard that you smoke a lot of dope."

"It's just that I have been having problems sleeping at night."

"Maybe it's because you are sleeping alone. Maybe you should start thinking about something else," JoJo said.

"Like what?" Rip asked.

"Like me."

"What about your father?"
"He's really not that bad, really."
Rip then heard JoJo's playful laugh and a giggle.
"Don't wait too long," she said. "Don't wait too long."
Then she hung up the phone.

CHAPTER 16

When it came time for the Stein Family Reunion, Rip was only too happy to be going to San Diego, and leaving the problems of being chief of the paramedic division behind. He needed the break. It would be sun, sand, fish tacos, and local beer. Rip really didn't think much about reunions. His family never had them. But it would only be for one night. What could go wrong? In Rip's mind, absolutely nothing. Get a little buzz on, meet Jan's relatives, charm Mother Stein, leave early, walk with Jan on the beach, have a toke and enjoy the evening. And he certainly liked the expectations of having sex with Jan again. Rip felt he had it all down.

And Jan did sleep with Rip the night before, just to make sure that he made it to the airport on time. The Stein Family Reunion meant that much to her. She even went through his closet to make sure Rip would look "California smart." Jan wanted to look good in front of her family, and was paying for everything. As for Rip, the softness of Jan's body during the night brought back those good feelings of sensation and fulfillment. Rip thought maybe in the morning he would get another chance. He woke up humming "Fun, Fun, Fun" till Jan told him to knock it off, and like the song, took his T-Bird away. She was having none of it. The softness of the night was over. After Jan made coffee, she told Rip to get dressed because they had to get to the airport, even though they were early. There would be no seconds.

The reunion was being held at the Hotel del Coronado, or sometimes called the Hotel Del. Rip always liked history in the condensed version, and reading the pamphlet, the Hotel Del was his kind of place. It was a hotel with a history. The Hotel del Coronado had a great view of the ocean. Its main restaurant featured fresh seafood and oysters and it had a great bar. Lots of different bottles of old scotch. Great presidents like Harrison, McKinley, Taft, and Wilson stayed there, and Ronald Reagan when he was a Hollywood star. In the 1920s it was Hollywood's playground. There was gambling and drinking during Prohibition. And it was right on the ocean. Rip was psyched. Though faded, the hotel still had a sense of elegance. The bartenders still wore ties. And although the pours would be smaller until the tips got bigger, Rip looked forward to room service for those late-night munchies.

While on the plane, Jan watched Rip looking out the window at the clouds as joy came over his face.

"Look at that cloud," Rip said to Jan. "Doesn't it look like the Pillsbury Dough Boy? Kind of like Hogwash. I met him once. It does kind of look like him."

"Don't forget that this is the Stein Family Reunion," Jan reminded Rip, needing him to focus on the task ahead.

"I am aware. When the stewardess comes by let's get drinks."

"Just don't get too comfortable."

But Rip was too happy to let Jan put him in a bad mood. He remembered her sensitivity the night before after the day had worn her down, and that was enough to forgive her morning temperament. And they both knew it was not serious, but just a way of Jan saying thank you to Rip for going to her family reunion. Rip had even wrapped in plastic three joints of Reed's pot, and hid them in his shampoo bottle in his luggage.

"I looked up the hotel last night. Great old pictures. Great bar. Reminded me a little bit like the Gold Room in *The Shining*," Rip said.

"You're bringing up *The Shining* and my family reunion? What a great combination," Jan said, shaking her head.

"I'm not comparing them, but I do remember when Jack Nicholson walks into the Gold Room with that smirk on his face. Maybe even Lloyd the bartender will be working there. I'd go to the bar and Lloyd would say to me that my credit was fine and pour me a Johnnie Walker."

"You don't even drink Johnnie Walker, and it was Jack Daniels that he poured."

"Whatever. Hey, maybe we will meet Delbert Grady."

"Enough. Rip, this is my family's reunion and you're bringing up a horror movie? Let me tell you about horror movies. Real ones! When I was young my father set up a boxing ring in the basement, so if us kids had a dispute, we could box it out. I used to beat the hell out of my younger brother, Jerry Junior, until puberty kicked in, and he learned the Stein jab. Instead of going with the haymaker like he always did, my brother learned to jab. It's the Stein jab that always gets you. And nobody is better at the Stein jab than Mother Stein. The verbal jab is always the most painful. Growing up, my mother was a hammer always looking for a nail."

"Well that's funny. Laura used to say that every hammer doesn't need a nail. Kind of like the Zen of carpentry."

"Yeah and where is she now?" Jan wasn't warming up to the occasion.

The stewardess came along with the cart to take their drink order.

"Jack Daniels please," Rip asked.

"We only have Johnnie Walker," the stewardess told Rip.

"That will be fine," Rip replied.

"I'll have the same," Jan said.

The stewardess gave them both their drinks and some packets of Planters peanuts.

"Oh, could you make them doubles?" Rip asked. The stewardess left an extra airport bottle for the both of them. Jan paid in cash.

"I can learn to like these things," Rip said, taking a sip.

"Yes, and you can move down to Southern California and become a Republican."

"Jan, we are going to have a good time. I promise you. Chief Rip Ridley will make everything right."

"Yeah, Chief Rip Ridley." Even Jan snickered on that one.

"Jan"—Rip tried again to make nice—"we had a good evening last night. And we are away from work. Soon we will be in nice digs with room service. The reunion is only one night. How bad can it be?"

"You don't understand," Jan said, trying for Rip to see her point of view, "the closer we get to San Diego, the more it comes back to me. The years of my mother's constant needling, her constant criticizing, her controlling nature. Like those stupid letters with her waves of negativity, and her badgering little jabs. 'Why do you eat so fast?' 'Why did you get your hair cut?' 'Why aren't you as pretty as your other sisters?' 'Why aren't you married?' 'Why are you a medic?' 'Why don't you let your hair grow?'"

"Why don't you just ignore her?"

"There are some things in life you can't ignore, and one of them is family. And you know what the worst thing is?" Jan poured the second bottle into her glass after quickly finishing the first.

"You mean there is a worse thing?"

"Yes. I'm afraid that I'm becoming just like her. Am I?" Jan asked Rip.

For Rip that was a dangerous question. Duderonomy appeared on his shoulder.

"Say the right thing, Bwana," he whispered in Rip's ear. "Say it!"

"Of course not," Rip shot back. "You're sensitive and independent."

For the first time on the plane Jan almost felt good about herself.

"Awesome," Duderonomy said, then disappeared.

"I just have to remember no haymakers," Jan said to Rip. "Haymakers mean I have lost my temper, and then my mother comes back with the Stein jab, as if to say, *I got you*. Then there is a quiet period, and you go back to your corner, but then the next round comes, and the jabs come back even harder. It's like she takes your will to fight back. I remember the time she found out that my father was having an affair with a Black woman. We could never watch Tarzan movies again."

"And you are telling me this because…?"

"Because your job is to make sure I don't lose my temper. They think I'm the emotional one."

Imagine that, Rip thought to himself.

"No matter what Mother Stein says to me, and no matter how angry I get, if I lose my temper then she wins, and my mother is not going to win this time."

"And why are we going again?" Rip asked.

"Rip, it's my family reunion, and there is a part of me that for just one time, I want to be accepted for who I am."

"Well now I know what my job is."

"I just thought I should tell you before we got there."

"You could have said it before we got on the plane."

"Hey," Jan said, raising her voice, "we had sex last night. Wasn't that enough?"

People in the seats around them turned their heads, and started to stare.

"It's okay," Rip said in a quieter placating voice to the stares. "Family issues. We all have them."

The stewardess came by, and Rip ordered another drink. Rip thought the stewardess was nice enough, but Jan thought she was giving her the stare, like she was being annoying, and that did not help.

"Is this Red or Black?" Jan asked the stewardess when she came with Rip's drink, even though the label of the Johnnie Walker airport bottle was red striped.

"It's Johnnie Walker Red."

"Next time we would like Black," Jan said.

The stewardess gave Rip his drink, and gave Jan a look like *Don't tell me my job*, and went to the back.

"Black is smokier with a deeper flavor," Jan told Rip. "Steins know their Johnnie Walker."

Once landed, Rip and Jan dropped off the luggage at the hotel. Rip noticed that the room had two double beds. He saw that as a bad sign. Would he be sleeping alone tonight? But their room had a view of the ocean, and that was a plus. Rip thought that maybe he should get Jan stoned before the reunion, and then nothing would matter. It always worked for him. When Rip took Jan to a fish taco joint and they had a few beers, he brought it up to her.

"Fish tacos and cabbage slaw. What could be better?" Rip asked. "And a local beer. Bottled in the San Diego area."

"What is this about?" Jan's feelers were up.

"Jan, I just want you to have a good time. Enjoy the moment. Maybe, just maybe we should get stoned before the reunion tomorrow night. I got three joints hidden away in my luggage. No security is going to stop me from having fun."

"Get stoned? At the reunion? Are you crazy? And you brought it on the plane? What do you think my mother would say if we got busted at the airport going to the reunion?"

"Actually, it was in the shampoo bottle in my luggage, and we didn't get busted. I learned how to hide it from Reed. If my luggage got searched then I knew nothing about it. It was my roommate's shampoo. Chip Hogwash is his name, and I am ready to sign a sworn statement."

"Two nights left," Jan said to herself.

"Listen," Rip tried to reassure her, "I understand the badgering, the past… All families are fucked up in their own way. Martin Mull used to say that a family is like having a bowling alley installed in your head. My family was more like a bowling alley in your stomach. Always hearing the noise of the pins rattling around like indigestion. That was my family."

"Martin Mull? What are you talking about?"

"I'm just saying, let's make this family thing an in and out deal, just like the burger. Hello, goodbye, see you later. Hello, I must be going."

"Haha. Very funny. This is not *A Night at the Opera*, Groucho. I never told you about the Stein Family Trail of Tears."

"There were Indians?"

"No. The Stein Family Trail of Tears. At the reunion, my mother gets Cousin Billy, with his Jerry Lewis infatuation, to be the emcee and after dinner, one by one, he tells everybody about how fucked up their lives are, and he just tears you apart. He always wanted to be a comedian, so he takes it out on us. Every year it's the same stupid jokes. 'A medic, really a medic? What does a medic do, Mother Stein? Save the homeless? She could have at least been a nurse.' My mother sits there in her wheelchair, glass of wine in her hand, and she laughs at everything he says. I just want to punch him so hard. And you'll be happy to know he dresses and looks like Jerry Lewis. You know when he started getting fat during his telethon days. I think he even puts black shoe polish on his hair."

"Oh yeah, I remember you bringing it up. Your Cousin Billy. Are there celebrities to handle the phones?"

"No Rip, there are no celebrities to handle the phones. It's not a real telethon."

"Like *King of Comedy*," Rip replied.

"Whatever, but every year it's the same thing. At first the reunion starts out fine. But then it's like my mother knows when everybody is half crooked because she is half crooked too, and then, after everybody has eaten, and the plates have been cleared, it's the Stein Family Trail of Tears. One by one little Cousin Billy tears us apart, and the drunker my mother gets, the more she loves it. So, Cousin Billy lays it on."

"What about the other ones? The rest of your family. Why do they put up with it?"

"They have learned to live with it, and my mother has money. Lots of money. Everybody wants their share."

"How old is Cousin Billy?"

"Around twenty-five. I don't know."

"Well I'll just get Cousin Billy stoned," Rip said logically.

"For God's sake Rip, he dresses up like Jerry Lewis. Getting stoned is not going to change him. Anyway, they threw Cousin Billy out of pharmaceutical school for sampling too many of the drugs he was supposed to be prescribing. Now he's in and out of rehab."

"Well then this should be easy. Me and Jerry Lewis will be smoking a joint before this Trail of Tears. He will be too stoned to remember any of his jokes."

"So that's what you were doing in the bathroom for so long this morning."

"Just a few puffs. Getting into the right frame of mind."

"I thought I smelled it. Just don't let my mother see it."

"Hey, you're talking to Chief Rip Ridley of the paramedic division. I will be so sweet with your mother that I will win over her cold, cold heart. I know how to do it. After a few drinks, and with my charm, she'll forget all this reunion nonsense."

"Rip, Mother Stein may be in a wheelchair but she never forgets."

"Jan, even though she is your mother, she is an old lady in a wheelchair who drinks too much. I'll have Jerry Lewis stoned, and your mother drunk on reunion night when I get done. The Stein Trail of Tears will be like *A Night at the Opera*. The joy will be unconfined. I think we should talk about tonight."

"Don't start before the reunion."

"But…"

"No buts, Groucho. Nobody enjoys themselves until after the reunion."

"But…"

"It's reunion sex, and it's only after the reunion is over. Get it?"

"How romantic."

That evening, when night started to fall and the sun dipped gently into the ocean, Jan calmed down a bit. Rip and Jan walked along the beach. They shared a joint under the pier and held hands and shared a kiss. For a short time, it was as if they were really a couple on vacation. Up in the hotel room Rip ordered a bottle of champagne to be sent up on ice. As she walked around in the hotel room in her underwear, Rip really liked Jan's body. It wasn't like Laura's body that was built for wild sex, but a body that could be tamed only by the night. This was his window of opportunity. Seeing how hard Rip was try-ing to make the evening just right, Jan showed the softness that only the night could bring on.

On the day of the reunion, Rip kept calling it *A Night at the Opera* until Jan told him to knock it off.

"Focus, Rip. Focus."

"I'm focusing."

Jan made sure that Rip looked good at the reunion. Summer jacket—dark blue, tan pants, and light blue shirt with a Grate-ful Dead designer tie. One that Jerry Garcia probably would have never worn. It wasn't tie-dye, but the person who de-signed it was certainly high on something. It was gold with dripping colors of red and blue. But the tie was a limited edi-tion, which gave Rip a certain flair. Jan was wearing a red bur-gundy dress with a low back. Rip thought she looked great and told her so.

The reunion started at three o'clock in the afternoon with hors d'oeuvres and drinks in the Crystal Room known for its historical architecture. On stands around the room were placed pictures of the Stein family in chronological order. There were the wedding pictures of the Stein parents, their first house, the kids growing up, the family on vacations. Real Norman Rock-well stuff. Everybody was always dressed up in the pictures. There were even pictures of Father and Mother Stein with ce-lebrities. Ronald and Nancy Reagan were in some of them; Wayne Newton and Perry Como, too. There was none of Jane Wyman, though. Rip thought to himself that his family never took pictures. They wanted to forget their past. While Jan went to the little girls' room to powder whatever, Rip looked at the pictures, and saw them as the family's attempt to show that their lives were picture perfect.

Looking around the room there was a stage with a four-piece band. The band looked old and tired, doing gigs on the side to pick up some extra money, and willing to play anything for a paycheck. Mostly it was Muzak with a touch of jazz, as if somebody was adding spices in a bland sauce just to give it some flavor. It was a band that after a few drinks nobody would be listening to anyway. Near the stage was a large framed picture of Father Stein with his handlebar mustache on one stand, and another blown-up picture of his signature on another. Rip thought that the picture of his signature was kind of weird.

When Rip was looking at a picture of Ronnie and Nancy with the Steins, Cousin Billy came up to him. At first glance, Cousin Billy reminded Rip of some creepy kid in a Jerry Lewis tuxedo with no redeeming features. He was pudgy, with a round face, but so was Jerry Lewis during his telethon days. And Rip thought that the hair on his head had to be some kind of hair piece. He had gold buttons down his fluffy white shirt, and big gold cufflinks. His hair was obviously darkened and pressed down with some sticky substance.

"You know Nancy killed Jane," Cousin Billy said to Rip. "That's why there are no pictures of her."

"You must be Cousin Billy," Rip said, trying to ease into whatever side could be good. "Maybe Jane got the best of the deal. Don't you think?"

"It's William, and I make the jokes around here," Cousin Billy protested.

Maybe there's no good side to Cousin Billy, Rip thought, but he made his pitch anyway.

"What does William do when you don't have any gigs?" Rip asked him.

"What do you mean?"

"You know, to relax. Can't be Jerry Lewis all the time. You're a comedian, which means you are an artist, so is there any reefer madness in Cousin Billy's life?"

"It's William, and are you trying to get me stoned?"

"Well yes… Does William smoke a little doobie every once in a while? I mean if you dress up like Jerry Lewis you got to puff the magic dragon sometimes."

"I'm still on probation."

"Oh yeah, the pharmacy thing."

"So, Jan told you?"

"Listen," Rip said, "nobody likes these reunions. Why don't you just lay off Jan and have a good time?"

"Sorry. Can't. Mother Stein thinks it's funny, and Mother Stein has all the money. She laughs when I tell the jokes. And everybody laughs too. Poor, poor Jan. She just can't see the humor. And I don't need your drugs anyway."

"Well Cousin Billy, I guess everything I heard about you was right."

"It's William, I said. And I will certainly make sure I tell Mother Stein you tried to get me stoned, just getting out of rehab and everything."

"Great. Well, thanks Cousin Billy. Go break a leg or something."

"Now I am really going to tell her for sure," Cousin Billy sneered, looking snotty, and walked away.

Well that worked out fine, Rip thought to himself.

While trying to find a place to get stoned, Rip ran into Mother Stein while Cousin Billy was in her ear. She had a Black aide in a tuxedo wearing white gloves pushing her wheelchair around. She was holding a glass of white wine with both hands in her lap. Rip was kind of shocked because she looked so frail, though sinister, and she wore a gray satin dress like the ones in those old Hollywood movies. Rip thought she did look a little like Joan Crawford in her later years, with lots of makeup on.

"So, you are Rip Ridley," Mother Stein said to Rip. Jan walked up to them. She sensed trouble.

"Are you the one who offered William drugs, and came with my daughter?"

"Yes, but not in that order?" Rip said in his defense.

"Now, Mother Stein," Jan interrupted, "we all know Cousin Billy has been getting stoned for years. Isn't that true, Cousin Billy? But is this going to be another reunion where the knives come out?"

"Daughter Jan, always thinking the worst of her poor mother. I just wanted to meet your nice friend."

"Good. Let's try to have a nice reunion. And that goes for you too, Billy."

"It's William, and I can see why you were never her favorite."

"Are you a medic?" Mother Stein asked Rip.

"Rip is the chief of the paramedic division," Jan said to Mother Stein.

"Are you sleeping with my daughter?" Mother Stein asked.

"Yes, but we are only friends," Rip responded.

"All my other daughters are married."

Rip looked at Jan, and Jan looked at her mother, but before Jan could respond, Rip took her by the arm and led her to the bar.

"Very nice to meet you," Rip said, walking away.

"So, you tried to get Cousin Billy stoned?" Jan asked Rip.

"It was worth the try."

"I need a drink. This is only the beginning."

At the makeshift bar that was set up next to the empty trays where the food would be brought out, Jan ordered a drink from the bartender. He was a young blond-headed kid with acne, and looked like he was trying to put himself through college.

"Johnnie Walker Black," Jan said to him, "Black!"

"I'll take a Corona," Rip said.

When Jan saw the short pour she was getting, she looked at the bartender. "Fill it up. Don't short pour me."

The bartender looked at Rip, who gave him the *I think you should do it* look, and then he poured.

"Mother Stein gets sloshed on her white wine, and then she tries to control how much everybody else is drinking," Jan said to whoever was listening. It was as if Jan had a rolodex of all the past reunions that were starting to flip through her mind.

"Easy girl, easy girl," Rip said to Jan. "You got your drink."

When Jan wasn't looking, Rip slipped the bartender a twenty.

It was just then that Jan's two sisters came up to Jan. One looked very pregnant and the other looked very thin, almost bulimic. They were married with rugrats running around. Rip saw them as trophy wives who both looked very tired, trying to be as invincible as possible.

Introductions were given. Both of Jan's sisters were quite impressed by Rip. He was funny and good looking. Rip made the sisters laugh when he said, "I always wanted to come to the Stein Family Reunion. Jan speaks so highly of it."

After the introductions and the small talk, one of the sisters saw Jan ordering another Johnnie Walker Black and came up to her. "Let's give Mother Stein her moment."

"Mother Stein already had her moments," Jan said, shutting her down.

Rip saw the alcohol changing Jan's demeanor. It became darker, like the Johnnie Walker she was drinking. He tried to get her to go outside to smoke the joint.

"Let's just go to the beach," Rip pleaded. "There is a great little bar outside, and then we can come back when it's just about over."

"I'm staying here," Jan stated. She was making her stand. Rip started to see the reunion as a merry-go-round where you can never get off, and he didn't see any gold rings. He quickly got Jan something to eat when the hors d'oeuvres arrived from the waiters carrying them on trays. There was Beef Bourguignon on toast. Stuffed mushrooms. Shrimp balls. Some kind of cheese on crackers. Rip just wanted to make sure Jan had something in her stomach. He was coming to the conclusion that the reunion wasn't going to be an in and out thing. But still Rip stayed close to Jan, trying to calm her down, and trying to make sure she didn't have too much to drink.

The dinner was the usual reunion shitty fare. The food was set up in metal heated containers, with trays and plates in front of the line, and the desserts and the coffee at the end. Kind of like cafeteria prison style. There were dinner rolls, a meat dish, a fish dish, a potato dish, a rice dish, mixed vegetables, and the desserts looked very sugary. People remarked how good the food was, but it really wasn't. They were just drunk, or hungry, or both.

After getting the food, people found places to sit at the tables already set up in the middle of the room that sat eight. Rip and Jan found themselves sitting at a table of aunts and uncles, mostly with spouses, who worked for banks and insurance firms, and saw the food as a free meal.

And at first the free drinks and the free food put everybody in a good mood. The band kept playing something that imitated jazz. People had seconds. The wine poured. After the desserts were cleared away, then the speeches came.

First Jan's brother, Jerry Junior, came up, the one she used to fight with when she was growing up, and made all the gracious compliments and introductions that were usual in reunions. He talked about Father Stein, and how he was missed, and Mother Stein who was the pillar of the family, and how great it was to get together every year for the reunion. "So let's enjoy ourselves tonight." Jerry Junior talked about the great hotel with its history, and how good the food was, and of course the great band. He then went on to talk about Mother Stein's grandchildren—there were seven and another one was on the way. Applause rang out in the room.

"Father Stein would be proud," Jerry Junior said, raising his glass, looking up at the ceiling. "Keeping up with the Stein family tradition."

Applause rang out again.

"Of course, we have another tradition," Jerry Junior said. "William our cousin—we all know his talents—is going to come up and entertain us. Come on up, William."

A drumroll followed. A microphone and an amplifier were set up in front of the band for Cousin Billy.

"Eaaaasy now," Rip said to Jan, who was on the white wine.

Cousin Billy came out like he was doing the telethon in Las Vegas. His hair was slicked down a little blacker than when Rip first met him. Along with his black tuxedo and untied black bow tie, he wore lots of rings, and on his wrist was a big fake gold watch.

"My orchestra is not here yet, so I brought my other band," Cousin Billy said into the microphone, as the drummer accented his jokes with a hit on the snare or the cymbal.

"Let's give a big hand for the band today."

Everybody clapped and laughed, except Jan.

On stage, Cousin Billy, in his best Jerry Lewis impression, went through his family reunion monologue, as if he was playing the MDA telethon. He even looked behind his back a few times, wondering out loud where Les Brown and his orchestra were tonight. "I guess they got caught in traffic." The audience loved it. The aide even rolled Mother Stein in her wheelchair up front, so she could get a better view. She seemed to love this moment, and it was easy for Rip to see from her expression of laughing at his stupid jokes that Cousin Billy was her favorite. Mother Stein laughed and spilled her wine on the front of her dress, as her aide helped her steady her glass.

"Hey lady!" Cousin Billy called out, imitating Jerry Lewis. "Hey lady! It's Mother Stein. Well, just don't do something, sit there!"

Cousin Billy pointed to the big picture of Mr. Stein. "They don't make Republicans like they used to. You sure don't see a handlebar mustache like that anymore. Come on, everybody laugh. I need the applause. Always remember the drinks are free."

And the more the drinks came, the more Cousin Billy's audience laughed. Everybody was drinking and having a good time and Jan was drinking too. But for her it was not good drinking. It was drinking when somebody was looking for a fight. Rip slowly tried to move her drink away, and since she hadn't eaten very much, he put some dinner rolls that were left on the table closer to her, but she just pushed them aside and took her drink back. Nighttime had arrived, but her bedroom eyes were nowhere to be seen. Her lips were tight, and she just glared at Cousin Billy and Mother Stein.

"Now let's talk about the kids," Cousin Billy said, looking at the picture of Father Stein. "I like to call them Jerry's kids! Four kids. Four kids! Seven grandchildren and another one on the way! Do you think you people could take a break? If you ask me, you need to go out more. Go for a walk or something."

The drummer hit the cymbal.

"And how many accidents can Jerry Junior get into? Thank God he wasn't drinking. Eh? I heard he had so many accidents that State Farm has his picture on the wall for employee of the year."

This time it was a snare drum.

"And how coordinated is sister Amy? In that skiing accident I heard the tree got in her way. I even heard that her daughter had to teach her how to walk."

The dumb jokes went on and on. Even Rip was amazed that the family took it. But Mother Stein loved it. *She must have a lot of money*, Rip thought. But then it was Jan's turn for Cousin Billy's abuse.

"And how about Mother Stein's favorite daughter, Jan," Cousin Billy announced with a drumroll. "You know we have all been waiting for it."

"Don't do it," Rip whispered to Jan. "Don't do it. It's not worth it."

But Jan wasn't listening. Her angry eyes were still focused on Cousin Billy and Mother Stein.

"Still not married, eh Jan? Well, you do live in SAN FRAN-CISCO. Maybe...well I'm just saying, you know. Ladies night out! And a medic to boot. What does a medic do, Jan? Give out blankets? That's nice. If you're homeless."

Everybody laughed. With the alcohol swirling in her brain, it seemed to Jan that the laughter was a roar in slow motion.

"How about her friend Rip Ridley? Chief of the paramedic division. Yeah, sure. Does he have a preference for Mary Jane or what?" Cousin Billy said, taking imaginary puffs. "If you know what I mean. Are you sleeping together yet, or do I have to ask? And how about those letters, Jan? Do you still get them? I guess you do 'cause I'm the one who mails them to some fire station on Evans Street. Of course, I read them first. Father Stein would be proud. Well, maybe not. When are you going to get a real address? But hey, does anybody need a blanket?"

"Fucking Cousin Billy" was all Jan said. She got out of her seat, and when Rip touched her arm and told her to maybe just sit and get it over with, Jan said, "Don't," and headed for Cousin Billy.

"Give me that fucking mike," Jan said to Cousin Billy when she approached him.

"Whoaaaaa," Cousin Billy said. "We have a heckler."

"Knock it off," Jan said, and she was serious.

"Daughter Jan," Mother Stein said, "why are you causing a spectacle of yourself?"

"Spectacle? Every year this stupid reunion is a spectacle. I'm surprised Patty Hearst doesn't show up here."

"Wow, Patty Hearst, now," Cousin Billy said to the audience.

"I'll get to you in a minute." Jan pointed to Cousin Billy. He backed down.

"Daughter Jan, why all the drama? We are only having fun," Mother Stein said.

Jan faced Mother Stein like Mother Stein had never been faced before.

"Don't 'Daughter Jan' me. You want drama? I'll give you drama. Like all those stupid letters you write to me."

"Daughter Jan, I was just trying to be a good mother by putting you on the right path."

"Right path? Do you want to hear about the right path?"

Jan was out of control and everybody was watching. There was no more laughter. Jan went over and grabbed the big picture of Father Stein.

"Let's talk about the right path." Jan showed the picture to Mother Stein and everyone else in the room. "This is Father Stein. Yeah, you remember him, don't you Mother Stein? The girlfriends, the scandals with other women. He never spent a faithful day in his life, and you are writing me letters?"

Whoa! There was a silence in the room. One of the relatives at Rip's table leaned over to the person next to him and whispered, "This is the best reunion we ever had."

"Do you remember his Black girlfriend? The one who was younger and prettier than you? The one he put up in that nice apartment, and the one he dressed up in nice clothes. Where is your reunion now? And she was at his funeral, and you didn't say anything."

Jan's sisters, after the initial shock, came up to Jan to take the picture away and calm her down.

"Don't touch me," Jan said to them, and they backed off, too.

By this time Mother Stein was starting to clutch her chest, as if she was having shortness of breath.

"Are you having the same heart attack you had for the past twenty years?" Jan screamed, "Well no more of your stupid letters, and no more of these stupid reunions."

Rip saw Mother Stein as one of those ancient Greek statues whose arms and facial expressions have been worn off by the ravages of time. As Rip went up to the stage to gather Jan and lead her off, Cousin Billy tried to intervene. He seemed a bit shaken.

"Jan," Cousin Billy said, now looking a little less snotty, "it's just a joke."

"A joke? Give me that mike, you pill popper," Jan said to Cousin Billy, and she grabbed it, though Billy was not giving it up. It was all he had in life.

Jan tried to yank it out of his hands, but Billy yanked it back, and it became a tug of war. When Rip tried to lead her away, Jan let go of the mike while Cousin Billy was still holding it. The backlash of his feeble hands going back still clutching the amplified mike sounded like a cannon going off when he popped himself right in the nose with it, and then blood flowed everywhere. It wasn't a very nice picture.

"Maybe we should call a medic," Rip said, as he was still trying to lead Jan away.

"Wait a minute," Jan yelled at Rip. "No more letters, Mother Stein. No more stupid letters, and no more stupid reunions. I don't need your advice. And Billy, I know the Stein jab so watch your step."

Cousin Billy quivered and held a blood-soaked towel to his face. Mother Stein had passed out in her wheelchair. Her empty wine glass had fallen to the floor.

"Is she dead?" Rip asked Jan.

"She will never die." Jan looked to the crowd of relatives who had gathered around. "Does anybody have anything else to say?"

There were no takers.

"Well then call a medic because we are leaving."

Rip got Jan out of there and even waved as he was leaving, telling everyone what a pleasure it was to meet them. He didn't know what else to say.

"Knock it off," Jan told him.

Jan and Rip went upstairs, got their luggage, and headed for the airport. They smoked the last of Rip's joint in the cab, and at first the cab driver objected, but then Rip put a few twenties on the front seat, and they headed to the airport. At the airport counter Jan got two tickets one way to San Francisco. They dropped off their luggage, and going through the security line, Rip gave her his suit jacket to put on, but they still smelled of dope. With dried blood on the front of her dress, even security didn't want to fuck with Jan, looking like she just got out of a catfight, so they let them go. Nobody said a word.

Once on the airplane, Jan and Rip sat there in silence. Rip was going to say something to Jan just to try to brighten her up, but then thought to himself, *No, don't.* He didn't even need Duderonomy for that one. Jan had a tear in her eye, but was still defiant. When the stewardess came by with the cart, Jan ordered a Johnnie Walker, double.

"Do you have Black?" Jan asked the stewardess.

"We only have Red," she said.

Jan didn't reply.

"Do you still want it?" she asked Jan.

"Yes."

"I'll have the same," Rip said.

The stewardess looked at Jan, but after seeing the dried blood on the front of her dress, gave them their drinks and quickly left.

Rip and Jan sat in silence in the cabin. Both of them felt deflated like a flat tire on a used Cadillac. And it was that noise of the wobbling flat tire that Rip and Jan started to hear. From their window they could see the engines on the wing. It was so loud. For a moment Rip wondered, *How much do these airplane mechanics make an hour?* It had to be union.

A voice came over the intercom.

"This is the captain. Please go back to your seats and fasten your seat belts. We are expecting turbulence."

Maybe it was the shock of the reunion? Or just the alcohol? Or smoking Reed's pot? Or the combination of all of it? But that wobbling noise in the airplane got louder and louder, and then the annoying alarm sound kept ringing to fasten your seat belts, and then the lights went out in the cabin. The plane started shaking. The pilot said something over the intercom but nobody was listening. Passengers started screaming. Luggage went flying out of the overhead bins. The drink cart had tipped forward and the pitchers of ice water had spilled down the aisle. The oxygen masks dropped. Seconds seemed like forever. That was when Jan unhooked her seatbelt, braced herself, and stood up.

"Listen up everybody," Jan announced, "I am not having a good day. Do you hear me? This plane is not going down. I have waited too long to tell Mother Stein, my mother, what I really felt about her stupid letters, and her stupid reunion, and today was that day. And I'm not letting it go to waste by going down with this plane. Do you hear me, everybody?"

Jan pointed her finger to the heavens, or really to the top of the cabin.

"And YOU up there, I know I'm not one of those starving kids in Africa, or one of those people who have to drink bad water every day, or have some terrible debilitating disease with flies on me, or even walk the streets of San Francisco every night because I'm homeless. And even though some people may consider my life privileged, I have feelings too. I am a pretty good medic and I enjoy being a medic too, and this plane is not going down today. Do YOU hear me up there? Yeah, YOU! This plane is not going down. I'm not afraid of dying, but not today."

Heads that were once down looked up, and were all staring at Jan. And then, as if from the hands of God, the lights of the cabin went back on, and the plane started to even out, and the shaking stopped. There was even applause in the plane, and Jan took it as if directed toward her, but everyone else saw it as a relief that the plane hadn't crashed.

The stewardess came over and asked Jan to "PLEASE sit down."

"She's sitting," Rip said, as he helped her back into her seat.

Mother Stein didn't die but she was taken to the ER for observation along with Cousin Billy, who had a broken nose. Jan was never invited to any more reunions after the incident, and never received any more letters either. One of the sisters even sent Jan a picture of Cousin Billy with hospital tape all over his broken nose. Jan put the picture on her locker at work. After the incident Cousin Billy went back into rehab, and went into therapy for his infatuation with all things related to Jerry Lewis. Mother Stein never spoke of Daughter Jan again. And Jan and Rip never talked about the Stein Family Reunion or the Stein Family Trail of Tears. Rip did mention it to Reed, when they were smoking a joint at Reed's house, as he always had a party after the first harvest.

"So, her Cousin Billy really dressed up like Jerry Lewis?" That seemed to amaze Reed the most about the events of the Stein Family Reunion.

"Yep," Rip said.

"Kind of like *King of Comedy*."

"That's what I said."

Between tokes, Rip and Reed came to the same conclusion that sometimes confrontation is a good thing and shouldn't be avoided, especially when it came to families. And according to Jan's sister, it was agreed upon by the siblings that Cousin Billy was never going to be allowed to tell any more jokes again at the Stein Family Reunions, and that the reunions were probably going to be kind of boring, and not the same, without Jan being there.

PART THREE

CHAPTER 17

The Whoppers for Jesus meetings could not have been better for Crack Addict Eddy, and he should have been happier. Jesus had fixed Eddy up with a job as a custodian at Burger King, and renewed his driver's license, and now he had a bank account with twenty-two dollars in it. Eddy even tried to get off the crack pipe, and slowly the color of his face was starting to get back to normal. Not the normal that most people have, but the normal that said he wasn't on the crack pipe every day, though the scars of the past remained. And Jesus took Eddy to Goodwill, and bought him clothes that he could wear to work that didn't make him look like he was a crack addict who lived in a van. Eddy was so proud of his secondhand Levi's slacks and his two plaid shirts that he hung them beneath the sword he called Redemption. But for Eddy, there would always be moments of weakness. The urge was never far behind, though he tried to hide it from Jesus. For Eddy, the crack pipe had become such an intricate part of his life that he didn't want to hurt Jesus' feelings. But the emptiness that he felt when he wasn't using could never be filled by religion. He never told anyone, not even at the Whoppers for Jesus meetings where you were supposed to confess all your misgivings.

And living in a van in Hunters Point, the crack pipe was always right around the corner. During the day Hunters Point was a quiet neighborhood. But at night the crack pipes came out. The crack houses opened up, and crack dealers came out, looking for aliens. Eddy even dreamed about crack pipes. They were shaped like little candy canes, dressed in cowboy hats and boots, and sang about Tender Crisp Bacon Cheddar Ranch sandwiches, just like the commercial from Burger King. But it wasn't the Black cowboy singing to him. It was the crack pipes. It was the tune that played in his head when he woke up in the morning, about a train of nice young ladies comin' by with nice cabooses. The crack pipe was never far behind.

And in those moments when Eddy had it bad, and he hadn't given in to his urges, he would pull out Mercy, his guitar, and strum those lonesome cowboy songs of his past. That helped him get by sometimes, but it did not help ease the pain.

It was Effin who first thought that maybe Eddy was starting to slide a bit trying to stay clean. He would see Eddy walking the streets slumped down, pushing his shopping cart, collecting empty bottles and cans, looking like he had just lost his best friend, which was the crack pipe.

With Jesus leaving for his trip to Mississippi to be ordained as a preacher, Effin didn't want to say anything to him about Eddy. But Effin wasn't very good at keeping a secret. And if he didn't say anything, it was certainly written on his face that something was up, especially if you knew him as well as Jesus did. Finally, Jesus, sensing that Effin had something to say, but couldn't quite say it, confronted him in the yard when he was smoking.

"Okay," Jesus pressed Effin, "out with it."

"Out with what?" Effin asked, not knowing how obvious he was.

"You must know something that you don't want to tell me."

"I got nothing."

"Tell me."

"Okay, I know how much this trip to be an ordained preacher means to you, and I didn't want to bring up anything that may not be so good. It would kind of be like putting a jinx on your trip."

"So?"

"It's Eddy. I think he's back on the pipe. And I mean like he was before."

"I know Eddy slips sometimes, but I believe he has the faith. And he knows he can always come to me when weakness overcomes him."

"Well, if it's between faith and the crack pipe, the crack pipe is going to win."

"And how do you know that?"

"It's just the way he carries himself," Effin tried to explain. "When you're around it's different. He tries to show his thanks by being a little cheerful, but when I see him and you're not around, he looks like he just lost his best friend."

"Will you look after Eddy when I'm gone?" Jesus asked Effin.

"Sure. I'll let him in the yard, but is there really anything else I can do for him?"

"Just talk to him for me. I'll talk to him too, before I leave."

"I'll try, but I ain't no savior."

"I'm not asking for you to be a savior. I'm just asking you to talk to him when you see him. He isn't a bad guy."

"Sure," Effin said. "Okay."

Before Jesus went down to Mississippi to be ordained as a preacher, he took Eddy, Flat Nose Joey, and Sequoia out for Whoppers and fries and Diet Cokes. He talked to all three how things were going to be better once he was an ordained preacher. That all they needed was faith. Jesus also talked to Eddy privately, and Eddy promised him he would do everything in his power to try to stay clean. And then he talked to Joey who promised he would treat Sequoia better, and help Eddy if he started to give in to his weaknesses. Though maybe that wasn't the best idea because Joey was high on everything he could get his hands on. But Jesus thought it wouldn't hurt to try.

Being ordained a preacher was a big deal for Jesus. Preacher Dan had even called Jesus to tell him that the flight had been arranged for him to fly into Memphis, and then his people would meet him at the airport, and they would ride the bus to Yazoo County, Mississippi. It would be a long bus ride, but for Jesus, it was like Mecca. And once a year, for those who had been touched by his ministry and followed his spiritual guidance, Preacher Dan would invite them on his annual trip to the Holy Land. Of course, they had to pay, but since it was a group, it was discounted. The Holy Land! Where it all began. Jesus was excited.

On the day Jesus was to leave, Effin even took a supply van and drove him to the airport. It was a quick drive on Route 101. Jesus wore a suit that he had picked up from one of his Goodwill trips when he went with Eddy to get him some clothes. The suit was black, and it fit. He actually bought two suits and a tie that was also black. His shoes were from Thom McAn. He had packed his old Samsonite suitcase with the clothes and the toiletries that he would need. In The Church of God's Guiding Light, cleanliness was close to Godliness. It had been a while since Jesus had flown anywhere. Once to Las Vegas, and another time to a weight lifters convention in Los Angeles. But those times were in the past. For a long time, Jesus never had anywhere to go until now. Since Effin had a city vehicle, he could park at the curb in front of the airport without being towed, and went inside with Jesus, and watched him get his ticket. Jesus was thankful for Effin driving him, and Effin was only too willing to do it, and thought it was great that they were breaking the rules.

"Look after Eddy for me," Jesus said to Effin. "Let him in the yard to get the empty bottles and cans."

Effin promised he would.

Then Effin and Jesus shook hands, and Effin watched Jesus walk through the security line. Effin watched Jesus go all the way in, and then Jesus waved, and he was gone.

Watching Jesus walk to the terminal, Effin was a little touched. Not the crazy touched, but the one where he knew that Jesus was his only friend at work, and he was sad that Jesus was leaving, if only for four days. Effin had never seen anybody off at an airport before, and never remembered the one time he flew in a plane when his mother took him on a trip to see relatives in Chicago, when he was very young. Now, his mother didn't take Effin to see anyone anymore. She just didn't know how he would be received or react. It was better that way.

As for Jesus, it was off to Preacher Dan's ministry of The Church of God's Guiding Light in Mississippi. When Jesus arrived at the airport in Memphis, two of Preacher Dan's people were there to meet him, and took him on the bus. They called themselves Brother Taylor and Brother Johnson, and they wore identical black suits, black shoes, white shirts, and thin black ties. Jesus would see that everybody who worked with Preacher Dan wore the same suit. And if you were a woman and were a helper, you wore a habit like nuns did without the coif, only a handkerchief on their heads. Everybody addressed Jesus not as Jesus or even Charles, but as Brother Wilson.

Preacher Dan and an aide greeted Jesus when he got to The Church of God's Guiding Light. There was a wooden church, a one-story building that looked like a schoolhouse, two smaller buildings that looked like barracks, and a brick building with a large antenna on top. There was also a lot of land around. The Church of God's Guiding Light seemed to be out a ways from everywhere and mostly the roads weren't paved.

But for Jesus to meet Preacher Dan, it was like meeting one of the Lord's disciples. Preacher Dan was a dark-skinned man, as was everybody in the congregation. His hair was cropped very close to his head, but it shined. His lips were thin, giving him the appearance of being detail-oriented. His eyes were small, but he had a bright and inviting smile. He was a tall man, but thin. The fact that Jesus was slim from his fasting was looked on by Preacher Dan in a good light. It meant that he had sacrificed. Preacher Dan also wore a black suit, but being the senior preacher, it was of a finer cut than the other members. Preacher Dan hugged Jesus when he first saw him, and called him "Brother Wilson soon to be Preacher Wilson." Then Preacher Dan brought everybody over in the congregation to meet Jesus. The congregation formed a circle around them, and Preacher Dan proclaimed, "Look at this man, who like us was once a sinner. He has come all the way from California to join our congregation." Then the circle closed, and everybody raised their hands proclaiming, "Praise the Lord." For Jesus it was a Hallelujah moment.

After a good night's rest in a bunk that was housed in what looked more like an army barrack, which he shared with the other men in the ministry, there was to be a Mass, and then breakfast. It was proclaimed a special day, and everything was about Brother Wilson being ordained.

In the church, during Mass, Jesus sat in the first seat of the first pew. The two young men who greeted him at the airport sat next to him. Preacher Dan said Mass. And during the sermon, Preacher Dan told the congregation how important this day was. A new member was about to join The Church of God's Guiding Light. Jesus, who was once Charlie and was now Brother Wilson, was soon to be Preacher Wilson. And though it was a hot and humid day, Jesus did not mind. Whenever Preacher Dan brought up that a new member was joining the congregation, everybody said "Praise the Lord" and "Hallelujah" again. In Holy Communion, Jesus got up and knelt in front of the steps that led to the altar, and was the first to receive the host, which was considered an honor.

After Mass and breakfast, Jesus was brought into a room in back of the church, and there he stood in front of the committee who would oversee his worthiness for his ordainment. Sitting at a long table, there was Preacher Dan, an aide, and three elders who wore white robes over their white shirt and black ties and black pants. There were no women on the committee. The main elder was very old, bald and had a long beard of white hair. The other two elders, who were younger, sat on either side of him and listened. They were in their mid-fifties, same dark faces, same white beards, same bald heads, looking like religious bookends. They would both be taking notes.

Jesus was nervous. He stood in front of the committee in his black suit, and even though the windows were open, he started to feel the Mississippi heat, and the humidity. He started to sweat a bit, and wiped his brow with a handkerchief. And his shoes hurt. But then Preacher Dan spoke with such kind words, as if knowing what he was thinking.

"Don't be nervous, Brother Wilson. We all have had those feelings. But you are amongst family now."

After Preacher Dan spoke to him, Jesus started to relax.

The first question the committee asked Brother Wilson was if he had met all the educational requirements, which meant he paid the money for the online courses, and if he had passed, which he did. When taking the course, if Jesus had any problems with any of the curriculum, he would call the 800 number, and they usually walked him through the process. Slowly Jesus' nerves calmed down, and he was able to focus. It was explained to Jesus by Preacher Dan that the ordainment process was to see if he had the convictions to follow the word of God. And that there would be a probationary period of three years where more studying was required along with yearly visits. It was also explained to Jesus that he was going to be assigned to one of the smaller branches that had opened up in Northern California, and Preacher Dan wanted him to continue his work with the homeless. It was not every day when a potential member had claimed to hear the voice of God. Jesus would be required to attend Mass at his assigned branch, and on certain Sundays preach the word of God at the pulpit. Learning to preach the word of God was a slow process, but considered essential. It was also the hope, Preacher Dan told Jesus, that a branch of The Church of God's Guiding Light would one day be opened in Oakland, and that Jesus would be a part of it. But first, at this meeting, he needed to disclose everything about himself.

"Tell us about your sins of the past," the older elder spoke to Jesus.

Jesus brought up the fact that he been fond of fornication in the past. Now, he just scratched himself when he had impure thoughts, but sometimes they lingered and crept into his dreams at night. There had also been lapses in religious judgment, though he didn't bring up Rip's picture on his desk of Laura, or his Christie Brinkley poster, and the effect they had on him. Jesus did bring up that before he found religion, he only cared about pleasures of the flesh, simple gratifications. He told the committee that there was a time when he lifted weights in the park, showing off his muscles, and winked at all the girls who passed by, hoping that they would wink back at him.

"What made you want to change?" the older elder asked.

Jesus went into a long confession about how he felt the presence of God one night during a Burger King commercial.

"Burger King?"

"Yes sir, I was watching *Family Feud.*"

"*Family Feud?*"

"The TV show, sir," Jesus replied.

"And what happened?"

"I was touched by the presence of God."

"During *Family Feud?*"

"Actually, it was during the commercial."

"Do you like Burger King?"

"I have a weakness for it, sir."

"Well I have to admit, sometimes I do too. But please call me Elder Hicks. You are amongst friends. Please tell us about the voices you heard."

"It was after I felt the presence of God come over."

"Did you believe it was a voice from God?"

"I'm not sure. But I heard, 'Help the…' Then I didn't hear anything else. But then later I had a dream, and in my dream, Jesus told me to help the homeless."

"What did you learn from this dream?"

"It made me realize that I was a sinner, and like Jesus I wanted to be a messenger for the Lord my God."

"That must have been some commercial."

"It was Elder Hicks."

There was light laughter.

"So, tell me what happened next?"

"After I felt the presence of God, I would sit at night with the lights out and the radio on, listening to the religious programs. One night all alone, I started listening to Preacher Dan's radio show, and it touched me. Preacher Dan was so kind. I listened to his preaching, and I listened to the tapes, and after talking to him on the phone, I went through the course. Then

I started working with some of the homeless who parked their broken-down vans near our station house. It's called the Evans Street Station. We have meetings in Eddy's van, with Eddy and some of the other homeless people. They are addicted to drugs. But I got Eddy a job, and I am trying to get him off those drugs."

"Did it help?"

"I do not know, Elder Hicks. Effin, the guy I work with, says I'll never make a difference, but I try, and I guess Eddy helps me face my weaknesses, too. Now there are four of us in these meetings. Sometimes I read scriptures, and we talk about what led us down our paths. It's a long journey."

"Amen," everybody said.

"Do you still have urges to sin?"

"Yes I do, Elder Hicks."

"What do you do when these urges come over you?"

"I pray. Sometimes I call Preacher Dan."

Preacher Dan nodded to confirm that he had received the calls.

"And how did you come to be in this room today?"

"I want to change my life. Until I felt the presence of God, and heard Preacher Dan's voice, I really never believed in anything that was important. I wandered aimlessly. But then listening to Preacher Dan, I felt that he was talking to me to follow the word of God. And it impressed me that I could pick up a phone and call the number, and talk whenever I needed someone. Sometimes I talked to Preacher Dan himself. That's when it came to me that I could be a messenger too. I never thought that I could be anything, but now this world has opened up to me. I am willing to sacrifice."

"Do you still go to Burger King?"

"Yes, sir. I have to admit I do, Elder Hicks."

"Well I have to admit," Elder Hicks proclaimed, "sometimes I do too. But the fact that you are willing to accept God into your life, and have acknowledged your weaknesses, I find very impressive. Are you familiar with all the requirements while on probation?"

"Yes, Preacher Dan explained them to me."

"Are you willing to follow them?"

"Yes, sir, I mean Elder Hicks."

"Are there any objections in this room to Brother Wilson being ordained?" Elder Hicks asked the committee.

There were no objections.

"Then it is agreed upon. Brother Wilson is now to be addressed as Preacher Wilson. Let us go, and be baptized."

They all left the room.

Jesus stood with Preacher Dan in the Yazoo River. They had both taken off their suit jackets and rolled up their pant legs, as everybody in the congregation looked on. Preacher Dan said a prayer, squeezed the nostrils of Jesus' nose, and dunked him backward, and with his baptism, the sins of the past were washed away. Jesus was impressed because Preacher Dan, after taking off his suit jacket and shoes, wore the same white shirt and black tie and pants in the water, and didn't even mind that he had gotten wet. When Jesus brought it up almost apologizing, Preacher Dan said it was such a small price to pay for him coming into the fold.

"And," Preacher Dan finished, as they were both given white robes to wear, "I found out the hard way that shoes in water have a tendency to shrink."

Then Preacher Dan laughed, seeing that Jesus had left his shoes on.

Charles…Jesus…Brother Wilson became Preacher Wilson on that day. Then the congregation sang, "Oh Happy Day."

For Jesus, it was his moment. He believed.

When Jesus got back to San Francisco, Effin was waiting for him in the supply van at the airport. For Jesus it was as if all his demons that had chased him all his life had gone away. For Effin, he had never seen Jesus so happy as when he came back from Mississippi, a preacher with a certificate.

"So, are you bona fide now?" Effin asked Jesus.

"I was ordained."

"A real preacher?"

"Well yes, but for three years I will be on probation. They want me to continue my work with the homeless."

"Did you mention the Whoppers for Jesus meetings?"

"I just said I work with Eddy and a few of the homeless."

"It would have been cool to mention it. Whoppers for Jesus. What did you have to do?"

"After Mass they brought me inside a room with Preacher Dan and some of the elders, and asked me questions about my calling to be a preacher."

"Was there a written test?"

"No, they just asked me questions."

"Like what?"

"Questions about my past, and what led me to want to be a preacher."

"Did you pass?"

"Well they gave me a certificate and called me Preacher Wilson."

Jesus took out the framed certificate that he had brought with him on the plane, and showed it to Effin while he was driving.

"Well at least it ain't xeroxed."

"Thanks."

"Did they baptize you?"

"Yes, in the Yazoo River."

"Was it all muddy and stuff?"

"No."

"Did they give you a bathing suit?"

"No, I just took off my suit jacket and rolled up my pant legs and after it was over, they gave me a robe to put on. I think I was supposed to take off my shoes, but I was so nervous I forgot."

"So, you had to walk around wet all day?"

"No, because later I changed into another suit."

"You went down there with two suits?"

"Yes."

"Wow, I only have one suit that my mother bought me. I never wore it though. But I'm proud of you. People say they are going to do something all the time, but you did it. Took a plane ride and everything."

Effin had a tear in his eye.

"Were these elders pretty old?" Effin asked.

"Some of them were pretty old, but not Preacher Dan."

"Where they Black?"

"There were no white people."

"Did they have any pictures of Jesus?"

"Of course they did. It's a church."

"Did Jesus look like Charlton Heston?"

"He didn't look like Charlton Heston, but the devil did."

"Really?"

"No, I'm just messing with you. But Jesus was a lot darker than any picture I've ever seen around here."

"Wow, a Black Jesus. What would the pope say?"

"They didn't talk about him. It's non-denominational."

"What's that mean?"

"It means the pope has nothing to say about it."

"Is there a cost?"

"Ten percent of what I make."

"Before taxes?"

"Yes, why?"

"They could have at least let you take taxes out first."

"So, you are proud of me?" Jesus asked.

"Yeah, I am."

"Thanks. How's Eddy?"

"I'm sure he's fine."

Jesus saw the concern on Effin's face.

"Did he come by to pick up the empty bottles?"

"Yeah, sure," Effin said, but he was lying.

While Jesus was gone, his van was still there, but Eddy hadn't come around to pick up the empty bottles and cans that he usually did like clockwork. Effin wondered how he was going to explain this to Jesus. He had given his promise to look after Eddy, but Eddy didn't show up. Effin didn't go looking for him, but he did feel that maybe something bad had happened to Eddy. It wasn't like Eddy had any relatives to visit, or any other place to go, and there had to be a reason why he didn't come around, and Effin didn't think it was a good one. Those few blocks in Hunters Point were his life. But Effin didn't want to ruin the moment for Jesus, so he didn't say anything. Riding north on Route 101, Effin didn't make eye contact with Jesus.

"I'm sure he's fine," Effin said. "He's fine."

CHAPTER 18

But Crack Addict Eddy wasn't fine. His van looked abandoned, and he hadn't shown up for dumpster diving, which was a lucrative deal for someone who collected empty bottles and cans all day. After two days of Eddy not showing up, Jesus confronted Effin in the yard. Effin confessed that he hadn't seen Eddy since Jesus left for Mississippi.

"Why didn't you tell me?" Jesus asked. Effin could see that Jesus was angry. Angrier than he had ever seen him before, and he just came back from preacher school.

"At first I really didn't notice that he hadn't come around. Then I saw that the dumpster was full," Effin tried to explain to Jesus. "I was afraid to tell you because I felt that I kind of let you down. I mean, fuck, I let down everybody, but I never meant to do it to you. And you were so happy becoming a preacher, so I didn't say anything. I just thought he would show up. They always do."

Effin lit the last cigarette from the pack, and then crumbled the pack up and threw it on the ground.

Jesus eased up a bit on Effin.

"I'm going to go find him," Jesus said.

"Do you want me to help you?"

"No, you just look after the warehouse, and if anybody asks, I'm on a run. Can you do that?"

"I can do that." Effin was still feeling bad.

"Please, do what I ask you to do. Okay?"

Effin nodded.

The first place Jesus went to was Burger King where Eddy was hired as a custodian, thanks to Jesus sticking up for him. When Jesus asked, he was told by the manager that Eddy hadn't shown up for work in the past few days. Jesus didn't have to ask if Eddy had been fired because someone else was doing his job. Jesus took the van on a run, and drove all around, mostly where the homeless congregate, but he couldn't find Eddy. Jesus checked, but the ambulance crews hadn't transported him, and he called all the hospitals, but Eddy hadn't been admitted. Finally, Jesus asked Flat Nose Joey and some of the others at Camp Willie if they had seen him. Since he didn't get the response that he wanted, Jesus put out the word that somebody better start talking, or he would start towing some of the clunkers that had been parked forever around the station. Towing clunkers was an easy thing for Jesus to do. There were usually tickets on their windshields, and the cops owed Jesus some favors for the rubber gloves and bandages and tape and disinfectants, and all the other stuff he let the police have when they came by. For the police, it was easier to just come by the Evans Street Station, and pick it up, and not have to fill out all the paperwork with their precinct. After two days of putting out the word, driving around looking for Eddy, and not finding him, Jesus towed a few of the clunkers.

That got Camp Willie's attention. Flat Nose Joey came up to Jesus with Stuttering Sam. They sent word through Effin that they wanted to talk when he was outside smoking, and met Jesus with Effin at the Fairfax gate in the yard.

First, Stuttering Sam tried to explain what had happened to Eddy, but Sam had been on the pipe all night, which made his stuttering worse. It wasn't that his stuttering was that bad, but it was in his head that he was going to stutter, and then somebody was going to make fun of him, so he stuttered.

"Eddy bback on the ppipe," Stuttering Sam said, not looking Jesus in the face when he said it. "Itt's jjuust…"

"It's just that he's fucking embarrassed that you may be mad at him. That he had let you down," Flat Nose Joey took over.

"That's why he hasn't been coming around and, well… Somebody stole his fucking guitar, Mercy."

"From his van?" Jesus asked.

"No, fuck no," Flat Nose Joey said. "He just passed out on the street from being up for two days, and somebody fucking stole it. He told me that he just went off when somebody stole his guitar, and he couldn't get those voices out of his head."

"See, I told you crack pipes can talk," Effin said, almost proud of himself, and Flat Nose Joey and Stuttering Sam nodded in agreement that crack pipes can talk.

"So, you saw him?" Jesus asked.

"Yeah." Flat Nose Joey nodded. "Just for a little bit. But when he heard you were coming back, he felt bad and slipped away. He was hanging out around city hall near the library. Do you want us to try to find him, and talk to him?"

"No, I'll find him."

"Ccan we pi-pick up the ca-cans?" Stuttering Sam asked.

"Yes. Effin will let you in. But just for today. But spread the word that if Mercy doesn't show up tomorrow, I'll be towing some more vehicles, and it won't be just clunkers."

"What do you mean?" Flat Nose Joey pleaded. "We didn't take it."

"You are going to roust them, aren't you?" Effin asked. He didn't care who heard.

"You really going to call the cops?" Flat Nose Joey asked.

"Get the cans and go," Jesus told him.

"But we didn't do anything. We fucking came to you. That's kind of fucked up, man."

"Do you want the cans or not?"

Both Flat Nose Joey and Stuttering Sam shut up after that.

"Those are the rules."

Effin was kind of amazed by this new Jesus acting like a preacher, getting his congregation in order. Effin let them in, and waited till their dumpster diving was over, and then let them out.

When Effin got back into the warehouse, he saw Jesus looking dejected.

"Hey, even Gandhi had bad days," Effin said, not wanting to make it worse for Jesus. "You really going to call the cops?"

"Yep. Sometimes a preacher has to know how to get into people's business."

"Wow. This Preacher Dan really must have made an impression on you. Hell, when the police come and roust them, I may even light up the barbeque. What are you going to do now?"

"I'm taking the van for another run."

Jesus took the van, and again went driving around the city looking for Eddy. There were always deliveries during the day, like picking up backboards from the hospitals that Effin usually did, but now it was Jesus. And for Jesus it was personal. Eddy was his first convert, and now he had to bring him back into the fold. He knew that Rip wouldn't care as long as all the work was getting done. And no matter what anybody said about Effin, he would always cover for Jesus.

Jesus drove to city hall, Civic Center Park, the wharf, underneath the freeways…but no Eddy, anywhere. The word spread throughout Camp Willie that the guitar had better show up, and quick. At first nobody did anything. Then Jesus had another two vehicles towed. He was serious.

That was when the holy trinity of Camp Willie—Flat Nose Joey, Stuttering Sam, and Sequoia—asked Effin for another meeting with Jesus. They met at the Fairfax gate in the yard again.

"We asked everybody," Flat Nose Eddy said to Jesus. "The guitar is gone."

"What do you mean it's gone?" Jesus asked.

"We heard they pawned it to buy some stuff." Flat Nose Joey didn't want to tell Jesus it was pawned for drugs. "It was just lying there, and when something ain't nailed down, then somebody is going to take it."

"Did they say which pawn shop?"

"No, but people don't go too far to pawn stuff. Can we go through the dumpsters?" Flat Nose Joey asked.

"Not until I get back the guitar."

"But we brought you information."

"But you didn't bring me back the guitar."

Jesus went back to driving the van, looking for Eddy, and started visiting pawn shops looking for the stolen guitar. They all had guitars but not Mercy. Jesus had no luck until, driving slowly on the Great Highway, he finally saw Eddy at Ocean Beach, near the parking lot. Eddy was sitting on the steps down from the walkway, looking out at the ocean, eating a Whopper, and drinking a Colt 45. When Jesus got out of the van, Eddy looked embarrassed as he ate his Whopper. Near his feet was a weather-beaten sleeping bag. Being near Sutro Heights Park and the ruins of Playland, there were a lot of places to crash for the night. Though Eddy did look worse for the wear. Jesus walked up to Eddy, and sat next to him.

"I went everywhere looking for you," Jesus said to Eddy.

"I'm back on," Eddy admitted, meaning the pipe, "but I guess you know. Flat Nose Joey came by, and said you rousted some of the clunkers."

"Until I get Mercy back."

"They didn't take it. It's not their fault. I passed out. I guess I also lost my job at Burger King. I felt they kept looking at me like I was a junkie. I could never handle people just staring. I know I'm an alien."

After finishing his burger, Eddy opened up to Jesus. They were both sitting on the steps, looking out at the ocean. Eddy didn't look at Jesus when he talked, only at the waves, sipping his Colt 45.

"I once had enough S.S.I. money saved up to buy a boat that I was going to live on, and fish and crab for a living. I knew a guy near Half Moon Bay at Johnson Pier who was going to sell it to me. We even went out sometimes, and I picked it up pretty easily because I always knew fishing. The boat needed a lot of work, but I thought that I could do it. But just when I had the chance, I used the money on dope instead. I always wished I had bought that boat, and then I could have sailed out to the ocean and never be seen again, and nobody would have ever known what I had become."

"There are other opportunities. The most important thing is that you don't lose faith."

"Are you a preacher now?"

"I am."

"I guess I failed you."

"I'm here to take you back."

"They didn't have to take Mercy. Mercy and Redemption and my van is all I got."

"What if I get you another one?"

"Nothing will ever take the place of Mercy. Some things matter. My mother sang to me playing that guitar. She showed me the chords on how to play Hank Williams songs. Her favorite was 'Hey Good Lookin'.' It made her feel so good listening to it. And she never had a lot of smiles."

"Then we will have to find it. I have been going to all the pawn shops, but most didn't even want to talk about it. They all had guitars, but not Mercy."

"Did you go to the pawn shop across from the Goodwill store on Mission?" Eddy asked. "It's Tom Thumb's Pawn Shop. He doesn't ask questions where you got the stuff. I went there when it first happened, but that little guy first told me to show him some money, and when it wasn't enough, he called me a dope addict and told me to leave the shop."

"I went there," Jesus remembered. "Yeah, a little man. But when I started asking about a stolen guitar, he didn't want to talk to me, either. Kind of rude, too."

"That's Tom Thumb."

"Well I guess we got to go back there. Let's get in the van and go."

Eddy picked up his sleeping bag, and got in the passenger seat of the van.

"Are you still in for the meetings?" Jesus asked as he was driving.

"I'm damaged goods."

"We are all a little damaged." Jesus turned up Point Lobos. "That's why I turned to God."

Tom Thumb's Pawn Shop was on Mission Street near Van Ness Avenue, across from the Goodwill store, next to the Chinese restaurant. The owner, Tom Thumb, was a dwarf who stood on a box behind a counter to speak to his customers. Nobody knew his real name, and nobody cared. The windows were barred and smudged. The pawn shop was always locked, and Jesus and Eddy had to be buzzed in at the front door to gain entrance. Once inside, Tom Thumb was waiting for them behind the counter. Though it was illegal, he carried a gun in a holster, around his waist. From the wrinkles on his face, he looked like he had lived a tough life, and resented everything. He wore a cowboy hat, had on cowboy boots, and on his belt was a big silver buckle. He didn't look like he shaved much either.

Tom Thumb's was the perfect pawn shop for somebody who wanted to unload something with no questions asked. He trusted nobody, and would never let the cops in the shop when they came by to see if anything he had bought was stolen. One time an undercover cop came by, looking for some stolen items, and tapped on the window. When Tom Thumb wouldn't answer the door, he flashed his badge. Tom Thumb just flashed one of his badges, from the inside of the same window, that someone had just pawned, and finally the cop went away. Two-bit stolen stuff was not a big priority for law enforcement. Just wasn't worth the hassle. Jesus approached him at the counter.

"We are looking for a guitar that my friend had stolen."

"You were here before, and I'll tell you again. I don't take stolen stuff, and I don't have your guitar." Tom Thumb frowned, putting his hand on his hip where he had his gun. "Maybe you got the wrong pawn shop, and maybe you should just turn around and walk out the door."

"We just want it back." Jesus put one hundred dollars in twenties on the counter. "No questions asked."

Tom Thumb looked at the twenties.

"No questions asked?"

"No questions asked."

"What's it look like?"

"It's a Martin," Eddy said, "a little weathered. *Mercy* is etched on the back. I had it done after the last time."

"The last time what?" Tom Thumb asked.

"The last time it was stolen."

Eddy put ten dollars on the counter.

"That's all we got," Eddy said.

"Wait here," Tom Thumb warned, "and don't touch anything. I got cameras."

Even Jesus could see that most of the cameras were fake. They were put up on the walls to look real. The only ones that were real was the one near the register, and the one in back of the shop, pointed toward the front door. Tom Thumb went into the back, and when he came out, he was holding Mercy. He put the guitar on the counter, and took the bills.

"Now both of you get going. I don't need anyone saying that I take stolen stuff."

For Tom Thumb, everything was a standoff. He leaned over the counter, trying to look big, and again put his hand on his gun. Eddy picked up his guitar and headed for the door. When Tom Thumb buzzed the door, Jesus followed Eddy out. Once outside in the open air, Eddy had a tear in his eye. He held Mercy close to his breast, like a long-lost friend.

"I'm sorry I let you down," Eddy said to Jesus.

"I know you are. Let's get back into the van, and I'll drive you back to Evans Street."

"You didn't tow my van, did you?" It was his idea of a joke.

"Why would I? It's my church, you know. But if you leave again, I'm going to. A preacher got to do, what a preacher got to do."

They both laughed, and then Eddy started coughing. It was probably the first time that Eddy had laughed in a long time.

When word got around that Eddy was back with his guitar Mercy, Camp Willie breathed a sigh of relief. Even the towed clunkers found their way back. They had been fixed up just enough by their owners to pull into a parking space, and some broke down again. Sometimes they had to push their vans into the parking spot. But it had cost one hundred dollars to get them out of tow, and they had to pay the parking tickets owed. Jesus had sent his message.

For the time being, Camp Willie was back to its usual self. Effin used to say that if Camp Willie was a person, it would be on life support. Eddy was allowed to dumpster dive again for the empty bottles and cans, and Jesus again started holding his Whoppers for Jesus meetings in Eddy's van. At first Flat Nose Joey didn't want to go back, as he was still mad about the towing, even though his van wasn't one of the clunkers that were towed. But Sequoia wouldn't shut the fuck up about the meetings because she liked them, so they started going again. They even brought Stuttering Sam with them, who didn't mind because it's hard to give up a free Whooper with fries and a Diet Coke. And sometimes, when Stuttering Sam had spent the night on the pipe, he had trouble completing his sentences when talking about himself. But Jesus made sure that he tried to finish his sentences, and Flat Nose Joey wasn't allowed to make fun of his stuttering. Flat Nose Joey still wasn't too happy about going to the meetings again, but he was smart enough to figure out that maybe it was better if he stayed on Jesus' good side, and he did like those Whoppers and fries. Most of the time he just sat there, eating, saying nothing.

"Looks like your Whoppers for Jesus meetings are back on," Effin said to Jesus one morning in the warehouse. "You still mad at me?"

"I was never mad at you."

"Well you had a right to be. But I thought you ought to know something." This time Effin was serious.

"What?" Jesus asked. Effin didn't have the usual sarcastic look about him. He followed Effin out to the yard.

"I just thought you should know that things around here are changing."

"In what way?"

"Well you heard about the merger with the fire department, right?"

"I heard."

"Well, my mother works for city hall, and it's even been in the newspapers. The merger is going to happen. We're going to be under the fire department. I even heard Chief Ridley is gone. They are going to bring in somebody else."

"Does Rip know?"

"If he reads the newspaper he knows. But there is something else."

"What?"

"My mom said that they're going to bring in Chief Brady. You know, the old guy who walks funny, and gasses up here, and smokes cigars. He's going to be the new CD1. He's the one who had Camp Willie towed before. Well, he's going to run the merger. My mom said the first thing they are going to do is to get rid of Camp Willie. Even before the merger."

"Get rid of it?"

"Clean it up. And I don't mean only the clunkers. My mom said there have been too many complaints. They are even going to red tag the curbs where you can't even park vehicles on the street anymore with NO PARKING signs everywhere."

"Are you sure about this?" Jesus' face became stern like he was thinking about his next move. Effin thought that Jesus was thinking more like a preacher now than just somebody who worked in the warehouse.

"I just thought I should tell you since I didn't do a good job looking after Eddy."

"Thanks."

"Is there anything I can do?"

"No," Jesus said in a soft voice, "it will be fine."

"But I just thought..."

"It will be fine." Jesus turned away and walked back into the warehouse, into his office and closed the door.

CHAPTER 19

The world got a lot smaller for Rip Ridley, and for everybody else at the Evans Street Station. An article in the *Chronicle* confirmed that the supervisors had signed off on the merger between the paramedic division and the fire department in the new fiscal year, which was just around the corner. It was front page news, and the headline *Paramedics to Merge with SFFD* was bigger than the headline of Bill Clinton and Boris Yeltsin getting together, and that was for world peace.

Rip was bummed. Rip always thought that maybe all this talk about a merger would go away. But now the merger was going to happen.

"You know something will always come up, Bwana." Duderonomy tried to cheer him up. "Not every wave is going to be the perfect one. You need to ride this one out."

"Ride it out?"

"Yes Bwana, just ride it out."

"And then what?"

Even Duderonomy didn't have an answer for that. Nothing could get Rip out of his dark mood. He thought about bumming a cigarette from Effin, but didn't want to go down to the yard. With the newspaper article, the word was out.

When Jan came up to his office, just to see how Rip was taking it, she saw him at his desk with that faraway look in his eyes, like he was distant from everyone around him. Jan went around his desk, and from behind ran her hand through his hair, then leaned over and kissed him on the cheek. Then she left the room. When Reed came up to Rip's office, he brought a baggy of pot. "I took this out of my own private stash. I think I found the perfect bud. I've been working on the right ph for the soil. I call it Dreamland."

"Dreamland?"

"Yeah, Dreamland. You'll find out when you smoke it. It should help you with your sleep."

Rip opened up the baggy, sniffed the freshness, and bobbed his head. "Thanks."

But still, at the end of the day, all Rip ever wanted was to be chief. He knew the end had arrived when Chief Brady came into his office to make his demotion official. *But at least*, Rip thought, *Chief Brady came up alone, while Lieutenant McGuire fueled up in the yard.*

Chief Brady took a seat across from Rip, who was still sitting at his desk.

"Well you must have heard," Chief Brady said, "but city hall sent me over here to tell you anyway. I'm surprised that Hogwash didn't call you himself. I thought he might have enjoyed it."

Rip said nothing.

"But for Christ's sake, Ripley, you had to expect it would happen. But I'm not here to rub it in. The fact that you didn't try to sleep with my daughter, like everybody else does, I'm going to give you a break. You were right to stay away. Probably the only thing you did right. I certainly don't need any hippie grandchildren in my life, if you know what I mean. And I know about her late-night calls to you."

"You tapped her phone?" Rip asked, bringing him out of his funk.

"I didn't tap it. It's my daughter. Since I owned the building, I offered to pay her phone bill. It just comes to me. Of course, I see what calls come in and what calls go out. It's the fatherly thing to do. I was happy to see you kept your distance. But I have to ask you. Where do you want to end up?"

Rip saw it as a trick question, so he didn't answer.

"Hogwash did make it clear that there are not going to be any more training films. Didn't seem to be a big fan."

"I don't know," Rip admitted.

"Give it some thought. Maybe training. It's going to be out on Treasure Island. It's got a nice view, and everybody leaves you alone. Let me see what I can do. Nobody wants to be in those RC vehicles in the middle of the night in the Tenderloin when it's raining."

Rip thought to himself that everyone seemed to know what he was thinking before he said it. Rip didn't have a poker face.

"I'll give you a few days to clean out your office before I name your replacement. But no hard feelings. It's the only way that it could have gone. But look at it my way. You are going to land on your feet somewhere. Fewer problems. Fewer worries. I got fucking medics merging with the fire department. Fucking medics! Oh well. At least it's a bump up."

Chief Brady got out of his chair and hit the desk one time with his knuckle lightly, as if to say goodbye, and walking to the door, turned around.

"Oh yeah," Chief Brady added before he left, "got the word from city hall. They want the homeless encampment that surrounds your station cleaned up, which means everything has got to go, and they want it right away. I'm making the phone calls today to get all the city agencies together. Everybody has an agenda. Going to make it into a no parking zone. We will need two ambulances to stand by. It should happen very quickly. I will get your cooperation in this?"

Rip nodded.

"Good. See, Ripley, I'm not a bad guy. If this goes well then you may just be on that island. Things just didn't go your way, that's all. But I need those ambulances."

Rip nodded again.

"Good. But if you get on that island, you better get that haircut."

Rip watched Chief Brady leave his office. Rip thought he had a little bounce in his waddle as he walked away.

On the day of the detail, Rip thought that Chief Brady came into the yard looking like a conquering Roman hero in a bad Hollywood movie. Rip was prepped on what to do by email.

Assign two ambulances for the detail, clean up the yard, and have supplies ready, especially rubber gloves. And assist Chief Brady in any way that he deemed necessary to complete the detail. It was supposed to go down exactly at noon.

All the departments were there with their supervisors. Park and Rec, sanitation, public works, and City Tow were all there to clean up the mess created by Camp Willie, and once it was cleaned out, red tag the curbs and install NO PARKING signs. Nobody would ever be able to park around the Evans Street Station again without being towed. Even social workers came from the health department to help with any transitionary issues that the move might cause the city's homeless. They were even offering beds in run-down hotels. Rip assigned two ambulances at the corner of Mendell and Newhall for any medical emergencies. Everything was set to start. But…where the hell were the police?

"For Christ's sake." Chief Brady looked at his watch, smoking his cigar in the yard of the Evans Street Station. As he paced, his limp was more pronounced. The detail was for noon, and it was a quarter past. And Chief Brady wasn't one to hide his emotions. As he paced, he puffed on his cigar, and the smoke swirled around his head then drifted upward. He knew that this detail would be seen by Hogwash as a clear indication of his ability to get things done. Chief Brady knew the political game, and the eyes of city hall would be on him. He didn't like the players, but he did like the announcement in the *Chronicle*, with his picture from an earlier time in the fire department, that he would be the new CD1 of the fire department. His pride was on the line.

"Where the hell are the cops?" Chief Brady growled at Lieutenant McGuire. "They got to be here so we can get this thing moving. That Captain Sherman is doing this on purpose. An Irish cop would have moved them out by now." Chief Brady stopped pacing for a moment. "He knows about my promotion, and now he's pissing on it."

"He will be here, sir," Lieutenant McGuire tried to reassure him. "It's his detail too."

"Yeah, but it's my ass," Chief Brady barked.

Rip came out to the yard, but after taking one look at Chief Brady and the army of city workers that had been assembled, he didn't want to stay around very long. He was going to be run off soon, too.

"Did you call Captain Sherman?" Chief Brady walked up to Rip.

"We called," Rip lied. He really hadn't.

"Then call again."

Rip walked away, and when he went inside the warehouse, Effin and Jesus approached him.

"Is it over?" Effin asked.

"Seems that way," Rip said.

Jesus had a forlorn look on his face knowing his congregation was about to be moved along.

It was also kind of sad for Rip. The homeless weren't the ones who were trying to demote him. They were a little messy, but they had to live somewhere. He was friends with some of the homeless at Ocean Beach when he was surfing, and Rip got to know a few who were ex-surfers whose lives just went another way. They shared joints sometimes in the parking lot. Maybe Laura's Zen had rubbed off on him a little more than he thought.

"I got some hot dogs left. I'm going to light up the grill," Effin said, thinking there was a few bucks to be made. Then he looked at Jesus making sure he wouldn't mind.

"Go ahead."

"Good."

Like dark clouds before a storm, the homeless knew the eviction was coming. It wasn't like they hadn't been thrown out of every place they had ever lived, including some out of their own homes. They had that hollow look on their faces of being the unwanted, of being an alien. The homeless formed little groups to talk about their next move, where they would go and park their vehicles for the night. Their voices were muffled except for a few "fucking assholes." During the day those yells fell on empty concerns. But even Chief Brady knew that this detail was going to take a few hours, and if it got too late, no good could come out of it. He knew there was more cover at night for bad things to happen, or at least hold it up. And he wanted everything to go down smoothly.

A police car came into the yard and pulled up to Chief Brady. The cop in the passenger seat rolled down his window and spoke to him. There was a shooting down the street, he said. After they wrapped that up, they would come down.

"There's always a shooting," Chief Brady snapped. "This is Hunters Point, for Christ's sake. I need you guys here."

Chief Brady's plea fell on deaf ears.

"Just let them write the report, and let's get moving."

"What can I say?" the cop said in the police car. "I'll express your concerns to Captain Sherman."

The driver of the police car tried to keep a straight face as they drove away.

Lieutenant McGuire walked up to Chief Brady.

"It will be fine, sir," he said, trying to reassure him.

"It's that Captain Sherman," Chief Brady sneered. "I know what he's doing. Just because he's Black and grew up in the neighborhood, he wants to make everything look official. It's a shooting, for Christ's sake. The guy is probably dead. There's always a shooting in Hunters Point."

Chief Brady knew that, since Captain Sherman grew up in Hunters Point, there would be no shortcuts. There would be people who remembered him in the crowd growing up, and seeing Captain Sherman, they saw him as one of their own, and he would pay special attention to the details, or at least go through the motions.

"Why did it have to be today?" Chief Brady said, showing his frustration.

Effin brought out some hot dogs and buns and bottled water that he had stashed away, and fired up the station house grill. For condiments, he had a bottle of mustard, one of relish, and little packets of ketchup from Burger King. Effin charged anyone who wanted a hot dog and a bottled water seventy-five cents. Everybody knew the routine about putting the money in the tip jar, which was an empty Folgers coffee can. It was house policy to always charge the amount of the meal to whoever was in, but Effin always took advantage. He even wore a stained apron that said, *Your opinion is not in the recipe*. Nobody cared that he made a few bucks off it. But if Effin didn't hear those three quarters hit the bottom of the coffee can, he would charge a dollar. "I don't make change," he would say.

When Chief Brady came over and took a hot dog and a bun off the grill, and didn't put any money in the can, Effin didn't say anything, but he was a little pissed. "Effin Penguin," he said underneath his breath. Rip also got a dog on a bun, but Effin told him it was on the house. That made Rip smile. Effin gave a hot dog on a bun to Jesus, who put some mustard on it, walked over to the gate where Eddy was looking through, and gave it to him. Since Eddy had come back, his van still hosted the Whoppers for Jesus meetings. But looking at Eddy's appearance, it was obvious from the ashen color of his face that the crack pipe had been coming around more often.

"I guess this is it then," Eddy said to Jesus, taking the hot dog.

"It may not be," Jesus told him.

"I'm sorry I let you down."

"You didn't let anyone down. There is always redemption."

"Redemption," Eddy muttered. "Redemption."

"When this is over, I will come find you. We will find another way."

Eddy nodded, and went back into this van. Jesus thought he was just getting his things together in order to leave. But Eddy, once in his van, sat on his mattress, and instead of getting ready to leave, picked up his crack pipe and lit the rock he had gotten from Flat Nose Joey that morning. He had wanted to do it that night after he had settled somewhere else, but with all the commotion his nerves were rattled, and the crack pipe was calling.

As the day went on, Captain Sherman was still at the crime scene, and nowhere to be seen around the Evans Street Station, which only rattled Chief Brady even more.

"Sherman is sure taking his sweet fucking time. He knows how much this promotion means to me."

"He will be here," Lieutenant McGuire said to Chief Brady, who was no longer smoking, but chewing on the end of his cigar.

"Fucking Sherman" was all Chief Brady could say.

At three o'clock, Captain Sherman finally rolled into the yard with two more police cars.

"Jesus, Sherman," Chief Brady said to him when he got out of the car, "where the hell have you been?"

"I'm sorry, Chief. I had real police work to do, instead of this hand holding that city hall has got me doing. Heard you got a promotion."

Captain Sherman had two years left, and belonged to the I Don't Give a Fuck Club, which meant he was on the fast track to retiring. He was an untouchable, and would only stay on the force if he got an inside job with a bump up. And he was a little jealous that Brady got such a big promotion. And he always did see Chief Brady as a prick. Loudmouth Irish prick. Racist too. But who wasn't? But he still wasn't going to go out of his way.

Chief Brady sensed the resentment, and he would have felt it too, if it was Captain Sherman who was getting the promotion, so he calmed down a bit.

"Do you think we can get these vehicles out of here before it gets too dark to red tag the curbs?" Brady asked. "I'll owe you."

"Well since you put it like that, my men are on it," Captain Sherman said, knowing that Brady really wanted this promotion, "but you may have some problems with the red tagging. I think your Picassos are leaving."

Chief Brady saw the city workers packing it up. The health workers were already gone.

"What? They can't be." Chief Brady walked to the gate, and seeing them leaving, went up to their supervisor who was holding a clipboard next to his city vehicle.

"What the hell is going on here?" he screamed, spitting tobacco.

"Well…" The supervisor looked like a college boy with his brown curly hair and glasses and his gray city shirt untucked. "It seems like the city is not paying overtime for this detail, so we're leaving. The crews are going back to headquarters to do what they have to do, and clock out. We'll come back tomorrow, but we can't do anything until all the vehicles are gone. But if approved, we will come back tomorrow, after you have finished up."

"But you got to stay. It will screw up all my plans."

"If you get them out tonight," the college boy said, "we will finish it up tomorrow."

"But you can't."

"That's all we can do."

"I don't need you tomorrow. I need you here now. Do you understand?"

"Well, tell it to the mayor. We'll leave you some temporary NO PARKING signs, and some of your guys can put them up. Staple them up to some sawhorses. But there is a safety issue here. Only when all the vehicles are towed, then we clean up the trash, and red tag the curbs, and put the permanent signs up. You know city policy. And since no one is paying us overtime to stay around, and all the vehicles are still not towed, that's all we can do. Our hands are tied," he said, raising his hand and giving the *Let's move out* twirling finger signal to his crew. With the sound of city vehicles starting up, they pulled out.

Lieutenant McGuire carefully approached Chief Brady.

"Let's just work with the police, and get the homeless out of here, and put up the temporary NO PARKING signs. That's all we can do for now. We will call the mayor's office and get the people to clean up tomorrow. City Tow will stay around all night if needed."

City Tow was under contract, and not under city time. Each tow was another invoice. They would stay around, but with the late starting time, a bottleneck of untowed vehicles started to form.

The cops in the police cars came out, and started going down the street hitting the sides of the vans and other vehicles with their batons, telling the homeless to move it out.

"I don't want anyone to leave until all these vehicles are off the street, and we have these signs up," Chief Brady yelled to anybody who was willing to listen. Nobody was really listening.

Some of the vehicles were able to start, and left right away, but others that couldn't start were tagged to be towed. There was the commotion of vans trying to start, with puffs of smoke, and the rattling of rusted tail pipes, and engines idling and sputtering, and starters trying to turn over, making high-pitch screeching noises. Chief Brady was not happy. It was going to be dark soon, and there were not enough tow trucks, since they waited so long, which meant that there would still be some broken-down vehicles left on the street when darkness fell.

After a few hours, Captain Sherman told Chief Brady that his boys were finished for the day.

"But I still got vehicles that haven't been towed," Chief Brady said.

"But you don't have the tow trucks. And it's getting late. Call down tomorrow, and we will finish it up," Captain Sherman said. It wasn't his promotion.

"Tomorrow? This is the mayor's detail."

"Hey, to show you I'm not a bad guy I'll give you one more hour. That's all I can do, but then we are out of here."

Chief Brady looked at his watch, and walked away. It was already past six o'clock, and the evening was starting to fall, and there was still so much that had to be done. Chief Brady counted ten vans and some broken-down cars that were still parked on the street, along with all the trash. And the temporary NO PARKING signs were not up yet.

"For Christ's sake, did you request more tow trucks?" Chief Brady asked Lieutenant McGuire bluntly. He was pretty hot.

"I made the phone call twice, sir. But once they get another call they leave."

"Well at least tell the police to get that one." Chief Brady pointed to Eddy's van. "It's right near the gate."

Chief Brady, unable to control his anger of the classic fuck-up that his detail had become, walked up to Chief Rip Ridley. He was looking to vent, and found the perfect target.

"For Christ's sake, what happened, Ripley? I heard your supply guy was able to get some of these clunkers out of here. Is he smarter than you are? Why are there so many left?"

"It had something to do with a guitar," Rip said.

"A guitar?"

"It was a Martin."

"A Martin, a fucking Martin! It could have been a brass band as far as I'm concerned. But the directive from city hall was clear. And all you did was watch from the sidelines. You didn't even make the calls, did you? You could have helped putting up the signs. But you did nothing. You just wait. I'm going to get these homeless out of here if it takes me all night. And then I'm going to find the deepest hole to stick your ass in where you are going to hate every day of fire department life. Do you hear me, Ripley?"

"I think I'm already starting to feel that way, Chief." Rip walked away.

"You don't know how bad I can make it for you. You can forget about the island," Chief Brady yelled.

Rip didn't care. He was tired. Everybody was tired. He was going to be moved out anyway. And Rip knew enough, when the time was right, to try to find an exit the way everybody else was doing, and not stay around to be a whipping boy. No good could possibly come out of staying around.

It was a simple tap on the side of Eddy's van with a baton by a cop to get his vehicle moving, but Eddy never got out of the van. He heard the tap, but the crack he was smoking had kicked in, and the paranoia came back to him. It was the time of day, when evening started to fall, that always made Eddy feel edgy anyway. Being homeless and smoking crack—and living in a van—does that to you.

But to poor Eddy, the tap sounded like the knock on his bedroom door his father would make with his fist, when he came home late, drunk, and he was going to take a beating. As Eddy grew up, he started taking the pills that he found in the medicine cabinet to hide the pain. When he needed more pills, he would break into pharmacies. Always washed down with Royal Gate. It was as if the crack pipe had always been waiting for him.

Sitting on the bed, Eddy looked up at the sword, Redemption, that was hanging on his wall. At first, he just wanted to hold it. He took it off the wall and cradled it in both arms, rocking on his mattress. *Redemption*, he thought. *Redemption*. He cried. There was another tap on the van that was louder, and a warning from the cop to move it out, now. It was getting dark, and the outside lights of the Evans Street Station came on, as they were on a timer. The fog also started drifting downward. Drops of moisture fell to the ground.

Jesus, seeing that Eddy was not coming out, walked to his van. He was going over to Eddy's van to help get him to move, but he stopped for a moment when Eddy came out of the back of his van holding Redemption. Everybody stopped as Eddy made his way into the middle of the street, swinging the sword with both hands over his head.

"Weapon!" a cop yelled. Guns were drawn, and now all eyes were on Eddy and his sword.

"Stay away," Eddy started screaming. "Stay away."

"Eddy, stop," Jesus yelled, as he started making his way toward Eddy to get him to put down the sword.

One of the cops, with his gun drawn, blocked his path and said, "Don't. We will handle this."

"I can make him put down the sword," Jesus pleaded. "Please Eddy, put down the sword," he yelled, but Eddy wasn't listening.

"It's too late for that now," the cop said. Then four of the cops with guns drawn slowly approached Eddy.

That was when Eddy started swinging Redemption, no longer over his head but from side to side. He wasn't swinging at anyone. He was swinging at everyone. He was swinging at everything that he had become in life. At all the crack pipes that had whispered to him in his weakest moments. At all the empty bottles of Royal Gate. He was swinging at his dead father who beat him until he had to leave. He was swinging for all the pain his mother had to go through, before they finally took her away. He was swinging at every misfortune that had ever paved his way to self-destruction. How he had let down Jesus, who had gotten him a job, and seemed to care. How, in life, he had become an alien, and he knew now he could never be put back into human form. He had finally snapped.

With Redemption in his hands, over his right shoulder in a military stance, he let out a yell and advanced toward the cops. The first shot took him down, but others followed. His body fell back in slow motion, and the sound of the steel of the sword falling out of his hands to the street could be heard in the night air.

There was an eerie silence after it happened. One of the cops kicked the sword away from Eddy's body. Two medics came over with a defibrillator, but Eddy was dead. As they worked on him, Jesus walked over to Eddy's body, and kneeled next to him. He touched Eddy's arm. Eddy's shirt was riddled with bullet holes. He had become a useless pulp. Little puddles of blood had formed on the street and ran down to the gutter. The chalk line of Eddy's life had been filled in. His body had become cold. On the ground, his face was turned away from the station, but looked as if he was at rest.

"Move on," a cop told Jesus. "This is a crime scene."

"I could have saved him," Jesus said.

"Well you can't save him anymore."

Effin walked up to Jesus, and led him away from Eddy to the yard.

"Fucking circle jerk," Effin yelled at the cop.

"What did you say?" the cop asked.

"You heard me."

"Come here, boy."

"No," said Effin, "I'm looking after my friend."

A voice came from the yard.

"We got a man down!"

At first, it was thought that it was a ricochet from one of the bullets, but then it was clear that the man down on the ground was Chief Brady, moaning, clutching his chest, wrestling with the pain that came in waves. He was having a heart attack. Eddy, as in life, was forgotten.

Rip was the first one to reach Chief Brady lying on the ground. In his pain, Chief Brady squeezed Rip's hand.

"Fucking medics," Chief Brady tried to say.

Then two medics came with the defibrillator. He still had a pulse, and was breathing.

"Get him to the hospital. Get him out of here, NOW," Officer Sherman screamed.

Quickly the medics worked on Chief Brady, packed him up, and put him in the ambulance, and the sound of the siren broke the silence of the night, as they drove code three to the General.

Everybody froze for a moment. Then more cops arrived.

CHAPTER 20

City hall did not wait to clean up Camp Willie. Within days, all the vans, and the cars, and the clunkers were gone, and the curbs were red tagged, and the NO PARKING signs were put up. All the trash on the streets and the sidewalks was cleaned up. The city even started planting trees along the streets. There were more patrols by the cops at night, and some of the crack houses were closed down and boarded up. Though it was only temporary, the few blocks around the Evans Street Station looked like they got a fresh coat of paint.

As for the merger, everything was put on hold. A new command staff would soon be announced, so officially Rip was still chief of the paramedic division. But it was just a matter of time before he would be replaced. As for Chief Brady, he lived after surgery. When he went home, he was told by his doctors to quit drinking, quit smoking, and start walking in the morning. But his retirement was a forgone conclusion.

As for Jesus, he didn't have the money for a burial plot for Eddy. But Jesus did have a friend in the district attorney's office who had a brother in the cremation business. Since the district attorney was always coming by for medical records and interviews with medics, and was always asking for favors on the cases he was assigned, he was only too happy to get his brother to give Jesus a deal on Eddy's cremation. Jesus called Preacher Dan, and they talked about cremation, and even though The Church of God's Guiding Light preferred burial, in the words of Preacher Dan, "We must always look after, in any way, the souls of the forgotten."

Jesus put up some pamphlets around the Evans Street Station that were titled *The Celebration of the Life of Edward Nathan Daniels*, the name on Eddy's driver's license, but everybody knew him as Crack Addict Eddy. Jesus even tracked down some of the homeless who once lived in Camp Willie before they were rousted, so they could take part. On the pamphlets was a picture of Eddy, when he was young, holding a fishing pole with his mother, that Jesus had found in Eddy's van when trying to locate any relatives in old cards or letters. There were none. On the pamphlet was a date, a time, and a meeting place: Ocean Beach on Sunday at noon, where Jesus would spread Eddy's ashes into the Pacific Ocean.

On the day of the celebration at Ocean Beach, in view of the Cliff House, people started showing up in the parking lot for the spreading of Eddy's ashes. Ocean Beach was known for its fierce undercurrent and unruly weather, but today there wasn't a cloud in the sky. It was a beautiful day with calm waters, like the postcards they sold in the gift shop at the Cliff House.

There was Jesus and Effin and Flat Nose Joey, Stuttering Sam and Sequoia and a few others of the homeless who had once lived at Camp Willie. A few of the medics from the Evans Street Station also came. Rip came, but stayed in his car near the PEOPLE SWIMMING AND WADING HAVE DROWNED HERE sign as he looked out at the ocean. Word finally came down in email from city hall that he was being relieved from duty as chief of the paramedic division for future assignment.

As Jesus walked on the beach toward the ocean waves, with the urn of Eddy's ashes in his hand, everybody followed except for Rip who got out of his car, and stayed near the walkway. That was when JoJo walked up to him. She was in blue jeans wearing a Ramones T-shirt. *God, she looks great*, Rip thought. *Really, really, great.*

"I thought you would be here," JoJo said.

"You came all the way here?" Rip asked.

"I just live in the Sutro Apartments on 48th."

"With a view?"

"Well yeah, my father owns them."

"Oh yeah. I know. How is he doing?"

"He is home driving everyone crazy. He asked about you."

"He asked about me?"

"I think he kind of liked the fact that you just didn't lay down and let city hall walk all over you."

"Well I got the email from city hall telling me I am going to be reassigned, so I guess it didn't do me a lot of good."

"I heard you called my station house asking for me."

"I didn't leave my name. I thought maybe you would call me," Rip said, looking a little shy. "But yeah, just to tell you that I was sorry about your father. So, you knew it was me?"

"Rip, there are no secrets in the fire department. And I wanted to call you. Just with everything happening, and the changes..."

"Changes?"

"I'm going to be reassigned tomorrow."

"So am I, after I meet the new chief and show them around. Lay of the land kind of thing. But they haven't told me anything. I don't expect much."

"Don't be too hard on whoever it is. You should see my father sometimes. It was nice you called." JoJo touched his arm.

Rip looked at her shirt.

"The Ramones, eh?"

"Yeah, my Beach Boys shirt was in the wash."

"Where should I call next time? If it's okay?" Rip asked, not wanting to be rejected again. JoJo laughed at his vulnerability.

"It took you long enough to ask. You were always running away from me."

"Well, your father..."

"My father is going to retire, and he doesn't run my life."

Duderonomy showed up on Rip's shoulder.

"Kiss her," Duderonomy whispered. "Kiss her."

Rip pushed him off his shoulder.

"And I never knew what you saw in me. I thought maybe it was just another fire department joke."

"It was no joke. Do you have a pen?"

"Yeah." Rip smiled.

JoJo told him her number, and he wrote it down on the back of his hand.

"Sometimes I don't have paper," Rip said.

"Well I have to go clean out my locker. Call me." JoJo leaned over and kissed Rip on the cheek, and then Rip watched her walk away in her blue jeans.

"Nice." Rip grinned to himself.

"Kind of like blue jean baby," Duderonomy said, appearing on his shoulder again. "I told you she liked you. I told you. Does she make you forget Laura yet?"

"She makes me forget," Rip said.

"So, are you going to see her?"

"Yes."

"Just don't lose her number," Duderonomy warned.

When JoJo left, Rip watched Jesus, with Eddy's urn in hand, walk to the water's edge. Those who came to show their respect to Eddy followed him. Jan and Reed drove their ambulance in the parking lot, but didn't get out. Jesus wore the same black suit, the same white shirt, the same black tie, and the same Tom McAn shoes that he wore when he went to Mississippi to become a preacher. The urn that held the ashes was made of porcelain. It was white with a blue cross painted on the front. It was a nice touch. After Jesus took off his shoes and gave his jacket to Effin to hold, he walked into the water up to his waist and held the urn high as the waves splashed against him. Jesus turned around to face those who had come. He raised his voice over the sound of the waves. Everyone watched him from the shoreline.

"Edward Nathan Daniels was my friend, though we may know him by other names. Eddy, who lived in a van, pushed a shopping cart, and collected empty bottles and cans to be sold for scrap. Eddy, who loved Whoppers and fries and Diet Cokes, and his guitar Mercy that his mother had given him. Eddy, who strummed cowboy songs on lonesome nights when he didn't have a friend. Eddy, whose demons sometimes whispered to him, and were never close behind. Eddy, who told me once he loved the ocean, and wanted to buy a boat so he could sail away. Eddy, who would listen to the sirens from the ambulances late at night. Eddy, who never knew how much he brought to other people's lives, and how much he brought to mine. Eddy, who once told me that he wanted to find God, and now is with him. In accordance to what I think your wishes might have been, Edward Nathan Daniels, I spread your ashes to the ocean. I'm going to miss you, my friend. May God have mercy, and wash away all of our sins."

As Jesus spread Eddy's ashes into the ocean, he quoted Ecclesiastes 3:1-2. "For everything there is a season..."

Turn! Turn! Turn! Rip thought to himself, being a big Byrds fan. It was a nice touch.

Jesus filled the urn with saltwater from the ocean, and washed away the remaining ashes. The tide came up on the sand and soaked his Tom McAn shoes.

"God bless Eddy, and all our souls," Jesus said, walking out of the ocean with Eddy's urn, to the wet sand, and picking up his shoes, shook off the water. Effin gave Jesus his jacket.

"Would anyone else like to pay their respects to Eddy?" Jesus asked.

Sequoia spoke up first.

"Every snowflake is unique and different. I guess it's the same with raindrops too because if every snowflake is different, and they are just frozen rain, then that would mean that every raindrop has to be different too. We are all unique and different, and so was Eddy. But Eddy was one of us. He was our raindrop."

"Why the fuck are you talking about raindrops?" Flat Nose Joey whispered to Sequoia. "Eddy ain't no raindrop."

Jesus came over and touched Flat Nose Joey on the shoulder, and he quieted down.

"Yes, he was," Sequoia yelled, and started crying. "He was a raindrop, and whenever it rains, I'm going to think of him. And Mumbles ran away. When the cops came, Mumbles left.

And now I can't park there to look for him. Eddy was a holy spirit, and Mumbles is too. But now Eddy is gone, and so is Mumbles."

One of the lesbian medics walked up to Sequoia, and told her she would look for Mumbles, and look after him if he showed up.

Finally, to everybody's surprise, Flat Nose Joey spoke up.

"Fuck it," he said. "I'm sorry. Sometimes I say the wrong things. But Eddy meant a lot to me too. People think because we're aliens that we don't have feelings, but he never made fun of my nose. Other people did, but not Eddy. He always called me Joey. I'm going to miss him. Eddy told me, when he was working at Burger King, that he could see it in the faces of others that they just saw him as another junkie. Well I'm a junkie too, and I know about people looking down at you, and feeling worse when they do. But Eddy was my friend and…" Flat Nose Joey stopped and put his arm around Sequoia to stop her from crying. "If Eddy was a raindrop, then I'm a fucking raindrop too."

"I'll ttthink of hhimm," Stuttering Sam said. "We rrre all rainnddrops."

When no one else spoke, someone gave out yellow and white flowers that they had bought at Safeway, and everyone took some and then tossed the flowers into the ocean. Most came back to the shore, but some followed the retreating waves out into the ocean. Then Jesus gave out pamphlets with the words for "Will the Circle be Unbroken?" Jesus started it off, and then other voices joined in. Nobody really knew the words, even though they were written down, but everybody knew the chorus. It wasn't the Carter Family, but it sounded nice. When the song was finished, Jesus thanked everybody for coming, and that was the end of Eddy's celebration.

When everybody started to leave, Effin walked up to Jesus when he was putting on his wet shoes.

"I guess this makes you a preacher now," Effin said.

"I don't know what it makes me."

"Well I thought it was a damn good speech. Damn fucking good."

"You could have said it in a better way."

"I guess I could, but I ain't. You want to go for a Whopper? I'll buy. There's a Burger King around the corner, near Safeway."

"Sure."

"You are going to do it, aren't you?"

"Do what?"

Effin had figured it out from the papers left out on Jesus' desk that he was leaving. And for someone who always filed everything away, it wasn't hard to find. Effin thought it was Jesus' way of telling Effin that he was going to leave.

"I saw the separation papers on your desk. You are going to cash out your pension, aren't you? You're going to become a full-time preacher."

"Maybe. Are you mad?"

"Fucking yeah I'm mad," but this time Effin didn't sound angry, only sad. "You are going to need a van too, you know."

"Why a van?"

"You are going to have to follow them. It ain't like the homeless have steady places to live. That's why they're homeless. It could be Whoppers for Jesus on Wheels. We can paint it on the side of the van."

"I'm not going to call it Whoppers for Jesus. It will be The Church of God's Guiding Light."

"Well, then maybe we can paint a lighthouse with a beacon, and maybe waves splashing against the rocks in the ocean on the side of the van."

"How do you come up with this stuff?" Jesus was impressed.

"I got my moments. But I know where you can get one of those old UPS vans. I can get it for you. Runs pretty good, too."

"And how are you going to do this? How are we going to pay for it?"

"Pay for it? This is Effin you're talking to. I don't pay for anything. It's just that I got a loser cousin who works at the shops for the city. Fucker owes me money. Got a gambling issue."

"An issue?"

"A gambling problem. And when he wins you don't see him. I may be angry, but at least I pay my dues. And he borrows money, and he never pays anyone back. You just have to take it. Every once in a while, he comes around with a black eye or something. But on the side, he picks up secondhand UPS vehicles, and fixes them up, and then sells them. Well, he's got one that he has been working on, and since he owes me money, I told him that we would call it even on the money he owes me, but the van is mine. That I was taking it. It wasn't easy at first, but then I know all his secrets, and I also know he was never going to pay me back anyway. It took some convincing, but he knows that Effin doesn't care, and I do have a tendency to mouth off about what he's been doing during the holidays when everybody is sitting around the table. Nobody wants to hear about your thieving relatives at Thanksgiving dinner. He even stole some tires from the shops for it. New ones with great treads. And he even put on a new coat of paint. They got buckets of paint in the shops, and my cousin has some quick hands. And he tuned up the engine with some better parts from some city vehicles he was supposed to be fixing. You know parts are all alike in those Fords. So, a few city vehicles break down because they got old UPS parts. He's been doing it for years."

"And you are going to do this for me?" Jesus asked.

"I already did. Well, almost. He still has to sign away the title. But he knows I can forge his signature. This is for looking after me, and all the other things. I already took the keys, and parked it in my mom's garage. If I hadn't, he would have already sold it."

"But I can't accept anything stolen. I'm a man of the cloth now."

"Why would you care? You didn't take it. And you know, as well as me, that it's the way the city is run. I ain't accepting no, or I'll call that Preacher Dan."

"You're not calling anybody," Jesus said, and finally he looked at Effin and said he would take it.

"Now you're talking. You know your shoes are all wet and your pants are too."

"I know."

"But I do think Rip is right about cashing out your pension. And I know something about mistakes."

"Well, you're not the only one who thinks that way."

Together they crossed the Great Highway toward the local Burger King.

"Where did you get the urn?" Effin asked.

"At Goodwill."

"Was the cross painted on it?"

"Sure was."

"Then it must have been made for Eddy."

Jesus was surprised that Effin never asked about Eddy's sword, but he figured he was thinking about it.

"The cops have the sword," Jesus finally said.

"I never asked about it. I have respect…" But then Effin thought for a moment. "Did they say when they are going to give it back?"

"No, but they will. I made some phone calls. I will let you know."

"That's kind of nice," Effin said. "I once heard that a preacher has to know how to get into people's business."

"Is that so?"

"Yeah, I think you said it."

"Maybe I did," Jesus said. "Maybe I did."

CHAPTER 21

The night before Rip was to go to work and meet his replacement, he couldn't sleep. He lay on his bed, hands folded underneath his head, looking up at the ceiling.

Like his office, Rip's bedroom was a little ying, and a little yang, and a lot of his past.

On the wall, near the entrance of the bathroom, Rip had a Bill Graham's Winterland concert poster called *The Sound*, with a voluptuous naked woman featured on it, surrounded by the names of the rock groups playing with the dates. Also hanging on the wall was an early promotional picture of Dennis Wilson in a candy-striped shirt. On the wall at the head of his bed was a poster of the Silver Surfer.

And though Rip loved comic books with superheroes like Batman, Superman, Wolverine, the Fantastic Four—the list went on and on—even more than Aquaman, Rip loved the Silver Surfer. Like the Silver Surfer, Rip saw himself as noble, but tormented. Treasuring freedom above all else. In his mind, sacrificing his individual liberty for the greater good. And he certainly felt, mostly when he was high, that he could rearrange molecules. Though the molecules at the Evans Street Station were rearranging themselves.

Rip also had a killer comic book collection on the floor of his closet. Some early editions of all his superheroes. But unfortunately, Rip was a late-night stoner, and his comic book collection was torn and tattered, with grease stains from eating fried food, burritos, pizza, Cheetos, and all the other snacks that went along with the late-night munchies.

Around the room were knickknacks of mementos of his past: a signed baseball by Willie Mays, miniature figures of soldiers that he had painted as a kid, an old heat lamp that he had once used for his tan, and during puberty to clear up his acne. There was also a little wooden statue of Buddha that Laura had given him, and there was a surfboard in the sand carved from lava from Hawaii. Hanging on the wall was driftwood Rip had picked up on the beach. There was a bookshelf with books from college, paramedic school and on surfing. There were also books with lots of topics for dummies. Then there were all the books that Laura gave him that he never read, but he kept them for the little handwritten messages she wrote inside the title page, when she still loved him.

And Rip had a killer LP collection when LPs really mattered. He had LPs of the Beach Boys, The Byrds, the Grateful Dead, Jefferson Airplane, Quicksilver, *Sgt. Pepper's Lonely Hearts Club Band*, *Blonde on Blonde*, Blondie, *Surfer Rosa*, The Tubes, The Ramones, Django Reinhardt, Dead Kennedys, Iggy Pop, Nirvana, Dick Dale and the Del-Tones, and even the Screaming Trees. His most prized possession was the Peter, Paul, and Mary's single of "Puff the Magic Dragon."

In Rip's bedroom was his dad's favorite stereo. It was a His Majesty's Voice stereo player from the sixties, with a decal of the famous dog Nipper listening intently to a wind-up Edison Bell cylinder phonograph. The stereo was the mark of quality. Rip took it when he had finally moved out of his father's house, and had his own place. It was after one of his dad's emotional outbreaks about Rip's mother leaving him for another woman.

When Rip's phone rang that night, he had just put on "In My Room" by the Beach Boys from the *Surfer Girl* album. He dug the harmonies at night. Wearing his comic superheroes cotton pajamas that he had bought at a Comic-Con convention in 1990 in San Diego, Rip was just about to go to bed. He really liked wearing them at night. Rip thought it was JoJo calling, so he picked up the receiver quickly. But it was his dad, who never called at night unless there was some problem.

"Dad, it's late and I got to go to bed. Why are you calling?" Rip asked.

"What is that? What is that I hear?" Rip's dad asked defiantly.

"What is what, Dad?"

"That music! The sound! The quality! That's my 'His Majesty's Voice' stereo with the decal of Nipper, isn't it? I always loved that dog."

"I don't know what you are talking about, Dad. It's late," Rip lied.

"I always thought you were the one who took it. It only made sense since your mother never played it. Then I thought maybe her girlfriend, or whatever you want to call her, liked it because of the quality."

"Dad, leave Mom alone. She's happy now. And if you really want to know, I did take it, and you are not getting it back. I have my own LP collection."

"Yes, I remember. Your Beach Boys surfer collection. Your Dick Wilson wannabe drummer fantasy magical mystery whatever tour, isn't it?"

"It's Dennis Wilson, and maybe it is my fantasy. Is this why you called me?"

"I used to listen to Maurice Chevalier and Django Reinhart records on that stereo. Sometimes Dean Martin. He was good, but Jerry Lewis carried him, when they were together. Come to think of it, I'm missing my Django Reinhart record. You didn't take that one too?"

"Maybe I did, Dad, but it's late. Let's get to it."

"I just wanted you to know."

"Know what, Dad?" Rip asked.

Duderonomy showed up on Rip's shoulder in his nightgown and nightcap, having the look as if to say, *Can you finish this conversation tomorrow? I would like a little toke before I go to bed.*

"Well I just wanted to tell you, in case you hear it from someone else, that I'm back with the Gray Beavers."

"So, you missed the sex?" Rip asked.

Duderonomy shook his head, as if to say, *What else could it be?*

"Maybe. That and they needed my car. It's hard getting around the city to protest when you only have the senior pass for the Muni. You know how unpredictable the bus system is. And sex and revolution always went well together."

"Well, I'm not going to be a big shot anymore. I'm being demoted tomorrow."

"Really?"

"Yes, Dad."

"Those bastards! So, me joining the Gray Beavers again is not going to be a problem?"

"Protest away. Penis and all."

"Aw, the little fellow is happy again. Do you think I can get my stereo back?"

"Goodnight, Dad."

This time it was Rip's turn to hang up the phone. But then the whispers came to him from Reed's pot in the baggie that was on his white Scandinavian-style dresser. The dresser had come with matching nightstands. Growing up, they were the most cheerful pieces of furniture in the house, as everything else was in dark gothic style, so Rip kept it.

"Psst," Dreamland spoke to him, "I'm really good shit. You need to try me. Let me help you sleep tonight. I'm one of Reed's best harvests. He's been working on the ph of the soil. Even piped in some classical music while we were growing. My personal favorite was Mozart. Quite mad, you know. But call me Dreamland. I know you want to get to sleep tonight with no tossing or turning. I'm not harsh either."

Rip got out of bed, took his pipe out of the drawer of his nightstand, and opened the baggie and smelled the sweetness of the pot, then packed his pipe and lit it.

"Okay," Rip said. "But I want a nice peaceful rest."

"Yeah, yeah, I understand," Dreamland whispered softly to him.

"Finally," Duderonomy said.

After his last toke, and the light was out, sleep came over Rip like the fog in a Dashiell Hammett novel.

Rip dreamed that he was surfing the waves underneath the Golden Gate Bridge near Fort Point. It was peaceful. It was easy. Waves splashed against the rocks of the foundation of the fort. The seagulls sang, and Alcatraz was in the background. Rip was happier than he could ever hope to be. He laughed. He grinned. He giggled. Rip was wearing a wetsuit, and Duderonomy in his swim trunks and a tank top sat on his shoulder.

"This is great stuff," Duderonomy commented.

"I think tomorrow is going to work out fine," Rip reassured himself over the sounds of the ocean waves.

But beneath the waves, a silver hand came up and pulled Rip off his board, and beneath the waves by his ankle. Down, down, down Rip went as he gasped for air. Anxiety overcame him. The fish that swam past him had large eyes, and panicked, and swam away in fear. The peaceful, easy feeling was gone. Duderonomy hung on to Rip's ear.

Reaching the bottom of the ocean, Rip could see that it was the Silver Surfer who had dragged him down. For a brief moment Rip looked around. Four flounders were at a table playing pinnacle. Two sharks were sitting at another table covered with a checkered cloth, each holding a fork and knife, and a napkin tied underneath their jaws. They both looked hungry.

As fast as Rip went down, the Silver Surfer flipped Rip like a coin to the back of his silver surfboard, and with Duderonomy still holding on to Rip's ear, changed course, and upward they propelled, as Rip balanced on the back of the Silver Surfer's surfboard. They rocketed out of the ocean and circled the Golden Gate Bridge. Then they ascended farther and farther toward the clouds.

"Shit," Duderonomy complained, "you and your dreams!"

But Rip wasn't listening. The anxiety had left him. He was going through the clouds without a care.

"Just don't look down," the Silver Surfer said to Rip.

"What did he say?" Rip asked Duderonomy, who was still hanging on to Rip's ear.

"Don't look down."

"What?"

"Don't look down, Bwana," Duderonomy yelled.

"But why?" Rip asked.

Inadvertently Rip looked down.

"Never look…" the Silver Surfer tried to say, but it was too late. It crippled him, and they started a swift downward descent. As the descent picked up speed, the silver started peeling off the Silver Surfer's body and surfboard until he disintegrated. Rip, with Duderonomy hanging on, headed down to a little speck in the ocean. They both closed their eyes, and screamed.

Puff… Wham… Bam… They landed without a scratch on…Alcatraz Island. Rip found himself wearing his comic superheroes cotton pajamas, and Duderonomy in his nightgown and cap.

"You had to look down, didn't you?" Duderonomy asked, as he was now sitting on Rip's shoulder.

"I couldn't help it."

"Yeah, yeah."

"But why Alcatraz?" Rip asked, looking around.

"Why the Silver Surfer? I never saw him to be too exciting. Kind of one dimensional."

"Well, he never let me down before in my dreams."

"Jung said that dreams reveal more than they conceal."

"How do you know this?" Rip asked.

"Remember Laura? Well she had a subscription of *Psychology Today*. I used to read it sometimes. Some heavy stuff."

"But why did we land on Alcatraz?" Rip asked, looking around.

"Everybody creates their own prison, Bwana. Maybe the descent was really the fall, which means you are probably overlooking something."

"All that from a magazine?"

"Laura used to read it naked."

"But what am I overlooking?" Rip asked Duderonomy.

"The big picture, maybe?"

"What's the big picture?"

"The obvious, Bwana. Jung said that dreams have no inhibitions."

"Are you sure he said that?"

"Well, somebody said it."

With Duderonomy on his shoulder, Rip started walking the grounds of Alcatraz. It was barren and rocky. The pigeons were big, really big. Larger than people, and so were the seagulls. Mostly they kept to themselves, and minded their own business.

"I feel like food, Bwana," Duderonomy said.

"Me too," Rip replied. They kept walking.

When Rip got to the main cellblock, he saw his dad sitting in a chair in one of the cells. Though none of the cells were locked, he didn't try to get out.

"Dad, what are you doing here?" Rip asked.

"Ah, they got me on that Gray Beavers rap. They gave me Machine Gun Kelly's cell. I asked for Al Capone's, but some guy named Hogwash got it. But they did say that Kelly was a model prisoner."

"Dad, why don't you just leave?"

"You know I'm really not sure. Do you know a way out?"

"The cell isn't locked."

"I just can't take the chance now. I have to pick the right moment. Can I get my stereo back?"

"No, Dad."

"Why are you wearing those pajamas with all those comics on it? You look like a clown."

"Dad, it's my dream."

"Well, if I were you, I would dress better."

"Dress better? You always dressed like a French peasant."

"A French worker, not a peasant."

In the cell next to his dad's was Rip's mother in a nun's habit, knitting a long scarf of many colors from a big spindle. It seemed to go on forever, filling up the floor of the drab cell. Although in adjoining cells, Rip's mom and dad did not acknowledge each other.

"Ask him. Ask him," Duderonomy said to Rip. "Remember, no inhibitions."

"Why did you drive Mom away?" Rip asked his dad. "Why do you drive everyone away?"

"Do you think it's easy being me? I'm complicated," his dad said.

"Complicated? You only cared about yourself."

"What about you? You drove that Laura away. You live in some fantasy world with all the dope you smoke."

"Well I have a new girlfriend now. This time, it will be different."

"We all feel that way in the beginning."

"So, you are saying that I will drive her away too?" Rip asked.

"We all do. It's part of being a Ridley. We can't help it."

"I can change," Rip said, though not convincingly.

Rip's dad turned away from him and continued sitting in his chair, thinking. Just like the statue in France.

Rip walked over to his mother's cell. "Mom, it's me," Rip called out to her. His mother looked up, then went back to knitting.

"Do you remember me? I'm your son."

His mother did not acknowledge him.

"Mom?"

"Maybe she's in her own world now," Duderonomy said.

"I'll help you both get out," Rip said to his parents.

They both ignored him.

"Let's look around. Remember it's your dream," Duderonomy said, as they made their way down the cellblock.

In another cell were Laura and Tarzan wearing their Aborigine garb. Rip still couldn't get over her mangled hair. The cell was filled with brush and dirt, and Tarzan was making a mud hut. There was a stuffed dingo in the cell.

"You tried to kill Sydney, you know," Laura said to Rip.

"I didn't know they were going to give him nuts."

"You always make excuses for everything. It's never your fault, it just happens, right?" Laura asked.

"Why are you making a mud hut when you're in a cell?" Rip asked.

Tarzan raised his head, wondering.

"Don't listen to him. He tried to kill you," Laura told Tarzan. He went back to work.

"It was an accident. I can't believe you left me for him," Rip pleaded his case. "And your hair was always so beautiful."

"Well in case you never figured it out, I did sleep with my yoga instructor. And there were others, too."

Duderonomy shook his head as if to say, *I knew it.*

"You broke my heart," Rip said.

"You only think about yourself."

"I thought about you."

"Your idea of love is that we move to Marin and have children. Some adventure. You would work, and I would stay home all day. The perfect world for you. The others never questioned my hair, or my convictions, and neither does Sydney. They let me be who I wanted to be. You never knew how important that is to me. You're too much like your dad."

"Low blow," Duderonomy said.

"I am not," Rip proclaimed, then asked Duderonomy, "Is that true?"

"Maybe a little bit."

"Thanks," Rip said, sarcastically. "Why is the dingo stuffed?" he asked Laura.

"You and your dingoes. It makes Sydney feel more at home."

"We could have had something together, you and me."

"You only cared about yourself, and the sex."

"I cared about you, and the sex too."

"Did you really know me?" Laura asked.

"Is that a trick question? I thought I did. But not anymore. I could have never moved to the outback. I like modern conveniences. Electricity and running water. Toilets are important too," Rip said.

"So, you picked toilets over me."

"I picked modern conveniences."

"Breakups are never easy," Duderonomy told Rip.

"Did you ever read the books I gave you?" Laura asked.

"I tried."

"That's what I mean. It was always about you."

"That's not true." Rip's voice echoed down the empty cellblocks.

Laura turned her back on Rip.

"It's best we move on," Duderonomy said, so they did.

In another cell was Chief Tortellini. He had put on a little weight, grew a beard, and wore overalls. He was sitting in a chair, playing solitaire on a wooden barrel, drinking a beer.

"Why did you leave?" Rip asked him.

Chief Tortellini looked up from his card game and said, "Haven't you figured it out yet?"

"No, tell me."

"They don't want you to fix problems. Their existence depends on a certain amount of inadequacy. You are only there to be a mouthpiece, and take the hit for them when it is needed. He plants them, you know."

"Who? Plants what?" Rip asked.

"The newspaper articles. Hogwash does that to keep you in line. Did you resurrect my Homeless One Program?"

"Yes, I tried."

"And what happened?"

"They never really gave it a chance. Hogwash made it seem like I was attacking his policies."

"Well, were you? Why did you release it?"

"I didn't get the best advice," Rip said, looking at Duderonomy, who shrugged. "They are demoting me."

"Hogwash is good about that. You had to see it coming."

"What should I do?" Rip was desperate.

"Don't worry, they will figure it out for you. They always do."

"Why did you leave so quickly?"

"Because the badge wasn't enough. Did you take it out of my desk?"

"Yes," Rip said.

"Did you wear it?"

"Yes."

"Well, then you were happy. But for me it wasn't enough. I thought I could make a difference. Then it was becoming too much about me. It happened so quickly. I guess I learned some hard truths about myself."

Chief Tortellini went back to playing solitaire.

In another cell were Hogwash and the Human Resources Lady sitting around a table, looking over Rip's working file. Everything in the cell was in black and white like a 1940s movie, except for Human Resources Lady's pantsuit. It was garnet. There was a newspaper spread out on the floor with bold headlines, *Paramedic Chief Replaced.*

"Why does it have to be this way?" Rip tried talking to them. "Why do you get to control everything. What about me?"

"What about you?" Hogwash finally said, looking up at Rip. Human Resources Lady never raised her head.

"Can't you do the right thing this one time, and not be political?"

"Things would have gone differently if you would have cleared out the homeless camp, and given your friend Cherry Pie his three days."

"You know that's not true."

"Probably not. But you'll find out soon enough. Chief Brady was right. Either be a free thinker, or paramedic chief. You can't be both."

"Why can't I be both?" Rip really didn't understand.

"Because it doesn't work that way. There has to be a sense of order."

"But who makes these rules? Who makes this order?"

Hogwash looked at Human Resources Lady, and they both had a look of disgust on their faces, as if to say, *He just doesn't get it.*

"Sometimes it's a matter of doing the right thing," Rip said.

"Did you really try to do the right thing, or was it just about you being chief?" Hogwash asked.

"I tried. I had hope. Maybe if I had more resources."

"Really? Resources? Are you really going to go down that road?"

"Maybe it was a little about me. I'll admit that. But I really thought that I could do better."

"You and everyone else when they first get the job."

"Okay, I did like the uniform. I did like having my own bathroom, and the bump up in pay. And I did like going to Ashbury Market in my Class A uniform. But I really thought that I could make a difference. I really thought I could make it easier for everybody. And I know I am only one person but I really thought…"

"Bwana," Duderonomy whispered in Rip's ear, "they are not listening to you."

It was true. Hogwash and Human Resources Lady had gone back to looking at his file.

In the cell next to Hogwash, ticking clocks hung everywhere. *Tick, tick, tick, tick…* And it was getting louder and louder. Duderonomy put his hands over his ears. Then alarms went off, and it wouldn't stop! It had to be a prison break. But then Rip's dream started to fade away. Rip, with Duderonomy again holding on to his ear, drifted upward, away, as Alcatraz Island got smaller and smaller.

"Wait," Rip said, as everything started to fade, "I'm not done asking questions. I need to get some answers. I haven't figured it out yet. How did everything go so badly? This is supposed to be my dream. I need more time."

The dream was gone.

On the nightstand the alarm kept ringing, until Rip turned it off. Duderonomy woke up too. It was six thirty and Rip got ready to go to work. In the bathroom, Rip, with Duderonomy on his shoulder, brushed their teeth in unison, looking in the mirror. They both looked a little bleary-eyed. For Rip it would be time to turn in his chief's uniform. He did, though, plan to keep Chief Tortellini's badge.

"Reed really outdid himself with Dreamland," Rip said.

"I know," Duderonomy complained. "The Silver Surfer, really? Sometimes your dreams exhaust me."

In unison they gargled with mouthwash, and then spit it out.

CHAPTER 22

On the day Jesus was set to sign his retirement papers, Effin waited outside his apartment in a city van to drive him to the retirement board. Knowing that it was the day of Rip's demotion, nobody would say anything, or even wonder where they were.

Once Jesus had signed his separation papers, the city wrote the check for all the money that Jesus had contributed to his retirement, though they did take out twenty percent for taxes. Effin thought, but didn't say it, that Preacher Dan would probably get his ten percent, too.

But for Jesus and Effin, it was more money than they had ever seen before. And by taking it out, it meant that Jesus would never get a pension, and the ties were cut between him and the city. Not a lot of people do it, and the retirement board was only too happy to write the check. But Jesus did do it, and now he was without a job and off the city's books.

"That's a lot of Whoppers," Effin said, looking at the check, "and fries too."

After Jesus got the check, he put it in his credit union checking account, and then both of them sat on a bench on Market Street.

"I guess this is it," Effin muttered, lighting a cigarette.

"I'll be around," Jesus said.

"People don't come back. They just go."

"When I submitted my paperwork, there was an exit interview with Human Resources downtown. I recommended you for supervisor."

"They will never do it."

"I don't know. I said you were the only one who could do the job. And with the merger being official, the fire department is a lot angrier than you are."

"That's the first time I ever heard that."

"Well they are. The fire department didn't want the merger. They had a good thing. Now city hall is telling them they have to accept medics into their station houses, and the chief who was going to look after them is now gone."

"So, I really have a chance?" Effin asked.

"Maybe not."

Effin smiled.

"Well, I got something for you," Effin said.

"What?"

"The title for the van. My cousin signed it over. He cried at first, but he always cries anyway about something. But he wasn't going to get anything over on me. Now all you got to do is sign your part, and go to the DMV to make it official. Then I will drive you over to my mom's garage, and you can pick up the van. But you ain't worried?"

"I worried all my life over something or another, but I have surrendered to His calling."

"No health insurance. No pension."

"I know."

"Well if you need something, I can get it for you. Supplies, whatever. I got some at my mother's house, too."

"I know you do."

"Well let's go to the DMV," Effin said. "I guess I have to drive since you are no longer a city employee."

They both walked to the city van, got in, and headed for the DMV office.

Just about the time Jesus was accepting the check from the retirement board for more money than he had ever seen before, the new EMS chief (as the paramedic division did not exist) was arriving at the Evans Street Station. When Rip came in that morning and went to his office, no one looked him in the face. He was dead man walking. Jan was going to go up and say something, but when asking Reed, he didn't think it was a good idea, so she stayed away. Even Cherry Pie knew that he may have had some issues with Rip in the past when he was chief, but there would never be a better one. And he felt bad that he didn't invite Rip to Burning Man. Then everybody started circling, whispering that maybe they should do something for Rip at the end of the day, or at least take him out for a beer. But as they were talking, and circling, and whispering, the new EMS chief drove into the yard, and got out of the EMS buggy, and walked past them in the warehouse and then up the metal stairs. Nobody had told them that in the fire department, a chief was supposed to be saluted, so they just stopped talking and looked dumbfounded and stared.

It was Captain Barbara Brady, JoJo, in her new chief's uniform. JoJo was the new EMS chief.

"This is weird," Jan said. "Kind of like the *Twilight Zone.*"

The footsteps of Chief JoJo Brady to Rip's office were softer than what they had been in the past from other members of the fire department. Rip had been packing when JoJo knocked on the frame of the open door.

Rip looked up and saw her. He saw the chief's gold bars on her uniform, which meant she was permanent. It would take time to register. Had she let him down, too?

"I never knew you were a medic," Rip said, not knowing what else to say. One of the requirements to be an EMS chief was that you had to have a medic's license.

Chief JoJo Brady took off her cap, brushed back her hair, and closed the door behind her.

"My father was not too happy when I became a medic. But I did it anyway. What are you doing?"

"Waiting to be reassigned. I thought I'd clean out my office for the next person. I guess you are the next person."

"Did anybody tell you to clean out your office?"

"Well I thought..." Rip didn't know what to say. He looked at JoJo, and his heart was thumping, but now she was going to replace him.

"I'm not moving into here." JoJo looked around his office. "I'm going to headquarters. But I will need an operations chief. They are adding it on to the budget with the merger. Do you have anybody in mind?"

Rip was now sitting on the edge of his desk. "Well there are some good medics who would make excellent operational chiefs."

JoJo had such beautiful light green eyes, and Rip tried to avoid looking into them.

"I don't want any other medics to be my operations chief. I want you. Will you stay?"

"What about Hogwash, and your father?"

"It's my call. I made that clear taking the job. I would have called you, but I know my father monitors my phone calls, and I'm sure he would have done something to piss me off."

"You mean you knew?" Rip asked.

"Of course. I know my father. I didn't think it was a big deal. He plays those games." JoJo moved ever so closely to Rip. "A few years ago, I used to see you and that girl you used to go out with at the Cliff House, the one you and your friends tried to kill her boyfriend…Morningstar or whatever her name was."

"We didn't try to kill him. It was just an accident," Rip tried to explain, but even to him it sounded unbelievable. And once an incident becomes written in stone in the fire department, it never goes away.

"You were both drinking martinis and eating oysters. You must have liked her a lot because you never looked at me. Since I lived close by, I used to go there with my friends. I thought we could meet there tonight to discuss your new job description. We have a lot of work to do."

"So, you want me to be your ops chief?" A Dennis Wilson smile came across his face.

"I didn't have anybody else in mind. About seven?"

"So, I'm still chief?"

"Yes, you are still chief, Rip Ridley. If you accept it. I already submitted your name to city hall. It would take a lot of paperwork to change it. And I know you don't carry a lot of paper on you."

"What about us?"

"Us? I like that." JoJo smiled. "I don't live that far from the Cliff House."

"So, you are asking me to be your operations chief and meet you at the Cliff House tonight?" Rip just had to touch her hand, and it was warm, and it took a lot of restraint from both of them not to embrace in a passionate kiss.

"For Christ's sake, Ripley," JoJo said, imitating her father, "take the job."

"Okay," Rip answered, wanting so much just to kiss her. "I'll be your operations chief, and I would love to meet you at the Cliff House tonight to talk about..."

"Martinis and oysters."

"Yes, martinis and oysters."

"Then I will see you tonight at seven?"

"Yes, of course. At seven."

"And you can start wearing that badge you always like to wear at work."

"The gold one? You mean Chief Tortellini's?"

"You are permanent."

"Wow," Rip said. "How did this even happen?"

"Why would you even ask? I just explained to Hogwash and his buddies in city hall that it would be better for the sake of the merger that the EMS ops chief be one of their own. And then Hogwash called my father when he had gotten out of the hospital, and they had words."

"Words?"

"We will talk about it tonight. But my father stuck up for you. He told them that it could be worse, so I guess that was some kind of compliment. But he did say, and I quote, 'For Christ's sake, make sure he gets a haircut.' I kind of like it the way it is."

"So, he stood up for me?"

"Don't give him that much credit. He may not have done it if he was still going to be CD1."

"Does he know about us?"

"He suspects, but let me handle it."

"Okay," Rip said. "Okay."

They touched hands for a moment longer, then JoJo put on her cap and walked out of Rip's office. Her footsteps in the hallway hardly made a sound.

"You should have kissed her," Duderonomy said, appearing on Rip's shoulder. "She wanted it too. See, I told you it would all work out. Ride the wave, I said. Remember? Ride the wave."

"Actually, I thought you were taking the opposite view."

"Well sometimes you have to play the odds, and your dream didn't help. You got a lot of shit up there."

"Well, you are part of it," Rip said.

"Are you going to kiss her? Please do. I could use the dopamine spike. Talk about good vibrations."

"More *Psychology Today*?" Rip asked.

"Hey, Laura had a two-year subscription. What can I say? But just remember..."

"Remember what?"

"Fly low, Bwana. Fly low tonight."

CHAPTER 23

For Rip's meeting with JoJo at the Cliff House, he wore California casual attire. Rip read about it in a fashion magazine in his dentist's office after he had munched too hard on a pistachio nut, and broke an old filling. Rip wore a smart light blue collared shirt, tan trousers, and a beige suit jacket. Exactly like the model on the page of the magazine that Rip had torn out for future reference. For Rip this was certainly a future reference moment.

Rip went to the Cliff House early. He was humming "Barbara Ann" by the Beach Boys. His hopes were high. Looking out at Ocean Beach, he saw the orange sun setting on the blue horizon, and the smell of sea water was in the air. Old men were fishing from the deck behind the Cliff House, near the camera obscura. Taking it all in, Rip took a few puffs from the joint he had brought with him.

"Okay, Bwana, be cool," Duderonomy said, showing up on Rip's shoulder. "Everybody loves the cool Bwana where nothing fazes him. But let her set the pace. That's important. And don't be over-confident, or too desperate."

"Thank you," Rip said sarcastically.

"And don't lose your head over her green eyes. And don't look away when you talk to her. Did you know that only two percent of the world's population has green eyes? I find that quite appealing. And don't drink too much on the first date."

"It's not a date," Rip shot back, kidding even himself. "It's a meeting between friends."

"Yeah, some friends," Duderonomy said. "Call it what you want, but it's a date."

Before going into the Cliff House, Rip watched the seals catching the last bit of rays on a group of small rock formations off the south shore of Ocean Beach called Seal Rock. Laura always said in her Zen-like way, when they walked along the beach together, that if they were in Japan, the locals would have tied long ropes joining all of the rocks together, and made them a family. She once saw it in a movie. But today Laura was gone, and Rip liked them just the way they were.

Going into the Cliff House, Rip went straight for the bar. It wasn't crowded, and the bartender was an old surfer friend that Rip knew named Hunter.

"Rip Ridley," Hunter said, "looking good. You got anything planned for tonight?"

"Can you save the seat next to me?" Rip asked. "Waiting for a friend."

"Sure," Hunter replied, pouring an ice water for Rip, then placing another one in the space next to him to hold the seat.

"You've been surfing lately?" Hunter asked.

"Not as much as I would like to. How about you?"

"Not really. How did that merger thing work out? I've been reading about it in the papers."

"Not bad," Rip said. "Not bad at all. Can I get a vodka martini?"

"Shaken or stirred?"

"How did James Bond like it?"

"I think shaken, but I always make them the same way."

"Good enough for me."

"You still got that green wagon?" Hunter asked, mixing the drink.

"Sure do."

"You still see that girl you used to come in with? Laura was her name, wasn't it?"

"No. She's gone."

"Oh well," Hunter said, putting the martini in front of Rip with two olives on a Cliff House coaster. "This one is on me."

Rip lifted his glass to say thanks, took a sip, and looked out the bay windows at the ocean. Everything was good. Everything was just right. The waves were a little calm for surfing, but Rip did not have surfing on his mind. He felt he was finally on a roll, and nothing could change it. Sevens and elevens were coming up. He didn't need any snake eyes tonight.

That's when someone sat down right next to Rip in the seat he had reserved for JoJo. It was her father, Chief Brady.

"For Christ's sake Ripley, I thought we were friends, and now you're trying to hit on my daughter," Chief Brady said. "Did you think I wouldn't know about your little meeting tonight?"

"It's just between friends," Rip lied. "What are you doing here anyway? Aren't you supposed to be home resting?"

"I'm taking my walk. Doctor's orders. A little heart attack isn't going to stop me. But those bastards are going to retire me out. They give you so much time on worker's comp, and then they let you go."

"Well, thanks for recommending me."

"Why not, I thought. Hogwash and all those bastards, they can go screw themselves. I'll get a bump up on my pension now because the heart thing is considered a disability. But I still don't know about you working with my daughter. Did you sleep with her yet?"

"Not that it's any of your business, but no."

"Yeah, but you like her, don't you?"

"I do."

"That scares me, Ripley. But for Christ's sake, the least you can do is buy me a drink."

"I'm sure you aren't supposed to have one."

"I do it in moderation. And don't be a saint to me. I can smell the marijuana on you like it's your cologne."

"Give him what he wants," Rip told Hunter.

"Scotch. Top shelf, on the rocks," Chief Brady said, pulling out a cigar.

"And you're still smoking?" Rip asked.

"I'm making concessions. I don't light them anymore. But tell me, Ripley, was this getting together your idea or my daughter's?"

"I shouldn't tell you, but it was her idea."

"I was afraid of that. She's just like her mother. Probably did it just to spite me."

Hunter poured Chief Brady's drink, and served it on a coaster.

"How did you know I was here?" Rip asked.

"My daughter told me she was meeting you. But I didn't know it was her idea. I would have had some friends from downtown set up a bogus meeting so she couldn't make it, if I knew that. I still have some pull, you know."

"I'm sure you do. But I think your daughter is too smart for that."

"What do you mean?"

"She is right behind you," Rip told him, and she was.

"Well Dad, good to see you. It's nice to see you are following the doctor's advice by not drinking or smoking." JoJo came around and put her hand on the back of Rip's neck.

"For Christ's sake," Chief Brady said, looking into his drink after JoJo's show of affection toward Rip. "Well it was this guy here who insisted I have a drink, and my cigar is not lit."

"Do you expect me to believe that?" JoJo asked. "And you just happened to show up when I told you I'd be here tonight?"

"I was just going for my walk so I thought I'd stop by, that's all. He never did stop by when I was in the hospital."

"I guess that makes me oh for two," Rip said, but he was enjoying the interaction between JoJo and her father.

"Will you be joining us for dinner?" JoJo asked.

"No, no, I got to go anyway," Chief Brady said, feeling a little awkward. He was used to being the center of attention, but now the center had changed. Finishing his drink, he got up from his stool. "Congratulations, Ripley. Tell Hogwash I said hello."

"Do you want us to get you a ride home, Dad?" JoJo asked, as he was walking away.

"I'm fine. I know where I live."

JoJo took his seat.

"You told him about us meeting here?" Rip asked, surprised.

"Yeah, why not? It's good to get him out of the house. I knew he couldn't resist coming by, and he's been driving my mother crazy being home. When my father realized they were going to retire him out, he let Hogwash have it. He had nothing to lose. And then he stuck up for you. He told Hogwash to leave you alone. He told him, 'I know secrets too, and I got friends in the press.' Next thing I know I'm getting the call from city hall that I'm the new EMS chief. Then city hall told me to pick my own operations chief, that they were adding the requisition in the budget. When I mentioned your name, city hall never said a word."

"They must have been some secrets."

"They were."

"Well, it was good seeing him," Rip had to admit. "I had this dream the night before you came into my office that Hogwash was going through my files, trying to get something on me."

"I'm sure they were looking for some excuse to deny it. You didn't write a lot of memos, did you?"

"I tried not to. Only my homeless program."

"Probably for the best. I'll have what he's drinking," JoJo told Hunter.

Rip touched her arm. When he looked into her green eyes, his head was swimming. JoJo was wearing a short-sleeve silk V-neck maroon blouse and faded jeans, and Rip just wanted to feel his body next to hers. She carried a leather jacket that she put behind her chair. Her perfume had the fragrance of lilacs. Chief Brady was right. Rip's cologne was more like Dreamland. When they looked at each other, the anticipation for a good evening showed in their eyes. Even Hunter saw it while cleaning a glass and grinned.

"What are you grinning about?" Rip asked.

"Hey, I'm just here to serve the customer." Hunter served JoJo her martini. Hunter was a good bartender. Irish. He was always accommodating when he thought a couple were on their first date.

"Are we that obvious?" JoJo asked Hunter.

"Let me go into the back and bring up some more bottles."

"Do it," Duderonomy said, showing up on Rip's shoulder. "Kiss her. I need the endorphins."

Rip leaned over and kissed her. It had been so long since he had fallen for someone who cared about him too.

"Yes," Duderonomy said. Rip brushed him off his shoulder.

"Would you like to share some oysters?" Rip asked.

"Yes."

"Can we get some oysters?" Rip asked Hunter, when he came back with the bottles.

"We have a nice variety. Would you like to know what kind we have today?"

"No, just bring a bunch of them."

"Can I ask you a question?" JoJo asked Rip, after Hunter left to place the order.

"Sure."

"What's this Dennis Wilson fascination with you?"

"He was the cool one. I was never the cool one in school. He always got the girl. I always lost the girl."

"How do you think you are doing tonight?"

"The wheels are in motion."

JoJo smiled. Hunter brought place mats, bread and butter, and then the oysters. They dug in.

"Do you still want to be him?" JoJo asked.

"Well, yeah."

"I wanted to be a ballerina until I grew. There are no tall ballerinas."

Rip couldn't take his eyes off her.

"You're not looking at my freckles, are you? They used to make fun of me in school because of them. I used to try to hide them with makeup."

"Don't worry. My family is used to being made fun of. But no. I like them."

"Not to mix work into the evening, but they want to make that kid they call Effin the head of supply. I heard he's got some anger issues. Do you think that's a good idea?"

"Yeah," Rip said, after thinking about it for a moment, "why not? Give him a chance."

"Really? Well as operations chief, you're dealing with him."

"I know what calms him down."

They touched hands underneath the bar.

"And your father is going to be okay with this?" Rip just had to bring it up again.

"How many times are you going to ask? Leave it to me. He'll be fine. He means well. He's just afraid of the fire department stereotype."

"What's that?"

"Meet someone at the station house, start dating, get pregnant, marry, have an affair, get divorced."

"Do you get pregnant before or after you get married?"

"It's a fifty-fifty percentage. Don't you have that with the medics?"

"Sometimes. Mostly we just have affairs."

"Well that's nice to know," JoJo said sarcastically. "Can we have another drink and some more oysters?" she asked Hunter.

"On its way."

"But I'm a good guy," Rip said, wanting JoJo to know, and they kissed again.

Hunter brought over the drinks, took away the tray of empty oyster shells, and prepared the settings for the next round.

"And I didn't try to kill him either," Rip added, trying to explain.

"You will never live that one down. But isn't your dad with the Gray Beavers? Aren't they supposed to be older women who expose themselves? My father warned me about him."

"Only at city meetings about housing. It's a big issue with seniors. My dad drives them around, and sometimes has sex with some of them. I don't really want to get into the details. But yes, he's volatile. Thinks he's French. But that's another story for another day. I really can't explain it. But I'll tell you one thing: He is not getting his stereo back."

"What about your mother?"

"She knits and quilts. And she has a girlfriend who paints. They live on a farm in New Mexico. In the desert. She's probably the most normal one of the family. She seems happy. Ours is a different kind of family."

"Let me get this straight. Your mother is a lesbian, and your dad exposes himself with the Gray Beavers."

"Well, I warned you. It's a different kind of family. That's all. The neighbors used to call us the Addams Family when we lived in the Upper Haight."

"Well that kind of explains it."

"Explains what?"

"Why I picked you for my operations chief."

Hunter brought the oysters.

"You can never have too many oysters," Rip said.

"Remember I told you that I used to see you with that girl in the corner, near the window, when I was here with my friends?" JoJo asked, talking about Laura.

"And…?"

"Is she gone for good now?"

"So gone."

"Good."

After finishing their martinis and oysters, and leaving a big tip for Hunter, Rip and JoJo walked to the gift shop. Rip picked up a paperback on San Francisco, and read to her that San Francisco was founded on June 29 in 1776, and was fifty-two feet above sea level. He put it down, and picked up another one on the history of the Cliff House. "The first Cliff House was built in 1858 by a prosperous ex-Mormon," Rip read, and then put down the book, and picked up a glitter globe with the Golden Gate Bridge in the middle, and started shaking it, and insisted that he buy it for her. The lady in the counter wanted to put it in a bag, but JoJo told her no need, as she held it in her hand.

"Are we having fun yet?" JoJo asked.

"I am. But I want you to know that I don't want to be…"

"What?"

"A stereotype."

"I'm not quite sure what you are, Rip Ridley, but you are certainly not that."

"What about your family?"

"My mother left my father twice for his little firehouse antics. He hates to be alone. Then he started straightening out. That's why he worries about who I see. He has this sense of order that drives everybody crazy. I got my mother's green eyes, and her height. But I want to warn you that people with green eyes tend to be competitive, independent, creative, and devious."

"Is that true?"

"I'm not sure. I read it. But I thought you should know."

"Noted."

JoJo took Rip's hand, and they went down to the Musée Mécanique in the basement of the Cliff House. It was a blast from the past, with antique arcade games and mechanically operated musical instruments, and Laffing Sal always greeted you at the door. They couldn't stop touching each other on the arms, around the waist, on the shoulders…like they were in high school. The attendant saw them kissing behind one of the penny arcade games, and gave them the look, as if to say, *Maybe it's time to go.*

"I was just looking for the Maltese Falcon," Rip said to the attendant, as they were leaving. He ignored them.

"Well I hope you find the real one," JoJo said.

Then they were gone into the foggy, misty, golden San Francisco night. They both had a buzz going on. A good vibration. Rip left his wagon parked on the street, and then they made their way, hand in hand, up Point Lobos to Sutro Heights where JoJo lived. Underneath a street light, they stopped and kissed. It was near the Blue House, with the round windows on Balboa Street that looked like a boat.

As soon as they walked through the door of JoJo's apartment, they went straight to her bedroom. Their clothes were off before they laid down on the bed. The glitter globe found its way on the dresser in her bedroom.

JoJo did not hide her affection. Like Rip, inside she was swimming. They were all in. Even though the windows were open and a cool breeze came through, they were sweating. Rip had the taste of her lilac perfume on his lips.

"Does this mean we are an item?" JoJo asked as she lay naked next to Rip.

"I think it's official. In some countries we would be married."

Then they fell into a long embrace again, but this time it was smoother, softer, slower. Then with the sweetness of her lips, JoJo kissed Rip, then asked if he had found his Maltese Falcon yet, Dashiell?

"Yes, I have."

"Good," and then JoJo closed her eyes, and fell asleep.

Rip got up and went to the living room, and sat down in the easy chair near an open window, and finished the joint he had smoked earlier in the evening. Reed's Dreamland had become his favorite.

"See," Duderonomy said, showing up wearing his PJs, "I told you it was a date. A slice of life, like vivid details from the effect from one's environment."

"Really?" Rip asked. "Again?"

"I think it was the anniversary issue."

"Are you done yet?"

"I think so."

Rip finished the joint, and let the breeze carry the smoke out the window.

"My job is done here," Duderonomy proclaimed, disappearing. "Goodnight everybody."

From his chair, looking out the window, Rip could see bon-fires on the beach. He heard foghorns blow. Then Dennis Wil-son showed up sitting on Rip's shoulder. He was wearing that same candy-striped shirt. Like the poster, it was a younger Dennis, when his hopes and his dreams were still alive. Before the beard, and the drugs, and the alcohol, and the Manson thing got in the way. He softly sang "I Can Hear Music" on Rip's shoulder.

From the view of JoJo's apartment was the parking lot at Ocean Beach. After Dennis disappeared, Rip focused his eyes, and through the fog, he saw an ambulance in the parking lot. *Why are they there?* Rip wondered. It wasn't an area where am-bulances were posted at night. The phone was close by on the end table, so Rip called dispatch.

"This is Chief Ridley. What ambulance is parked at Ocean Beach?"

"Rip, it's me dude." It was Cherry Pie. "Congrats, man, I heard you're still chief."

"Thanks," Rip said.

"This radio thing is a good gig. I was toast being on the ambulance," Cherry Pie admitted. "I even like the night shift. Nobody fucks with me."

"Good. I'll make sure they don't change your schedule."

"It's good to be king again, isn't it?"

Rip had to admit it felt good.

"Hey, who is in the ambulance parked at Ocean Beach?"

"Oh yeah," Cherry Pie said, with a chuckle. "It's Arne Dib-ble doing his ride along with RC Suzy Pang."

"RC Pang and Arne Dibble? Really? Who approved it?"

"Who knows? It was on the schedule. Do you want me to give them another post?"

"No, no. Leave them alone for the night. What could go wrong?"

"Yeah, what could go wrong?" Cherry Pie asked. "What could possibly go wrong?"

In the ambulance, Arne was in the passenger seat, while RC Suzy Pang was in the back. It was a typical San Francisco evening with a cool breeze and fog. Arne felt a chill. He tried turning on the heater to warm up a bit.

"This ambulance is one of the old ones," RC Suzy Pang said to him from the back. "Sometimes the heater doesn't work. Help me back here. I'm setting up a sleeping bag so we can get a little sleep. It's going to be a long night, and I worked all day."

"A sleeping bag?" Arne asked.

"Arne, don't be shy. We need to get some rest."

"What if we get a call?" Arne asked. His voice broke.

"If we get a call, then we will run it. But I already talked to dispatch."

"What did they say?"

"They said come back here and help me."

"Let me make a phone call first." Before Arne had been cold, but now he was starting to sweat. He called his girlfriend, Ashley, from his Motorola. Her line was busy.

"Come on Ashley, please pick up the phone, please! Moment of weakness. Moment of weakness."

Arne hung up, and called again, but Ashley's line was still busy.

"Arne," RC Suzy Pang said, "please come here."

"One moment," Arne replied. His voice broke again.

Arne opened the window to get some fresh air. He started breathing heavily thinking about what Effin had said to him about RC Suzy Pang's reputation with rookies. *Grasshopper*, he could hear Effin's voice in his mind. *Grasshopper*. He tried calling Ashley again, but her line was still busy.

"Please, please pick up the phone," Arne pleaded.

"Arne, please put the phone away and come back here. It's going to be a long night, and if you keep the window open, I'm going to start getting cold."

One last time, Arne called Ashley. The line was still busy.

"What to do? What to do?" Arne asked himself. He put the phone away, rolled up the window, got up from the passenger seat, and slowly made his way to the back of the ambulance.

"Arne," RC Suzy Pang said. She was already in the sleeping bag wearing her Station 51 T-shirt, and must have only been in her underwear because her pants and boots were on the side. She sat up, and held out her hand. "Come over here, Arne. Don't be afraid. It's warm in the sleeping bag. It's not like I'm going to bite your head off. I promise, Arne… I promise."

ABOUT THE AUTHOR

Joe Mareschi lives in the Pacific Northwest. At age twenty, he left the East Coast on a Trailways bus traveling on Route 66 to California. Hitch-hiking, he found himself in San Francisco and the Bay Area, where he stayed for forty years. It was a great time.